TRINITY'S TRUST

MACY BUTLER

PARADISE PRESS

For Jimi and Leigh- my fearless and fun travel companions on our epic European backpacking adventure back in the summer of '97

CHAPTER 1

TRINITY

*T*he tart sweetness of the pisco sour did little to abate the bitter thoughts of Diego. For the past three days, I'd been trying to drown the memory of him and what he'd done. The blue expanse of the Pacific stretched toward infinity beneath the cover of cotton, offering me some hope that there were still possibilities beyond the thunderheads that had consumed me.

I checked my phone. Danielle was five minutes late, uncharacteristic of the efficient entrepreneur. I'd been dreading this meeting, but I owed it to her. I hated to leave her in the lurch, but I couldn't stay in Peru. I'd been tearful and nauseous for the two days I'd hoped to enjoy the exquisite cuisine in Lima but I'd left my appetite in Cuzco. It was time to head home.

Danielle appeared disheveled as she pushed past a waiter to plop her purse down in the seat across from me. I stood and she pulled me into a long hug. I hadn't realized how much I needed it, and didn't want her to let me go when she did. Her brown eyes, full of concern, met mine. "Hey there. How are you holding up?"

I inhaled sharply and nodded. "I'm alright." A lie I wanted to believe.

She studied my face before taking the seat beside mine. "What happened? Your messages were cryptic."

I hadn't wanted to go into the gory details of my broken heart. I still didn't. "I stupidly went and fell in love. And then it went sideways." It felt like a childish excuse for quitting my job. "I'm so sorry to put you in this position."

Her brow wrinkled. "Don't be ridiculous, Trinity. You stepped up when we needed you and you've given us six months. I knew you wouldn't be staying forever."

"Funny, I thought that maybe I might." My voice quivered at the possibilities I'd let myself consider with Diego.

"Who is this man? I'm assuming he's an asshole if he did you wrong."

"He is. But it's done." I tried to feign a smile as the waiter set menus on the table.

"You don't have to tell me if you don't want to."

I waited to reply until she'd ordered a drink and the waiter was out of earshot. "Long story short, we'd been seeing each other for four months before I ran into him at a restaurant a few days ago. He was supposed to be out on a trip—he has a tour company. But he was actually out to dinner with his wife and three kids." I nearly choked on the words.

Danielle's jaw dropped. "Oh dear. That's just awful. You thought he was single, I presume?"

"Well, he certainly never mentioned the wife and kids." I bit my lip but wanted to bury my face in my hands. "The worst part is that one is a tiny infant who was probably born while he was having an affair with me." Guilt washed over me like it was somehow my fault that he was a cheating wanker.

Danielle licked her lips after sipping her pisco sour. "How did he manage to keep that from you for months?"

I'd asked myself the same question a thousand times. "We both worked a lot so we got together in between. Or at least that's what I believed." I felt like such a fool. "I was probably naive. But at the time it didn't seem odd." Even all those nights he couldn't stay because he had to be up so early the next morning for a tour.

Her pained face was sympathetic. "What a dick. I'm sorry."

"*I'm* sorry you're scrambling to find someone to lead the next trip. I just couldn't wait three more weeks."

"I understand completely." Danielle held up a hand to stop me from apologizing further. "Don't worry, there are plenty of surfers in Lima. I'm interviewing three this afternoon." She took another sip of her cocktail. "So what next? Back to Australia? Or back on the road?"

"No, my travels are finished. Well, they will be after a quick stopover in Florida on the way." I didn't want to make the last stop, but I'd promised Max I'd visit the surf shop where he'd worked in the eighties—while a backpacker in his twenties like I was now.

"If you ever decide to come back, there will always be a place for you here. You've done a tremendous job. Our clients love you, and I do too." She reached across the table to lay her hand over mine. "You're a beautiful and vibrant person. It might not feel like it now, but I'm certain you'll find the right guy when the time is right."

Tears brimmed in my eyes. "Thank you. But I'm done with men."

Her lips pursed as she shook her head. "Don't be silly! You're still so young."

"I'm old enough to know better. Back to women for me." I took a bigger sip of the strong drink than I should have.

Danielle's eyes widened before she smiled. "Well, if that's what floats your boat."

"I've had more girlfriends than boyfriends in my life, none of whom ever lied about a wife and kids at home. But I'm not interested in either right now. It's time to get back to real life. I still have three more years of uni and after a year-and-a-half away, I'm missing home." I needed more long hugs from my mum. She didn't even know what I was suffering through. I couldn't bring myself to tell her when I'd phoned to ask them to book the ticket. She could tell something was wrong, but she didn't press. She was as happy as I was that I was going home.

"I bet. I'm sure you have a bright future ahead of you. And I'm sure you're doing the right thing. You'll get over this quickly. You're resilient."

I wished I had her confidence. "Getting home to my own bed is a good start."

We talked about the last few trips I'd done while sharing a ceviche that I didn't have an appetite for despite being my favorite. Danielle asked if wanted anything else before she asked for the check. I was tempted to order another drink, but alcohol hadn't helped me forget.

She pulled an envelope from her bag. "Well, tomorrow you'll be on your way and I'm sure the future will look brighter once you're home. There's a little something extra in there for you. Thanks for everything. And remember, the offer still stands if you ever want to come back to Peru."

I smiled up with surprise as I took the envelope. "Thank *you* for everything. Getting paid to surf was a dream come true. If you ever decide to branch out and start doing tours to the Land Down Under, I'm your girl." The chances of me ever setting foot in Peru again were nil.

"I have a good feeling that this is not the last I'll see of you. Take care of yourself in the meantime. And—fuck men. Just have fun and enjoy yourself. Everything comes in due time."

I nodded as I quoted my favorite poem. "The universe is unfolding exactly as it should."

She tilted her head and her smile widened in recognition. "*Desiderata*. I love it. Because it's true."

The irony that the poem was written by a man was not lost on me. It seemed like the universe had a bad sense of humor.

CHAPTER 2

I dozed in and out through two movies on the six hour flight to Miami. It seemed silly to go east before heading west to go home, but I'd made a promise. Max would take it as a snub if I didn't visit his old stomping grounds. And I certainly didn't want to fall into his bad graces if I planned to do any surfing when I got back.

Max taught me everything I know. It was the least I could do, even if it was a pain in the arse. Having a few days on my own to decompress and catch some waves would do me good. After meeting Diego, every surf trip was followed by a mad rush back to the mountains of Cuzco. It would be good to reconnect with the ocean—and myself—away from Peru.

My head bounced off the window, jarring me awake as the Tri-Rail train that had carried me from Miami screeched to a stop at its final destination in West Palm Beach. I still had a 40 minute bus ride to Jupiter. My backpack felt like it weighed twenty kilos when I shimmied groggily into the straps. I groaned as I flung my guitar over my shoulder, cursing Max under my breath. This had better be worth it.

I could barely hold my eyes open by the time I found the Greyhound bus for the last leg of the journey. I'd hardly slept the three nights since running into Diego and his family in Cuzco. Stepping into the broiling Florida heat, I felt like I'd been hit by the bus that finally left me at the station. Luckily it was only a fifteen minute Uber ride to the Drifter Surf Hostel.

From the looks of the facade, it was even more basic accommodations than I'd been expecting. At this point I'd be happy with a cardboard box. Thirty dollars a night for a bunk in a dorm seemed like robbery, but it was tough to be a backpacker in the US. Budget travel usually meant seedy establishments, yet as I walked in, I found that this place had a bohemian charm, which was further accentuated by the tattooed receptionist smiling up at me from the desk.

I propped my guitar against the desk and tried to force a smile. "Hiya. I made a reservation a couple of days ago. Trinity Timmermans."

The receptionist grinned as she scrolled the computer screen. "I love the accent. Where are you from?"

I took a deep breath. It was only the thousandth time in the past month that someone had commented on my accent. "Australia."

"Oh really? What part?"

"Forrester's Beach, near Sydney."

The young woman's green eyes lit up from under sun bleached bangs as she smiled. "I was in Sydney a few years back. Awesome surf at Bondi Beach."

"Yeah, I grew up surfing that break." Max had taken me there from the time I was eight.

"You're a lucky girl. I hope you're not expecting anything like that here. It doesn't compare."

'I'm not expecting much." I realized how bitchy I sounded and tried to recant. "I mean, I'm just passing through, and I promised an old friend I'd check out a surf shop where he used to work."

"Oh, yeah? Which one?"

"Slim's?" There was probably little reason to wonder if she'd heard of it since it had been open for decades.

Her face brightened. "That's *the* surf shop in Jupiter. It's iconic."

I chuckled. "So I've heard."

"You're in the Longboard Dorm—top of the stairs to the left. Pick any open bunk. Lockers are in the dorm."

"Great! Are the lockers big enough for this?" I held up my canvas guitar case before slipping it over my shoulder.

"Yep. Do you need a lock?"

"No, thanks, I've got my own."

"Good. Use it. The bathroom is at the end of the hall. Bring these back when you check out." She handed me a set of sheets and a towel.

The efficiency of the check-in process was like culture shock after over a year in Latin America. Moving back to the first world was going be interesting. On one hand, everything works and a schedule means something. On the other, everything is on a schedule and all you do is work. I'd been so anxious to get away from Diego that it hadn't even registered that leaving him also meant leaving the land of mañana. Even with all its chaos and disorganisation, the laid-back lifestyle focused on the important things in life. That, I would miss.

I sniffed the stack of linens as I scaled the narrow wooden staircase. At least they smelled clean.

Only three of the eighteen or twenty metal bunks with thin mattresses were empty. There was no shortage of budget travelers for the short supply of options in this surf town, especially when conditions were ripe for a decent wave.

I smiled and said hello to two guys listening to music on a small speaker between them on the bottom bunk of the beds next to the one I chose. I climbed the ladder to make the top bunk. I was tempted to lie down but knew better. If I napped now, I'd be out for hours and would be awake all night and ruined for tomorrow. And tomorrow I wanted to be out there for low tide at eight-fourteen a.m. to catch the wave at the inlet.

I fished my toiletries bag out of my overstuffed backpack and went to the loo. I let out a sigh of relief at the smell of bleach and the sight of the sparkling white tile. It wasn't nearly as bad as it looked from the street. First impressions aren't everything.

I washed my face and brushed my teeth before smoothing my unruly brown curls. I looked like shit, and didn't feel much better, but I was going to Slim's.

CHAPTER 3

ARLOWE

*S*huffling through a stack of invoices, I sighed and started punching numbers into a spreadsheet. Inventory was my least favorite task, but I disliked most everything about the actual running of the shop. It kept me from surfing.

The bell on the door jingled. I put a finger on the line on the invoice where I'd stopped and looked up to a bright-eyed brunette strolling toward the counter. Loose curls hung around her angel face. "I'll be right with you. Just a sec." I picked up a pen to mark the last item I'd entered.

"Take your time."

When I looked up she was taking a photo of the vintage board hung high on the wall behind the counter. "You like that one?"

"I do." She looked back to her phone to type. "But I was texting the picture to my friend back home."

I eyed her curiously. "A friend who's into vintage boards?"

"A friend who probably surfed that board when he was here thirty years ago. That's what I just asked him, in fact." Her pale blue eyes sparkled with her smile as she slid her phone into her pocket.

I grinned, leaning into my elbows on the counter. "How can I help you?"

"I'd like to rent some gear to go out tomorrow."

I nodded. "Where do you plan to go?"

She looked at me curiously as though I'd asked a trick question. "The inlet…"

At least she was familiar enough with the area to know that much. "That's the spot. Follow me." I waved her around the counter to follow me into the back room. "These are our rental boards. Do you see one you'd like?"

She perused the selection of beat up longboards on the rack before her face scrunched up. "Not really. Don't you have any shortboards for rent?"

My brows raised. "Ah, you surf a shortboard, do you?"

She stifled a scoff. "I do. Do you have any?"

"From the sound of your accent, and from your obvious confidence, I'll assume you know what you're doing. We don't usually rent those, but I can probably find one for you in my personal stash. Come with me." I showed her three shortboards against the wall.

"That one looks perfect." She pointed to the last of the three.

I chuckled and grinned. "Good choice. That's the board I surf most days."

She stepped back away from it like it was now off limits. "Oh. That's *your* board?"

"They're all my boards." I waved my hands in the air to indicate the whole shop before pointing to the back wall. "But these three are my personal boards."

Her blue eyes narrowed in a quizzical stare. "You rent your own boards?"

I grinned. "Not normally."

Her eyes narrowed further. "But you'd rent me your *favorite* board? Why's that?"

"Well, it *is* the best board in the shop. And I trust that you'll take care of it. Is that trust misplaced?" She seemed spunky enough to endure a little prodding.

"Trust comes easier for you than for me." She laughed. "You don't know me from Adam, but you're not wrong. I'll take care of your baby—or either of the other two. Just please don't make me surf one of those longboards."

I chuckled to hide the smile I couldn't suppress. "You can take my baby, as long as you promise to take good care of her. And leave a credit card for the deposit, of course." I flashed a smile that made hers spread.

"Thank you for trusting me." She pulled a wallet from her bag and handed me a card.

"Trinity Timmermans." I read her name off the card. "That has a nice ring to it."

She smiled but her subtle eye roll wasn't lost on me. "Thank my parents, I guess." Now I felt like a tool, but at least I didn't say what I was thinking—that I could thank them for more than her pretty name.

Instead, I offered her my hand. "I'm Arlowe. Arlowe Asher. Nice to meet you."

Trinity shook my hand more firmly than I expected from such a slight girl. "Sounds like both our folks are fond of alliteration. Nice to meet you, too, Arlowe."

"Do you want a guide for tomorrow?" I wanted her to say yes, not for the sale, but for the chance to take her out.

Her eyes dropped bashfully. "I'm afraid I don't have the budget for that."

I laughed as I led her back out into the store. "How do you know? You didn't even ask how much it costs?"

"Because I don't have a budget for much of anything after a year and a half on the road. And the US is killing me. Coming here was a big detour, but I promised a friend I'd check it out—the one I sent the pic to earlier. Anyway, lucky for me there's a west wind running tomorrow and low tide is at a reasonable hour. I think I'll be fine on my own."

I eyed her curiously as she walked around the counter. She didn't look old enough to have been "on the road" for a year and a half already, or to be so in-the-know for local conditions. "You've done your homework."

"Damn right I did. I've been praying for this west wind for three days now and I studied the tide tables before I planned my trip, just hoping I'd hit it right."

"With a name like Trinity, I'd guess that God listens. Thanks for that. I'm always praying for that west wind, too, but it's not often we get it."

Her pale blue eyes danced with a hint of mischief. "Don't let the name fool you. There's nothing holy about me."

"Good to know." Her sexy mic drop left me speechless. My cheeks flamed as I stammered to break the awkward pause. "Say, I'm taking some advanced junior students out tomorrow. You can join us if you'd like. No extra charge."

The rippling undercurrent of reserve melted away as the corners of her eyes creased. I must've said the right thing. "For real? That would be amazing. What time should I meet you?"

"Seven thirty, here. We'll go straight over. I'll have my baby loaded on the Jeep for you."

Blinking her blue eyes up at me with tilted head and hands on her chest, she looked genuinely grateful. "Thanks, Arlowe. I'm looking forward to it."

Not nearly as much as I was. A brief tinge of guilt rose up in me for feeling excited to see this enigmatic Trinity again tomorrow, when I had a date with Monica tonight.

Trinity turned to walk away but stopped short like she'd remembered something. "Do you have a loo I can use?"

The way she said loo made me grin. "Sure, right there." I pointed to the restroom door.

"Thanks." Her blue eyes lighting with her smile made my heart skip a beat.

My phone dinged obtrusively and I looked down. Surely Monica was some sort of psychic, I thought with another pang of guilt.

Sorry this is last minute, but I have to cancel tonight.

I should've been disappointed, but all I could do was shrug.

I waited for further explanation, but the phone was silent.

Was she waiting for a response? My first instinct was to say, "No problem," and call it a day. Our last date had raised a red flag. Only four dates in, she'd already started plotting the future trajectory of my life—as if who I was now wasn't good enough. That she sounded just like my dad as she suggested that I find a manager to run the shop, so I could get back into tech—where the real money was—had only made me bristle. Maybe I hadn't been so subtle after all. Could be she was smarter than I gave her credit for, ready to cut her losses. No matter—I had an early morning tomorrow.

When my phone dinged again, I was *sure* Monica was psychic.

I'm heading to Orlando this evening for work for a couple of days. See you Friday?

I guess we were still on then. I was ambivalent, but didn't want to be a dick. I'd planned to ride that merry-go-round for a few more spins anyway. I shook my head at myself. *Maybe I am a dick.* Whatever, it would all play out in its own time. That relationship's days had been numbered since day one. Same as all the rest. I had a knack for dating the wrong woman, which probably came from my lack of desire to find the right one.

Life was far simpler when I never let it get serious. But, for now, I'd stay on for another spin if she was game.

Sounds like a plan.

Trinity skipped out of the restroom. "Thanks! That saves me from having to find a decent public loo while I'm out exploring."

The corners of my mouth tugged into an uncontrollable grin.

I considered asking if she'd like to have a beer later now that I was free, but thought better of it. That would be a blatant dick move. She probably wasn't old enough to go to a bar anyway.

"Have fun out there. You should definitely check out the lighthouse."

"It's on my list." She turned on her heel, calling back over her shoulder. "See you tomorrow."

"I'm counting on it."

I looked down at the stack of invoices beside my laptop as the door jingled, wishing I was going exploring with her. At a mere twenty-seven, I was pining over my youth that seemed to be melting away in tedious tasks. I was supposed to be living the dream. That was the whole point of buying into the surf shop. Turns out it was just a sentence to be stuck in one place dealing with the same problems day after day. I guess that's why they call it work.

It was Trinity who was living the dream. She'd probably set off traveling around the world fresh out of high school. I knew from other travelers that the "gap year" was a rite of passage. In the US, it's straight to college whether you know what you want to do with your life of not. If I'd taken a gap year, I would have known better than to take a corporate job right out of school.

It took me four years of living a life I never wanted to realize it. That was sooner than most—most people never do. I'd unwittingly traded it for another job I wasn't excited to get up for most days. The days I got to surf made up for it, at least that's what I told myself. But the parts that felt like work took most of my time. Maybe one of the resumes I'd half-heartedly put out would land me a flexible consulting gig. I could find the silver lining in that, like hiring someone else to do this crap so I could focus on surfing. Or exploring with a much-too-young Australian pixie.

CHAPTER 4

TRINITY

J awoke fresh as the morning dew. I must've slept like a stone through any ruckus that may have occurred in the packed dorm. The two tall-boy beers from the gas station down the street had made sleep come easier. As had the promise of surf.

Arlowe's board glistened in the rack of his cherry-red Jeep. I was looking at the Jeep and not at the door when I ran into Arlowe on my way into the store—literally. My hand went up instinctively to block the impact, landing on his chest that felt firm through his tee. The scent of a manly soap mixed with the coffee on his breath. "Well, hello, unholy one."

I stepped back holding the door open while he and two kids who looked to be about twelve filed out of the surf shop. "Sorry, I'm still half asleep."

He took hold of the door, brushing up alongside me as he pulled out a key to close up the shop.

"No worries." He gave me a wink as he stepped past me onto the sidewalk and threw open the back door of the Jeep. The students eagerly piled in, then grinned at us expectantly. "This is Josh and Malachai. They've surfed the inlet many a time with me, but never in the pristine conditions we're expecting today. You are the good luck charm we've been waiting for."

My cheeks flushed. The compliment caught me off guard—especially since it felt like I was still swimming beneath a black cloud of bad luck—but I was more amused than flattered. "I'm not sure I've ever been called a good luck charm. So, thank you…?"

"Don't let him charm you, Trinity." A lanky older man wearing Lennon-style wire-rimmed glasses approached us from the sidewalk, grinning as he laid his hand on my back. My face must've shown the surprise that he knew my name. "Max told me you were coming."

I held out my hand with a wide grin. "You must be Slim." His silver waves of hair matched his goatee.

"The one and only. Max and I go way back."

"I've heard. He's the reason I came. He'd never forgive me if I didn't meet the infamous Slim."

"I wish I could say I taught him a thing or two, but the truth is Max was as good as I was, even at your age."

"Yeah, he's pretty amazing." I had a sudden warm feeling for Max as I said it. It would be good to be back home soon. "He taught me pretty much everything I know."

"I'm sure you're well-trained then. You might even show Arlowe a thing or two." He chuckled as he glanced Arlowe's way.

Arlowe's hazel-green eyes flashed briefly at Slim—with what

emotion, I couldn't quite tell—before he smiled my way and swung the back door of the Jeep shut. "I'm always open to learning new tricks, especially from a pretty girl."

Slim's narrowed eyes showed a hint of amusement. "As long as we're talking about surfing. No funny business. Max will have my head if you make this young lady feel uncomfortable."

"Gee, thanks, Slim. It's good to know what you really think of me."

I winced at Slim's admonishment, but he chuckled as he patted my back. "I'm just kidding. Arlowe is a gentleman. You're in good hands."

He wasn't kidding, though, and I was grateful for the warning after the way Arlowe had looked at me yesterday. I didn't want to have to fend off advances from a charming hot guy. In normal times, I'd have been all over the opportunity, but these heartbroken times were far from normal. His sun-kissed hair, piercing eyes, and bright smile made him just my type. That he looked nothing like Diego only helped up the temptation. But he'd been warned.

I said, "I'm sure he knows how to treat a lady."

Arlowe eyed me playfully as he chuckled. "Are you now?" A grin tugged at the corners of his mouth as he guided me to the passenger door. He chuckled as he swung the door open for me. "Your accent is infectious. We might all start talking like you soon."Arlowe squinted as his smile grew wider when he turned to the two kids in the backseat. "Right, mates?" His imitation of the Aussie accent was poor at best, but it merited a giggle from his students.

I rolled my eyes as I hoisted myself up into the passenger seat. "You're the one with the accent."

"It's all relative. I wish mine was as cute as yours." His brows waggled before he slipped his Aviator Ray-Bans over his eyes and closed my door for me, like a true gentleman.

Everything about him was pretty damn cute, but he probably knew that.

I helped Arlowe unload the boards from his roll-bar rack and we all marched down to the beach like ducks in a row. I waited patiently with Arlowe's favorite board under my arm while he helped his two students prepare. His hands-off approach demanded independence, and his compliments every step of the way had them grinning from ear to ear with confidence by the time we were ready to start. Arlowe was good. Very good.

I waded into the surf. "God, the water is so warm!" After the frigid waters of Peru, it felt like bathwater.

"Yeah, it's crazy warm this year. We're lucky we didn't get a hurricane this season with the temps this high." His knuckles tapped his board. "I'd knock on wood, but fiberglass will have to do. The season isn't quite finished."

I smiled wryly. "I hope you didn't just jinx us."

Arlowe flashed a grin. "Luckily we have our good luck charm. You guys ready?"

The kids nodded with excitement as they bellied up on their boards. I kept their slow pace as we paddled out to wait for a wave. Arlowe instructed them to get ready when we spotted a ripe swell approaching. They were up in no time, like little pros. Remembering being that age alongside Max every weekend and most days of the summer made me happy I came. I'd done it for him but I didn't realize how much I needed it for myself.

The kids impressed me with their skills on that first ride in and Arlowe was quick to point out everything they'd done well before bringing up what they could have done better. He was far more compassionate a coach than Max had been.

As we started to paddle out for the next wave, Arlowe grinned at me. "Don't feel like you have to hang with us if you'd rather shred on your own."

I smiled, a little relieved. "Thanks, I will if you don't mind."

"Not at all. Go, enjoy."

And I did. The first wave I caught was a big barrel that Arlowe let pass. The exhilaration of riding it made me forget the heaviness in my heart. I paddled as hard as I could to catch the next wave, and then the next. I was back at home in the ocean and nothing else mattered.

After several good rides, at least eight or nine, the kids were ready to pack it in. I'd have stayed out there all day, and I suspected Arlowe would too if he had the choice. I could tell by the almost forlorn look in his eyes when he watched me ride the last wave in.

"If you want to stay, I'll come back for you after I drop these guys." I was tempted but I didn't want to be any more trouble for him.

"No, that's alright. I still have exploring to do. And I plan to be back out here tomorrow morning...as long as you don't mind renting me your baby again."

"As long as you don't mind that I join you." He grinned as he cinched the strap tight over the board on the rack.

I liked the idea of surfing with a local who knew his stuff, even if he was a little flirtatious. "Do you have students again?"

"No, but I'd planned to surf anyway. It's supposed to be perfect conditions again tomorrow. But low tide is a little earlier so meet me at seven?"

"Sounds good. If it's okay with you, I'll just stay here for now. I want to get to the lighthouse museum before they close. I missed it yesterday."

"Oh, yeah, of course. You don't want to miss that. My dad used to take me there all the time. It's awesome."

Arlowe wasn't kidding. The lighthouse was truly awesome. The view from the top was staggering. The sun sinking over the Everglades to the west set the sky afire in deep orange and red. And looking out to the east, over the Atlantic, made my heart sing. My troubles in Peru seemed like a distant memory.

I decided to walk the forty-five minutes back to the hostel, stopping once at a 7-11 to grab two more tall-boys and a sandwich for dinner.

My phone dinged in my pocket as I climbed the narrow stairs of the hostel. I checked it once I set my loot down on my bed. Evie. I hadn't talked to her in nearly a year. Yet somehow she knew I was on my way home.

You're coming back!?

I smiled at the thought of her. Evie and I had been best friends through high school, and roommates our first year at Macquarie. That felt like a lifetime ago.

I cracked open a beer before I typed my reply. *G'day, mate!* It was nearly midday back home. *The rumors are true. How'd you know?*

Your mum told my mum

That a wasn't a surprise since I hadn't told anyone I was going home except my parents and Danielle. And I hadn't asked Mum not to tell anyone, so of course she'd blabbed. As far as she knew, my return was a happy occasion. She was probably shouting it from the rooftops after months of trying to persuade me to get my arse back home.

I rolled my eyes as I replied. *Of course she did. Sorry for keeping it secret. I was saving the surprise.* More like I was saving myself from the questions that were sure to follow.

So you'll be back for first term?

Evie would be nearly finished with university by the time I started back in January.

Yes! I've got a lot of catching up to do

Her response made me smile. *WE'VE got a lot of catching up to do!!!! Can we be roomies again?*

If you'll have me, fuck yeah!

My stomach fluttered at her answer. *Of course I'll have you!!*

I had been shite at keeping in touch with anyone but my parents after the first few months of my trip. I felt a little guilty for how self-centered I'd become. But my life was rich with adventure and there wasn't much I missed from back home until I'd gotten my heart broken.

Good! I'm looking forward to it.

We had a lot of good times our freshman year. That was some thing to look forward to for sure.

Me, too! I'll let you know when I get registered so we can put in the request. I hadn't let myself think about all there was to do when I got back. Getting home was daunting enough. But chatting with Evie stirred an excitement.

How've you been?

I bit my lip. I didn't want to bring her—or myself—down with the truth. *Great. Surfing Peru was a dream. And I'll be out shredding again tomorrow in Florida, so I can't complain.*

I can't wait to hear all about your trip! Can you FaceTime now?

I couldn't wait for the time I could talk about it without crying. *Sorry I'm in a crowded hostel. Let's talk soon though."*

I looked around at the empty dorm. It would be crowded in another couple of hours when everyone came to bed.

Okay, have fun tomorrow!

That was the plan. *You know it!*

Snuggled up on my bunk with my guitar, I strummed the songs I used to play in the Mezcal Bar back in Antigua. With all the backpackers out partying, I could sing and play without bothering anyone. I didn't want an audience, not there. As much as I yearned to return home, I would've given almost anything to be back in Antigua.

I tapped on my guitar remembering rehearsing in Dante's house while Lena tapped her foot and swayed. I missed them something fierce. I considered calling Lena, but I was still so embarrassed by what Diego had done, and how stupid I'd been. I couldn't bring myself to tell anyone that really mattered. It hurt too much. And, I didn't have it in me to tell them that I was heading home. Dante and Lena would surely try to convince me to return to Guatemala if they knew. Truth be told, part of me would rather be going back there than home. But I couldn't just waltz back in. They were together now, just the two of them, and having a baby. Everything was different now, for all of us.

CHAPTER 5

ARLOWE

The boards were loaded and ready to go at ten till seven. I was itching to get out there. It was the best waves we'd seen in four or five years. Trinity was a good luck charm, no doubt. The tropical storm that was still south of the Bahamas was the real reason for the ideal conditions, but I liked to think that she brought us the storm—the perfect storm that would give us epic waves while offering a wide berth.

Trinity showed up a few minutes early, which made me like her even more. Her ringlet curls framed her face in the amber morning light while she scanned the boards on the Jeep. "Wow, you're all loaded up and ready to go."

"No time to waste on such a perfect day. You ready?"

"I was born ready."

I was probably already on a surfboard by the time she was born, but I liked her confidence. She might be able to keep up with me after all.

Grinning as the wind whipped through her curls, Trinity held her hair back behind her neck as we gained speed. She looked as excited as I felt about the waves.

The parking lot was half full already. On these rare perfect days, the locals drop everything else to be there at prime time. I pulled a cooler out of the back, and a bag with a blanket and a couple of towels.

Trinity went straight for the cooler, flipping the lid open. "Coldies! And what's all this?" She rifled through the cooler and pulled out a wheel of brie and a bag of grapes. "How *bourgeoisie*."

"I like good snacks." I grinned. "Don't you?"

"I do. I'm impressed."

"Wait till you see me in action when I'm unencumbered by students."

"And your humility, that's impressive too." Her blue eyes rolled as she grinned.

She was a smart-ass and I liked it. "There's a fine line between cocky and confident. You're only cocky if you're not as good as you think you are."

"I suppose it remains to be seen then."

"Challenge accepted."

Trinity's competitive streak was evident as she paddled out. She wanted to stay a step ahead of me, and everyone else for that matter. Several other surfers bobbed on their boards as a few duds passed. She read the ocean expertly when the right one came along, kicking with all her might. I almost missed the wave, I was so busy watching as she muscled into position ahead of the other surfers vying for the same wave.

Turning at the perfect angle, she waited until the optimal moment to pop up to her feet. She carved along the wave's edge several meters ahead of me as the massive lip formed above us. Trinity controlled the board like it was an extension of her taut little body.

I was smiling ear to ear when I caught up to her. "Damn, woman, you claimed that wave."

She brushed off the compliment like it was sand on her feet. "Isn't that what you're supposed to do?"

Trinity did it better than most I'd ever seen. "I suppose so." I paddled hard to keep up as she turned right back around to chase the next one down.

With every wave I was more awestruck by her ability. She had more natural talent than anyone I'd ever seen and a tenacity that made me feel like a slouch. When I was gasping for air, she was on her way back out. She was relentless. I tried to hide my relief when she finally said, "I'm about ready for one of those coldies. How 'bout you?"

"It's beer-thirty." About fucking time.

Trinity placed her board on its side in the sand and waited for me to balance mine beside it. "God, it's so good to be back in the surf."

I tried not to stare as she dabbed a towel against the water droplets that glistened on her chest. "It doesn't seem like you've been away at all. Haven't you done much surfing on the road?"

"I did a lot of surfing the last six months in Peru. But it's good to be somewhere new."

"Well, coming from Australia via Peru, this probably doesn't compare. But right now it's about as good as it gets here." I sat down on the blanket, still winded, hoping she wouldn't notice.

If she did, she didn't comment. "I'd rather be here right now than either of those places."

My eyes wandered down to her abs as she stretched out on the blanket and I had to force my gaze back to hers. "Me too. But you must be excited to get back to the waves back home."

Trinity's lips twisted as she shrugged, popping open a can of beer. "Yes and no. I do miss the surf. And I need to get back to uni. But now that I'm actually on my way home, I'm not that excited."

It seemed like there was something she wasn't telling me. "So you took a year off after high school that turned into a year-and-a-half and now it's back to reality?"

"Close. I did a year of uni *then* took a year off—a year-and-a-half ago."

She was a little older than I thought, but not by much. "At least you're going back to college and not to work, especially when you have great surfing nearby. I'd call that ideal."

"For the last six months my work was surfing. That was pretty much ideal. Like you, I suppose. Lucky you, doing this for a living."

I chuckled. "On days like this, I can't complain a bit. So, you were surfing for a living in Peru?"

"Yeah, I led groups on week-long tours up and down the coast."

I raised my brow as I sipped my beer. I hadn't pictured her a leader, but she wasn't as green as she seemed. "That sounds like a sweet gig."

"Really sweet. I worked for a high-end agency so it was pretty luxurious. Not how I normally travel."

Her nonchalance inspired me to let my sarcasm flow, a refreshing change from choosing my words carefully so that they wouldn't be misconstrued. If you have to explain sarcasm, there's really no point. I'd given up with Monica. But I figured Trinity could take it. "And real life was calling you back so loudly that you had to leave?"

Her shoulders stiffened as she inhaled. "It ran its course. It was time to move on." Her short response made it clear she didn't have anything else to say about the matter but there was definitely more to the story. Maybe sarcasm wasn't in order.

"I have a feeling you'll land a sweet gig back home if that's what you want."

"I need to finish my degree, but if I can figure out how to get paid to surf while I do it, I'll be winning for sure."

"Manifest that shit! If you want it bad enough, it will happen. Like magic."

"Yeah, I suppose my life's worked out that way so far. That's how I ended up practically running a bar in Guatemala, which is where I landed the surf tour job. Did you manifest working with Slim?"

"In a roundabout way, I think I did. I grew up surfing with Slim, much like you with Max. Then I went off to college, studied computer science and got a job in tech. But the ocean always called me back. When Slim fell on hard times a few years ago—his wife had health problems and no insurance—

he almost lost the shop. So I took the money I'd saved for a house and bought into the shop. I hate to think I manifested his problems, but I was certainly ready to act when the opportunity presented itself. I helped Slim out of a jam and traded a corporate job for this. I'd call that winning."

"I remind myself frequently that the universe is unfolding exactly as it should. And I think you're right…being open to its possibilities is the key."

I loved her easy way and how naturally we fell into philosophical musings. "Funny, now it's real life that's calling me back. I guess everything comes full circle eventually."

Trinity's face twisted into a confused scowl. "What do you mean, isn't this your real life? And don't you love it?"

"I love the surfing, but there's a lot that I don't love about running the business. And while my tech skills are still relevant, I can make good money consulting. So hopefully I can pay someone to do the parts I don't like and get back to surfing."

Trinity considered what I'd said before she shrugged. "Surfing and tech. Doesn't sound like a bad plan if that's what you really want."

Something in her tone made me think she doubted that last part. Well, so did I. "I think a good plan is to get back to the waves before I'm tempted to open another beer." Or tempted to hit on her. She was the coolest chick I'd met in a long time —maybe ever. And she was off limits.

Already struck by her ability, the next waves left me astounded by her grace. Her duck dive technique was flawless. To do something well is one thing, to do it beautifully is another. This woman was a pinnacle of perfection. As much as I loved watching her, I felt like my legs might collapse if we kept on.

I was relieved—again—when she rode a wave all the way into the shore. She grinned as she shook the water out of her curls. "I'm starving. Let's break out that bougie cheese."

"I could use a beer after that last run."

"The last four were epic. Fuck, that was amazing! Best day I've had in a long time."

"Me, too." It was the best day in as long as I could remember.

Remarkably, Trinity still had a spring in her step as she pranced, board under her arm, all the way back to the blanket.

My legs felt like jello as I handed her a beer, before setting the food out on a wooden cutting board. "You're really good, you know. I don't think Max should get the credit for it, but I'm sure he's proud of your skills."

"Thanks. You're not so bad yourself. But Max doesn't doll out compliments so freely."

"I guess he doesn't want you to get cocky." I smirked.

"He's quite the critic—which always made me work harder to get better—so I don't begrudge him that." Trinity stretched out on the blanket, like a mermaid in her red bikini.

"Sounds a lot like Slim. It took a thick skin, but if it weren't for him, I don't think I would have fallen in love with surfing."

"I know exactly what you mean." People say that even when they don't have a clue, but she clearly did. She tilted her head, biting her lip pensively before she continued. "I fell in love with a town in Guatemala, or, I thought I did."

"The one with the bar?"

"Yep, Antigua. I really loved it there. I mean really, really loved it there. It was magical—cobblestone streets amid volcanoes. I had great friends and a fun job. I was there for months and it just kept getting better. But it's exactly like you said—the ocean was always calling me. When the tour job in Peru landed in my lap, I didn't think twice about leaving Antigua for Peru. As much as I could love that mountain town, it didn't have the sea. That's when I realized that I *need* surfing in my life."

My chest tingled with a deep breath of the salty sea breeze. There's nothing like the feeling that someone actually gets you. That Trinity felt the same made her perfect in my book. "Like I need air in my lungs."

She smiled as she said wistfully, "Or blood in my veins. It really is in our blood, isn't it?"

The sun was low enough in the sky to give her hair an auburn hue. Despite Slim's warning, all I wanted to do was touch her, feel the warmth of her skin against mine, the heat of her smile. But, much like catching the perfect wave, sometimes you've got to take a chance—even if it means risking a total wipe-out. I reached out and gave her hand a small squeeze. "For better or for worse, I think it is."

"I know, it's a tough life." She grinned as she wiggled her hand away and popped a slice of brie into her mouth. It didn't get much better than this. But the sun was on its rapid descent. If we didn't leave soon I'd be tempted to kiss her. I was about to suggest that we pack up when she asked, "Are you sure you want to get back into tech?" I detected a note of disdain in her voice, as if we were discussing returning to a drug habit or an abusive ex. Or maybe I was just feeling sensitive to the topic after my recent conversations with Monica.

"If getting back to tech means more days like this and fewer days that suck, then, yes." It felt like a logical argument. For all the good days I had now, there weren't many like this, and that was a fact. Was it a coincidence that Trinity happened to be here for it? More likely, she was what made the day truly epic. Her energy had the strange effect of filling me up while leaving me wanting more.

Trinity nodded pensively as she inhaled. "It's all about balance. If that helps you find your balance, then it's a good thing."

She got it. Completely. I grinned as I patted her thigh. "That's the tricky part." My self-restraint was slipping. I hoped she didn't mind.

"Always. But I'm sure you'll figure it out. You're smart like that." Sarcasm seeped from her smirk.

I'd been thinking of her as young—even a little naive—an obvious misconception. She seemed so far from either, I didn't know what I had been thinking. Her peach skin glowed in the last light. I didn't want the day to end. But I knew better. Between the fact that Monica was still in the picture and Slim had specifically told me not to fraternize with his lifelong buddy's prodigy, it would be a dick move all-around to continue this any further.

"As much as I hate to, I've got some work to finish up back at the shop."

"Back to the fun part, huh?" Trinity's eyes twinkled with her sassy smirk as she hopped to her feet.

"Right." I let my eyes linger on the dimples on her low back above her red bikini bottoms before I stuffed our towels into the beach bag. Fuck. She was hot.

Back at the shop, Trinity insisted on unloading and carrying her board despite my protests.

Slim greeted us from behind the counter with a wide smile. "Did you kids have fun?"

I put my board away, then turned to accept back my favorite one from Trinity. "The best kind of fun." That might not have been exactly true where Trinity was concerned, but it had been damn near perfect.

Trinity's innocent smile made my heart skip a beat—even if it was inspired by the spectacular waves and not the company—as her gaze swung to Slim. "You should have been out there."

"If you hang around long enough, I'll get out there with you."

I chuckled. "She might have to stay a while for that. I haven't seen you catch a wave in months."

"There's a lot you don't see." Slim winked, but we both knew he hadn't surfed in ages.

"Maybe next time?" Trinity winked back at Slim. "I'm keen to get back out there before I go, if the weather cooperates."

Slim looked doubtful as he pushed his glasses higher up the bridge of his nose. "That's a big if. The outer bands of that storm in the Bahamas may clip the coast in the next couple of days."

"I'll keep my fingers crossed. Though I can't complain after today." Trinity's gaze shifted my way as her lips spread in a smile. "Thanks. It was lovely."

I pushed my hair back and grinned. "The pleasure was all mine."

"Hardly. I'll stop by tomorrow and see how it looks."

"I'll be here, finishing inventory." For Slim's sake, I tried not to grimace.

CHAPTER 6

TRINITY

I was on cloud nine, practically floating back to the hostel. No wonder Max loved it so much here. The waves couldn't compare to back home, but there was something magical about the place nonetheless.

The lobby was alight with long-haired guys around a ping pong table covered in plastic red cups. There was nothing magical about beer pong. Tonight would be a good night to actually go out and check out that restaurant I'd been eyeing ever since I arrived.

I was relieved to find empty seats at the bar. According to reviews, the raw bar on the beach had the best oysters in town. A scattering of license plates and dollar bills with names and dates adorned the wall behind the bar, keeping me distracted while I waited for the bartender to finish serving two men at the other end. She was a cute blonde whose dark brows framed big brown eyes. She smiled as she rubbed a rag over the weathered wood in front of me.

"What can I get you, gorgeous?" A chill spiraled up my spine.

Dante always called Lena "gorgeous" and me "beautiful." As much as I loved Jupiter, what I wouldn't give to be back in Antigua with those two. I took a deep breath to try to forget. "Just a beer. And a dozen oysters please."

"Domestic draft is on special tonight. Bud okay with you?"

I shrugged with a grin. "Sure. Whatever saves me a buck."

"I hear you." She smiled as she held a tilted glass under the tap. "Where's that accent from? Are you a Kiwi?"

I chuckled and shook my head. "Close—relatively speaking. I'm Australian."

"Ah." She set a frosty mug on the bar. "What brings you to Jupiter? The waves?"

"Yeah, it's been amazing the past two days. I don't want to go home."

"I haven't been out, but I've heard how awesome it's been about a million times a day." She rolled her eyes, leaning onto her elbows on the bar. I knew the feeling, hearing about things you didn't really care about over and over from buzzed customers.

"I know exactly how you feel. I've been on your side of the bar."

"Yeah? I'm not surprised. You look like you could hold your own with a rowdy crowd."

I chuckled. "More than I care to repeat. At least Americans tip well."

As if on cue, even though he was too far away to hear, a guy at the other end of the bar called out, "Excuse me? Can we get some drinks down here?"

The bartender forced a smile their way before turning back to roll her eyes and whisper, "Not well enough to put up with their shit sometimes. But I shouldn't complain. It's not very professional of me, is it?"

"I won't judge." As much of a pain in the ass the drunks could be, I missed slinging drinks in the Mezcal Bar. I missed everything about my life in Antigua—especially Lena and Dante.

One of the guys at the end of the bar caught me watching the cute bartender serve them their drinks. I guess he took it as an invitation because he tapped his friend's shoulder and started my way. That I didn't miss.

He was not nearly as handsome as he probably thought he was, based on his confident swagger. He slid onto the stool beside me and leaned in far too close for comfort. "Hey there."

I tried to control my facial expression but my lip snarled despite my efforts. "Hi." I shot him a *Fuck off!* glare before spotting his sidekick approaching behind him.

The wanna-be suitor was undeterred. "What's your name?"

I raised a brow and glowered. "Betsy. Yours?"

"Carlos. And this is Alex." My eyes flitted only briefly to catch him as he patted his friend's shoulder like he was proud to make the introduction. "Where are you from, Betsy?"

There were so many ways to fuck with this wanker, but I figured shooting down his intelligence early was an efficient approach to emasculation. "Where do you think I'm from?"

His eyes narrowed but his face lit up in a playful smile like he thought I was flirting. "Sounds like England, maybe?" He waited expectantly but I shook my head and smirked. He looked confused when I didn't answer. "Close?"

"Not even."

"Of course. You're too hot to be British. Those girls are pale and have bad teeth. Well, where then?"

The blood rushed to my cheeks and I was tempted to defend every Brit I'd ever known, but it would be lost on Carlos. He was a real charmer alright. "The Land Down Under. You ever hear of it?"

"Get out. You are not Chinese." He chuckled toward Alex. "She doesn't look Asian does she?"

He was a moron and I didn't want to get any further into this dead-end conversation but I couldn't resist a snarky reply. "Strike two."

Alex looked embarrassed by his friend's stupidity. "I think she means Australia."

At least Alex had a neuron firing. "Bingo!"

Carlos chuckled like he'd known all along. "Oh, *that* Land Down Under. How long are you here?"

I looked up to the pretty blonde bartender with annoyed eyes as she set a plate of oysters in front of me before I answered him. "I'm leaving tomorrow." I'd hoped that lie would shut them up, but no such luck.

"Well, we should celebrate your last night!" Carlos called loudly after the bartender, who'd turned her back. "Can we get a round of lemon drops?"

I took a deep breath and looked away as I said, "No thanks,

I'm good." Girly shots with men who were pussies did not appeal.

Carlos muttered to his friend in Spanish, "*Que cabrona.*" He smiled and touched my hand on the bar. "Don't be silly. You should never turn down a free drink." He waved more emphatically at the bartender with the other hand. "Three doubles."

I eyed the bartender who was awaiting my response, then my gaze traveled to his hand before I jerked mine away. "No, thank you, really. I'm sticking with beer." I squeezed lemon onto an oyster and lifted it to my lips.

"You know, oysters are an aphrodisiac" Alex gleaned a flirty grin. "That can only be a good thing. Enjoy." Great, he was as much of a creep as his buddy.

"Thanks, I'll keep that in mind." I shifted to turn away from them as I sucked the first oyster from the shell.

Carlos ignored my rejection completely and repeated his order. "Three shots, beautiful. Doubles."

As much as I loved when Dante called me "beautiful", It flew all when Carlos said it—like he had some sort of claim on the bartender. I thought maybe I was overly sensitive, but she wasn't having it either. Her icy gaze leveled on him. "That sounded like a clear 'no' to me. Do you have a hard time hearing that word, Carlos?" She'd been listening closely enough to catch his name along with my refusal.

Carlos puffed out his chest. "I hear just fine. Did you hear my order?" He turned to mutter to Alex under his breath. "*Que puta.*"

"Oh, I heard you." She picked up a vodka bottle and started to fill a shaker. She poured three tall shots. "Have fun with that, you two."

Carlos pushed a shot toward me. "Go on. It's just a drink. Let's celebrate."

I took a deep breath, holding back the insults that came to mind, trying to be polite. "You make me want to celebrate leaving tomorrow. But I said no, thank you."

Carlos chuckled and handed Alex a shot. "*Idiota.*"

My cheeks burned with fury. "*No soy idiota, ni cabrona. Dejame en paz, por favor.*"

"*Ah, hablas español?*" Carlos seemed amused rather than deterred.

The bartender brushed her hair off her face before swiping Carlos' drink that wasn't quite empty from the bar and pouring it down the drain. "She speaks Asshole, too. Maybe you'll understand that better. Have your shots and move on, gentlemen. Find a new place to park or I'll get Jake to show you the curb." She nodded toward the broad-shouldered bouncer at the door.

Alex looked ashamed until Carlos punched his arm lightly. "Let's get out of here."

Alex threw back his shot. "You should finish those oysters. It might loosen you up a little. *Feliz noche.*"

"Good night to you, too." *And good riddance.* I rolled my eyes and turned on my stool to give them the cold shoulder. Why I responded at all was a mystery. But I was trained to deal with assholes like Carlos. It was part of the indoctrination as a a woman.

The bartender giggled after the jerks had gone. "The look on their faces when you spouted out whatever you said in Spanish was priceless." Her smile faded as her brow crinkled. "I'm sorry you had to put up with that, though. Some guys just don't get it."

I sighed. "Most guys don't get it in my experience." I shook a drop of hot sauce onto another oyster. The fuckwits nearly ruined my meal, but now that they were gone I could see why the oysters were held in such high acclaim. They lived up to the hype.

"Yeah, they're dumb. It's a y-chromosome trait." She cleared the abandoned shot glasses and handed me the one they hadn't touched. "You want that now that they're gone?"

"Sure." I puckered my lips after sipping down half the shot. "God that's sweet."

"It's a pussy drink. I guess they were hoping for pussy." She laughed before extending her hand. "I'm Jules."

Butterflies stirred in my stomach as her hand lingered. I don't know why, but I had a hard time holding her playful gaze. It had been a while since a girl made me feel that way. Since Lena. "I'm Trinity. Nice to meet you, Jules. Thanks for running them off. You didn't have to do that."

"You can clearly look after yourself. I just didn't want any trouble. And I didn't want to have to hear any more of it than I already had. They were dicks."

"Yeah, I'm done with dicks." My cheeks flushed as I willed myself to hold her gaze.

"I hear you." She smirked as she tucked the bar towel into her waistband, then poured herself a shot of *Corralejo* tequila. "Join me?"

I grinned. Offering me tequila definitely seemed like she was hitting on me. "If it's not sweet and citrusy, yes please."

Jules poured me a tall shot. "Guys like that will make you give up on men altogether."

I sucked down most of the shot, savoring the pungent burn that warmed my throat. "I've given up. I'm sticking to women." I wondered if I should have said it but if she was going to flirt I wanted to see where it might go. Maybe it was the oysters.

But she definitely had a spark.

"I've met a few that made me want to switch to the other team, too."

The other team? Apparently I'd read her all wrong. But for some reason I felt like opening up anyway. "I had one in Peru that did me in."

Her mousy scowl was adorable. "Peruvians are the worst! I dated one for six months—a total asshole in the end."

"Maybe he knew Diego. Sounds like they have a lot in common." I smiled before I finished my shot. At least she was on the anti-Peruvian-asshole team. I shook my head, worried that my gaydar was permanently damaged. Men had done that to me. Fucking men.

I scanned the room while Jules tended to other customers. The tequila was taking effect. I averted my eyes from two different men who seemed eager to catch my gaze. I needed to get the hell home before someone else tried to buy me another drink.

I stopped Jules as she hurried by. "I'm going to head out. I'll take the check when you have a second."

She smiled so sweetly that I doubted myself again. "It's on me. Have a safe trip home tomorrow."

I wanted to admit that I'd be around a few more days and I'd like to see her again, but that was just my pathetic loneliness coming out. A bitterness in my mouth made it hard to swallow. "Thanks. Take care, Jules."

I shoved a twenty in her tip jar when her back was turned before I headed for the door.

The wind had picked up. That could be good for waves. Hopefully the weather would be better than Slim had predicted.

The beer pong crowd had dwindled at the hostel with only the die-hards still standing. I smiled at the tattooed receptionist on my way past, but said nothing. I was in no mood to converse. Time to find my bed and dream about surfing.

CHAPTER 7

ARLOWE

*R*ain lashed against the store windows and it looked like dusk outside despite being midday. There was no point staying open on days like this, but Slim disagreed. He offered to come relieve me but I was already here. Besides, he had a wife to care for at home, and I still had inventory to finish. My mood was as gloomy as the weather when I heard the jingle of the shop door.

Trinity's smile brightened the room as she strode across the store holding her arms to her chest. When she got closer I saw the small white head of a kitten peeking out from her arms.

"Aww. Where'd he come from?"

"How do you know it's not a she?"

I shrugged. "It looks like a boy."

She held the drenched creature up to inspect its backside. "You might be right. It's too young to tell. I guess I just assumed that a dripping wet pussy would be female."

I nearly choked as I met Trinity's playful grin. She was a pistol. "I can't argue with that." I reached to scratch behind the kitten's tiny ear. "Poor little thing. Lucky it didn't drown. Rain's been coming down in buckets all morning."

Trinity kissed the cat's head softly before looking up. "It's like a bloody monsoon. I was waiting for it to let up all morning but I finally had to leave to get food. That's when I found this little thing in the gutter."

I patted the cat's head before wiping my hand on my shorts. "It's the outer bands of that storm out there. It'll pass."

"You think we'll be able to get out tomorrow?" She sounded hopeful.

"Not likely, but it depends on what the storm does. If it keeps moving north like they predict, Sunday should be good, at least."

"That's my last day to surf, so I fucking hope so."

"What do you plan to do with your dripping wet pussy in the meantime?" I couldn't resist.

Trinity's blue eyes fixed on mine, amused. "I thought maybe she could stay here."

That was a loaded comment. I wanted to say that her pussy was welcome here anytime, but that would be going too far.

"Oh, no. We can't have a cat. Slim's allergic." It was a lie but I thought it sounded like a good one.

Trinity held the cat closer to her chest with a worried look in her eyes. "Well, I can't take her back to the hostel. Can't she go home with you?"

I shook my head. "I definitely can't have a cat at home."

"Are you allergic too?" Her smart-assed grin faded as she looked back down at the kitten. "We can't put her back on the street."

I could be a dick when I wanted but I wasn't a heartless asshole. I sighed on my way to rummage through the gear room, emerging with a cardboard box and an old beach towel. "It can stay here tonight, but I'll have to take it to the pound tomorrow."

Trinity glowered like I'd suggested we dismember the kitten for fun. "That's horrible. You can't do that."

I held up my hands to defend the attack that seemed imminent. "I didn't pick up a kitten on the street. Don't make me the bad guy."

Her face twisted further into a scowl. "You'd have just left her there in the gutter?" Her accent made me smile despite her admonishing tone. She shook her head like she wasn't buying it but her taut lips relaxed. "You're too nice a guy for that."

At least she didn't think I was a monster. Although a nice guy probably wouldn't be eyeing her nipples through her wet shirt. I forced my eyes back up. "Don't worry, there's a no-kill shelter down the street. She'll be adopted in a day or two."

"So much for nice guy." She took the towel from the box, delicately rubbing the kitten to dry it. Trinity was crass, but she was a softie at heart.

Wishing I could rub her wet curls with the towel, despite my date with Monica tonight, only confirmed Trinity's assessment. "Yeah, I'm not that nice."

"Well, you were nice enough to take me surfing. But if you

insist on taking her to the shelter, I want to go." She looked down to the kitten in her arms.

"Please, come along. You'll see—she'll be taken care of there. And I'm sure they'll tell you the same thing I did. This little cutie won't have any trouble finding a home." I rubbed the cat's now-fluffy fur that was a patchwork of gray and orangish-beige splotches over white. I had to admit, it was cute. "By then we should know if we're going to be able to get out on the water for your last day."

"It would suck not to."

"I can't control the weather." I couldn't control anything. If I could, she wouldn't be leaving in a few days and I wouldn't have a date with Monica tonight. And there wouldn't be a stray kitten to worry about. "But I'm sure it will all work out."

Trinity blinked her long dark lashes, her eyes as blue as the sky had been yesterday. "I hope you're right. I'd hate for my travels to have a dreary end."

No matter how the weather behaved, the end of her travels was a dreary prospect indeed. "I'll put your request in with the guy upstairs." I glanced up toward the ceiling with a grin.

Trinity's gaze followed mine for a confused second before she realized I meant God. "If you have a direct line, I might have a few more requests."

"Oh yeah? What would you pray for?"

"I don't know, maybe that I wouldn't have to leave in a couple of days."

That made two of us, although probably for different

reasons. I wondered why she seemed reluctant to go home though. "I'd trade going to sunny Australia just before summertime for staying here for the winter."

"If I could send you in my place, I would. Mum wouldn't be pleased but she'd come around to the idea of an adopted man-child."

I chuckled. "I've been called that before but I'm pretty sure it was meant as an insult then." The last girl I'd have called a girlfriend definitely didn't mean it as a compliment when she said it during her angry break-up speech.

"Let me guess—she was jealous of surfing?"

I cocked my head and eyed Trinity while she lifted the kitten to her shoulder and nuzzled it with her chin, struck by her astute assessment. "Among other things."

She nodded knowingly. "Some people just don't get it."

"Most people, in my experience." Especially of the female persuasion. But Trinity understood my addiction to the sea because she suffered the same affliction.

"Yeah, well, fuck 'em." She kissed the cat's calico head while scratching behind its ear. "Right, kitty?" It purred like a motorboat before yawning an affirmative meow from her arms. Trinity's sweet smile at the kitten told me that taking it to the shelter tomorrow wouldn't be fun. It was hard to hold her tender gaze for the guilt that churned in my gut. Thankfully, she changed the subject. "So what's your plan for this rainy afternoon?"

"Catching up on work. I guess rainy days are a blessing sometimes. I can get shop work done without wishing I was out there." I glanced toward the storefront, the sidewalk barely visible through the sheets of water coming down in a persistent deluge.

"No one wants to be out there today, that's for sure. Anything I can help with?"

"That's sweet, but I wouldn't subject you to my private hell on one of your last days of vacation."

"I'm not doing fuck all else, and I'm happy to help. I could polish the rental boards if you like. I'm offering free labor. Use me!"

She wasn't trying to be cheeky but my dirty mind went straight to all the things I'd like to use her for—if she weren't off-limits and so young I'd feel like a creep. But I wasn't going to pass up the opportunity to hang out with her a little longer. "If you insist, I'll put you to work. But only on the condition that you let me buy you lunch."

Trinity's face lit up. "Deal. I'm famished. I tossed the soggy convenience-store breakfast sandwich I was trying to scarf when I found the cat."

She handed me the kitten while she folded the towel and placed it in the box. Catching my smile as it purred in my arms, Trinity grinned. "She's growing on you isn't she?"

I shook my head. "She's adorable, but no. No cats for me."

"I'm starting to think you have a pussy aversion."

I was starting to think her mind was as dirty as mine. Even if she wasn't flirting, the suggestive banter made me a little hard. "I don't have a problem with pussy. But a stray cat is a different story." I smiled and handed the feline over.

She kissed the kitten before placing it in its bed in the box then flashed a playful grin. "Maybe it's a commitment aversion then."

She'd hit another nail on the head. My eyes slanted but I couldn't help but smile. "You wouldn't be the first to say that either."

"I'm not surprised." She smirked as she wiped her hands on her shorts and scanned the room. "Where should I start?"

"Waxing boards sounds like a great place to start." I followed her into the back room. "You like pizza?"

She threw me a sideward glance with an exaggerated scowl. "What sort of question is that? Who doesn't like pizza?"

I grinned. "My kinda girl. You have a preference?"

"I'm easy. Surprise me." I tried to ignore the twitch in my cock that her comment had provoked while I scrolled to find Luigi's number.

Trinity laid out the board she'd borrowed on the work rack. "I'll start with your baby."

We worked for nearly three hours straight, breaking only once to inhale the pizza. The conversation flowed easily and always ended up back on the subject of surfing. I asked her to describe the best waves from back home, and it almost felt like I was riding them as she regaled me with details. I could picture her with the guys in that classic surf film Slim had shown me when I was a kid. They were living the dream—traveling from one wave to another along the western coast of Australia. I'd always wanted to be one of them. She already was.

"It sounds fucking amazing. It sounds like Paradise. So my

question is, why is it that you seem reluctant to return? I'm starting to think you have an aversion to real life."

She laughed but finished with a sigh. "That sounds highly plausible."

"I understand better than most."

"Maybe real life is overrated. I've loved being on the road. Even with a few hiccups along the way, it's been the best year-and-a-half of my life. It felt more like real life than my first year at uni, I'll tell you that. And *that's* what I'm going home to. It's a harsh reality after what feels like a whole other lifetime of freedom. *That's* what I'm not so sure about." Her blue eyes opened wide as she let out a tired-sounding huff. "Actually I'm pretty sure I'm dreading it miserably."

I studied her face for a second. She was serious. "Well, do you *have* to go back now? Why don't you just carry on working your way around the planet? There are worse plans."

"There most certainly are. But my parent's patience is running out. When the Peru thing finished, going back seemed like the logical thing."

Her explanation was a little cryptic, but she seemed to be grappling with her situation. I'd been pressured into decisions that were somebody else's idea of the "right thing" enough to empathize. "But now you're not so sure?"

The way she crinkled her nose before answering stirred something in my belly, or my groin, or both. "Not at all. But prolonging the inevitable seems—I don't know—immature."

"I've been called that a few times too." I chuckled. "But I'm a fan of prolonging pleasure and avoiding the not-so-pleasant."

She smirked. "Says the man in a hurry to get back into tech."

"Precisely, so that I can avoid the not-so-pleasurable aspects of my current situation."

"By replacing them with other not-so-pleasurable experiences." She nodded, pretending to understand with sarcastic exaggeration. "Got it."

Her sassiness was a bigger turn on than I wanted to admit. Especially since I had to meet Monica in less than an hour. "A change might be nice."

"But you worked in tech before and left it to come run a surf shop."

"And now I can have both—the best of all worlds."

"I don't know, I wouldn't trade this for being parked behind a laptop." She looked down at the board that she was putting the finishing touches on. "I'd even call it *pleasurable*. But you do you."

I chuckled. She had a good point. I had started to doubt my decision as soon as I sent out the first round of resumes. Even the mundane tasks were better than staring at a computer screen, especially in present company. "We'll see how it turns out. If I hate it, I'll quit." That approach had worked for me so far. "And if you want to prolong this pleasurable experience—and the dreaded inevitable return home—I'll give you a job. No joke. You're a hard worker, and know your way around a surf shop. You can start next week." Her narrowed eyes studied mine but I was sure she could tell that I was serious as a heart attack.

She let out a resigned breath. "I wish, but my parents would kill me."

"What are they going to do? Disown you?"

"Not support me financially when I do decide to go back to uni."

"You've been supporting yourself for over a year though. It seems like you have that part figured out. You're smart. You'll be fine."

"Well, thank you, Arlowe, for saying that." She seemed genuinely grateful for the acknowledgement. "You're right. I can take care of myself. But I'm an only child and they really want me to come home. I've stayed months longer than I'd planned. I feel like I *have* to go back sooner than later. Might as well be now. It's all set."

"Boy do I know how that feels. All the expectations land on the only child."

"You don't have any siblings either?"

"Actually, I have two sisters—in Chicago. But we didn't grow up together. They didn't actually know I existed until maybe seven months ago."

"What!? That's mental! How did that happen?"

"DNA registry. I did one several years back for fun, so my sister Kate discovered me when she did one last year. My father's short marriage to her mother ended badly. She cut my father off from them completely and he eventually lost track of her after several moves. It was sad, really. I knew they were out there somewhere but it never seemed real— until it was."

Trinity's jaw hung open while she blinked three times, staring at me in awe. "Wow. Meeting them must have been intense."

"Yeah. Kate came to visit us here first. Sally was pregnant at the time, and she wasn't really ready to meet my dad back then. She's older so she was more resentful."

Trinity rubbed her eyes. "Fuck, that's a load to process."

"It still is. Dad and I went to Chicago a few weeks ago to meet Sally and baby Asher." My lips turned up while uttering my nephew's name. He was a cute little bugger.

"Aw, it's as nice a proper name as it is a surname. I like that."

"Sweet, isn't it?" A buzzing vibration in my pocket interrupted my bliss. I was surprised to see the time when I pulled my phone out to glimpse the message from Monica. She was on her way to the restaurant. Fuck. I had to close up and get going. I'd lost track of time talking about babies and the meaning of life. I'd enjoyed it so much that I resented having to cut our time short.

I handed Trinity my phone. "Put your digits in there so I can touch base tomorrow about the conditions. Hopefully we'll get back out there before you go." A pang of dread stabbed me in the gut at the thought of her leaving and that I had to leave her now. "Sorry to kick you out, but I've got to run."

"Oh, of course. I didn't mean to keep you. I suppose it is getting late." She glanced out the window into the grainy darkness of dusk. "It's hard to tell. It's been grey all day."

"Hopefully tomorrow will be better." I grabbed my keys from under the register.

"I trust that you'll put in that urgent request with the one who controls the weather."

"I'm not sure he'll hear since I don't talk to him often, but I'm happy to ask on your behalf." A not-so-small part of me hoped her request for the Big Guy to keep her from going home would be granted as well.

Trinity leaned over to whisper into the fur behind the kitten's neck. "Sleep well. I'll keep working on him for you."

"Don't go getting the cat's hopes up. It's not staying." Neither of them was, but false hope was better than none at all.

CHAPTER 8

TRINITY

*T*he rain had let up enough to walk back to the hostel, but the weather sucked. After the shark feeding frenzy in the bar last night, going out on a Friday night held little appeal. I was in no mood to fend off another lecherous Latino. I wasn't in the mood for much of anything. I was feeling homesick again, but not for Australia. I was missing Lena and Dante.

I climbed up onto my bunk and slumped back into my pillow. I should've never left Antigua. Then I would have never met Diego. The three-way relationship with Lena and Dante might have resulted in the same broken heart if I hadn't left while it was still good, but it couldn't have been this ugly. At least what I had with them was real. My chest tightened with the familiar ache in my heart.

I'd put off calling long enough, and I needed a friend.

I could hear Lena smiling when she answered on the second ring. "Trinity! How are you, beautiful?"

"Hiya, gorgeous. I'm alright. But how are you?"

"Feeling like a cow and getting bigger by the minute."

Picturing Lena pregnant made me smile. "Rubbish. I'm sure you're stunning. Are you still feeling well?"

"Fortunately, yes. The second trimester has been a breeze compared to the first. I feel great, to be honest."

"That's fabulous news. I'm so happy for you guys."

"Thank you. I wish you were here though."

My chest constricted with the lump that formed in my throat. I answered shakily. "I do, too." More than she knew. "How's Dante?"

"He's great. I swear he's so excited about the baby that I have to wonder if he knocked me up on purpose."

A flutter in my stomach made me forget about Diego for a moment. "You guys are going to be great parents."

"I hope you're right. It's a lot of responsibility." Her voice quivered slightly.

"Nothing you can't handle, love. You aren't getting worried are you?"

I could picture her biting her lip as she paused. "Maybe a little. It's kind of scary to have a baby in Guatemala."

After seeing the dark side of the country, I didn't blame her. Hiding out from would-be kidnappers after they'd shown up at our front door had traumatized us both. But she didn't need to hear that.

"At least in Guatemala you have Maria. I bet she can't wait to get her hands on that baby." A full time housekeeper would make having a newborn easier. "And Miriam, too. She must be over the moon." I could tell

Dante's mother liked Lena from the start. It was one of the reasons I'd thought it was a good time to leave Antigua when I did.

I could hear Lena brighten when she answered. "It seems like she plans to be a very involved grandmother."

"Ah. A bit pushy, is she?"

"No, not really pushy. Especially since we made loose plans for a wedding."

"A wedding?" I grinned. My malaise faded with her news. "That's wonderful, love! Did you set a date?"

"Not yet. But we announced our plan to tie the knot when my mom was here a couple of weeks ago. We're thinking six months after the baby comes. Maybe by then I won't be too fat to fit in a nice dress."

"Oh, hush. You're not fat."

She chuckled. "You haven't seen me."

Her laughter made me miss her sweet smile. "True. It's been too long. How was it with your mum? How's she taking your decision to stay in Guatemala?"

"She would much rather I go home, but she loves Dante, of course."

"What's not to love?" That was the truth. For both of them. Which is why I missed them both so much.

Like she read my mind, Lena's voice lowered as she suggested, "Maybe you can come up for a visit before the baby comes? Surely you could squeeze in a quick trip between your surfing adventures. How is that all going, by the way? Sorry I've babbled about myself the whole time.

How is Peru? And the boyfriend? Are you still madly in love?"

The empty hole in my heart opened back up. "Mad, yes. In love, no."

There was a short pause before I heard her suck in a deep breath. "Oh. What happened?"

I didn't want to tell the story, but it poured from me in a torrent of words swallowed up by sobs. I took a deep breath to regain composure after I'd given her the synopsis of Diego's deception. "So, I left Peru a few days ago."

"You left?" Her voice strained with shock and concern. "Where are you now?"

"Florida. I'm on my way home. I fly out Monday."

"Home?" Her voice trembled in disappointment. "You're heading back to Australia *now*?"

"Yeah…well, Monday." I bit my lower lip, doubting my decision.

Lena tried to sound chipper. "I guess it's good that you're going home. At least you have your family and friends. I'm so sorry you're going through this, Trinity. What a fucking asshole."

The ache in my chest felt like a stake twisting through my heart. "Of the worst sort. But you live and learn."

Lena chuckled. "Hopefully we actually learn."

I rubbed my runny nose as I laughed. "Hopefully we actually live! That's the fun part." Trouble is, jumping into fun feet first can get you in over your head. Sometimes we have to learn the hard way.

"That's my Trin. God I miss you. I can't believe I won't see you before I'm a mom."

"I promise I'll do my best to make it back for the wedding. That should give me time to save up for another trip." I was already planning my next escape.

"You must be excited to get back to Australia, though. Right?"

"At first I couldn't wait to get back home. But now that it's happening, I'm kind of dreading it, to be honest. Going back to reality hit me these past couple of days. I'm not sure I'm ready for it."

"Maybe you should come back here for a while first and get yourself sorted."

"That could take years." I laughed to keep myself from crying again. I wanted to go back to Antigua, or stay here, or go anywhere but home. "I'd love to go back, but my parents would kill me."

"I only know what you've told me, but I'd bet that your parents wouldn't be too surprised if you change your plans again. They will support you no matter what."

"I'm not so sure about that."

"If my mama can accept that I'm getting married and having a baby in Guatemala, your parents will get over you coming back to Guatemala for a few months. Come now and stay until after the baby comes. Or longer—as long as you want."

Her offer was sincere, but things were different now. They were a family. And it was beautiful, something I didn't want to disrupt. I couldn't go back there. But the way her thoughts mirrored Arlowe's offer tugged at my mind. "The surf shop owner said the same thing about my parents today, after he offered me a job."

"A job? In the surf shop? You should do it! Oh my god, Trinity, that sounds perfect."

I chuckled. "A perfect way to prolong the inevitable."

"Well, if you aren't ready to go home, it's inevitable that you'll wish you hadn't. School, and everything else that you're going back to, will be right there waiting for you when you're ready."

I might not ever be ready to go back to all that. The thought of it made my stomach knot. "That stuff isn't going anywhere —that's for sure. But, then again, am I? I'm just wandering."

"Are you kidding me? You're going—everywhere. But you have to follow your heart. If it's taking you home, follow it."

My heart was a broken compass leading me in circles. "I can't hear my heart right now."

Empathy oozed from her voice. "Then you need to get quiet and listen. What did you tell me after Chase was gone and I was free but didn't know what to do? You said the world was my canvas and that I'd know which colors to paint when it was time."

I chuckled. "I can be wise when it's someone else's problem. Thanks for that. It's a good reminder."

"That's what friends are for. You know I'm here for you, don't you? Always."

I'd never have another friend like Lena. I'd never loved anyone so much. "I do know. And you know it's mutual. I'm here—wherever I end up—I'm here for you, too."

"Where are you exactly? You just said Florida. Surfing, I presume?"

"Yeah, I promised an old friend I'd come check out his old stomping ground. I'm in Jupiter."

"Fuck, I lived in Pompano, half an hour down the coast."

"That's where Chase lives?" The thought of him so close made my skin crawl. I'd never met the man who'd made our lives hell and scared the piss out of me while he'd hunted Lena down like an escaped pet, but I hated him just the same.

"Yeah, but don't worry. We haven't heard a peep from him. Dante has people watching him in Pompano. He has a new girlfriend. I think he's moved on."

I giggled. "If only he could see your belly he'd see how far you've moved on."

"I hope he never does."

"He won't. But I sure wish I could. Send me a pic of that pregnant belly in all its glory."

"Ugh. You might be shocked. But I will after dinner. Speaking of which—I should go. Dante has steaks on the grill."

"*Parilla*?" I loved our backyard barbecues. I missed them.

"Thank God he likes to grill. I can't be bothered cooking— something else I miss about having you around."

"My cooking isn't much more than avocado toast and eggs. You know that."

"I love that. And you. I miss you, Trin. Send me a pic, too. And keep me posted. Follow your heart."

"I'll let you know if it sends me any coordinates. Kiss Dante for me. And pat your belly to tell the baby hello from Aunt Trin. Are you guys ever going to find out the gender?"

"Nope! We want it to be a surprise."

"Wasn't having a baby surprise enough?" I grinned, wishing she wasn't so far away while we said goodbye. "I could never wait, so I admire your restraint."

"It will make it more fun. I learned that from you."

"I'm sure you're not referring to restraint, of which I generally have none."

"Sometimes restraint is more fun. Sometimes lack thereof is the better choice. You taught me to measure life in terms of fun."

If that was the impact I had on Lena's life, I'd succeeded. "What else can you measure by?"

"You tell me."

I stared at the phone for several seconds after the screen went black. What else was there but fun? The fun of surfing and even waxing boards with Arlowe in the shop was the light that had drawn me from the darkness of what Diego had done. I was not broken if I could still experience joy. But I was too broken to admit that part of the temptation to stay was to see how much more fun I could have with Arlowe.

CHAPTER 9

*T*wenty minutes late and I was in a rush, but not because I was excited to see Monica. Five dates in and the downward trajectory was already obvious. I'd consider ending it, but in my experience, women take it better when it's their idea. Otherwise they tend to make life a living hell. Needless to say, the prospects for a fun evening were as gloomy as the weather.

Monica waited at a table for two by the window, in a sexy low cut blouse that invited appreciation—while all I could muster was a vague sense of regret. She fixed me with a stiff smile. "Hey you. It's been a minute." She fondled the bottom of her Chardonnay glass like it might somehow sooth her mood. But it clearly wasn't helping.

"Sorry I'm late. I lost track of time at the shop."

"Oh yeah? What was so consuming in the shop? I figured it would be dead with this weather."

"It was. But that's why I lost track of time. I got busy with projects. The afternoon flew by until I got your text. Oh, and

I have a tiny kitten sleeping in a cardboard box in the shop." I hoped the mention of a kitten might lighten the mood.

But Monica's mouth twisted in a grimace. "A cat? Where'd you get a cat?"

"A customer brought it in. She found it in the gutter, but she's a tourist so she pawned it off on me. I'll take it to the shelter tomorrow, so someone who actually wants a cat can adopt it."

"Good. The last thing you need is a pet."

The hairs on the back of my neck stood at her display of entitlement. A few dates and she already thought she knew what was best for me? Nuh uh. Even if, in this case, she was right. But I didn't want to argue. "It's cute, though."

"Cute until it pees in your closet. I'm glad you're getting rid of it."

I'd better change the subject before I agreed that cute wasn't enough of a reason to keep something around. "How was Orlando?"

"Good. I mean, it was work, but good. Speaking of work, did you ever hear back on the resumes you sent out last week?"

My shoulders stiffened at the thought. "No, nothing yet."

"It's only been a week, but if you don't hear by Monday you should call to follow up." She finished her Chardonnay with a large sip and signaled for the waiter. "Should we get a bottle?"

I didn't want to be there that long, especially if her unsolicited advice was going to continue flowing freely. "I'll just have a beer. You ready to order food?"

"Sure." She picked up the menu. "Anything but pizza." Her nose scrunched into a scowl.

"You don't like pizza?" Not that I wanted it twice in one day, but still—who doesn't like pizza?

"No. It's too greasy."

"That's what makes it so good."

"Different strokes. But you should think about eating healthier. You're not in college anymore."

I wanted to tell her she should worry about herself, but I didn't want to start a fight, especially before I got some food down. "You choose, then."

The salad and Portobello Parmesan weren't half bad, even though vegetarian wouldn't have been my choice. I didn't really care by that point.

The rain rolled down the window in a steady stream. It wasn't letting up. The small talk while we ate felt awkward and boring and after-dinner options didn't look much better "It's still shitty out. We might have to call it an early night."

"That's fine by me. We can go back to my place and watch a movie." Her brows lifted suggestively.

Netflix and chill sounded like the perfect plan for these conditions, but I wasn't feeling it. I didn't see a way out, though, not without sounding like a total asshole. I briefly considered feigning illness but that would be a dick move, and hardly believable. But maybe I could plant a seed. "Sure, I can go for a little while. I'm pretty beat and have a busy day with Slim tomorrow."

Monica laughed dryly. "I won't try to keep you all night."

She hadn't responded well the last time I'd avoided spending the night.

I paid the check. At the restaurant entrance, we found ourselves huddled beneath the awning, not willing just yet to get caught in the downpour. Monica pulled me by my collar into a peck of a kiss. "See you at my place." We counted down from three, then sprinted in opposite directions for our cars.

For the two mile drive to her apartment, I tried to psyche myself up for some sexy time with Monica. How fucked up was that? Sure, we'd had good sex on our last three dates. Her amazing body and her desire to please made it fun. So why was I almost dreading this sure thing? Maybe because she was bitchy. And she didn't like pizza. Her amazing cleavage couldn't erase the tarnish of those flaws. But once my face was buried in it, surely I'd be inspired.

Monica opened a bottle of wine and carried two glasses over to the coffee table. "I don't have any beer to offer you. You'll have to settle for wine, I'm afraid."

Settling for anything didn't sound appealing, but I was along for the ride. "No problem. I'm easy." I took the glass and held it up to tap the rim of hers before taking a sip. "Did you have something in mind to watch?"

"If you want an early night, I'm happy to skip the Netflix and move straight to the chill." She took a long sip of wine before setting her glass on the table. Her hand ran up the inside of my thigh as she bit her lip and smiled. "I've missed you."

"Thanks. I've missed you, too." I wondered if I sounded as insincere as I felt. I shifted as she settled in under my arm and her lips found my neck. "There's an incentive trip to Key West in a couple of months that I'm on target to hit. So if you play your cards right, you can be my date."

The offer of a free trip to Key West would normally give me a hard on in itself, but even her kissing my neck and rubbing my thigh was getting no response in that department. The chances of me being around to make that trip with her in two months were pretty slim. "I love the Keys. Did I tell you my sister is getting married down there at Christmas?"

Monica sat up straight and pulled away to stare at me suspiciously. "You have a sister? I thought you were an only child."

Fuck. I hadn't even told her about Kate and Sally? I guess we hadn't spent that much time talking. Monica had a brother in Naples and had mentioned on our last date that we should have dinner with her parents when he came to visit in a few weeks so I could meet the family. I'd changed the subject. That was a milestone I'd learned to avoid. But I was embarrassed that I hadn't told her about my sisters. "Well, I was always an only child. I have two sisters from my dad's first marriage. I barely know them." I didn't feel like telling the whole story, and hearing it now would probably just piss her off that I hadn't told her before.

"Ah, okay. At least you're invited to the wedding. Christmas in the Keys sounds like Paradise. Maybe I'll be your date, if you play your cards right." She grinned wryly. "Two trips to the Keys sounds like double the fun."

She leaned in to kiss my neck again, her hand so high on my thigh that the edge pressed into my crotch. I let my head fall back onto the sofa and tried to relax into her kisses, but I was distracted by the lack of activity in my shorts. Not even the slightest tingle of excitement stirred.

She kissed a trail up my neck to my ear and then over to my lips. I leaned forward to set my glass on the table and ran my fingers into her silky hair. She gasped as I pulled her mouth hard onto mine. She liked it a little rough. That had been a big turn on from the start. But my groans were forced as I pretended to devour her, hoping that faking it would wake up my dormant desire. Still nothing.

Zip. Zero. Zilch.

I grazed her breast before slipping my fingers under the lace of her bra. But even with her nipple between my fingertips, I remained flaccid as she stroked me through my shorts. I squeezed her breast hard and bit at her lower lip, like I knew she liked it. Moans escaped her lips onto mine as she rubbed me harder.

She squeezed my cock before she pulled away from the kiss to unbutton my shorts. My first instinct was to protest so that she wouldn't see the sad state of my lack of erection, but she had my soft shaft in her fist and her mouth over mine again before I could think of a way out of it. Thankfully my body seemed to be waking up a little. But after several enthusiastic tugs, Monica stopped kissing me and eyed me curiously as she continued to pull on my lazy cock. "Are you feeling alright?"

She'd served me a segue on a platter. It didn't seem like any amount of stimulation was going to ignite my desire. I'd never not been able to get it up. Ever. I didn't have to fake it. Something must actually be wrong with me. "To be honest, I'm not feeling great. I think something didn't agree with me tonight."

"That's weird, we shared the same food."

"Yeah, I don't know. It's weird. But something's not right." That much was true.

"Aw. I'm sorry. Maybe I can make you feel better." She stroked my cock with a mischievous look in her eye and started to bend over but I stopped her with a hand on her shoulder.

"You know I love that. But I think it's better left for next time. Sorry, I was afraid I might be too tired."

Monica rested her head on my shoulder and released her grip, sliding her hand up to my chest. "If you're turning down a blow job, you must be sick. Or crazy."

"I might be both right now." I kissed her temple with a tinge of guilt. "I probably should get going so I can get some rest."

Monica didn't try to hide her disappointment. "Yeah, you probably should."

She walked me to the door and gave me a terse peck on the lips. "Call me when you're feeling better."

That hadn't gone well at all—worse than I expected. I'd hardly given Monica a second thought for the past few days, and she had already started to annoy me before that. But the extent of my apathy had me perplexed. My failure to perform worried me a little. Even if I wasn't *that* into a girl I could usually fake it for sex. And I *was* into Monica. Was.

I slid into my Jeep, and wondered what Trinity was doing as I turned the key. My cock pushed into the back of my zipper, half-hard in an instant at just the slightest thought. So, it was a software problem. The hardware was fine. But I didn't need an Aussie nymph on my mind. She was too young. She was practically a teenager, for Christ's sake. And Slim made it clear that she's off limits. She was leaving in a couple of days anyway. These are the things I told myself to help me resist the urge to call her.

Even if Trinity wasn't a real possibility, she'd made me rethink my strategy of dating the wrong women. I liked keeping my worlds separate. And picking girls that didn't like what I like, or do what I do, helped. But what I liked about Trinity was that she was into the same stuff as me. Maybe that's why talking to her was so easy. Hell, she already knew me better than Monica did. I shuddered that I hadn't even told Monica about Kate and Sally. What had we even talked about on those first four dates? Not a lot. Her work, mostly. And how she thought I should get back into tech. I rolled my eyes as I pulled up to the curb outside my apartment. No wonder I'd lost interest so quickly. I could barely remember ever having any interest at all.

I settled onto the couch with a beer and Googled until found the name of that film Trinity had reminded me of. *Morning of the Earth.* It was on Prime, for a price, of course. Nothing I ever wanted to watch was free on Prime. I groaned as I clicked the *Purchase* icon. Maybe it would quench my Aussie thirst.

CHAPTER 10

A dim light peeped through the curtains, providing scant illumination for the darkened dorm. I checked my phone. Half past eight already and no sign of the morning sun. I considered stalking over to the window to get a better look, but didn't want to disturb a roomful of surfers finally catching up on some sleep.

The rain had kept most of them in all night, so the party in the lobby went late. I estimated most of them went to bed between two and three. Drunk people cannot be quiet. It's impossible. But the funny thing is that they think they *are* being quiet. Loud whispers and fits of giggling as they stumbled around in the dark. I couldn't be angry. I'd been one of them many times. There were things about backpacking that I wouldn't miss. Hostel life was one of them. I grabbed my toiletries bag and tiptoed into the shower.

Coaxing the last drops from my travel-sized shampoo, I cursed that it wasn't nearly enough to wash my mop of wiry hair, and I still had two days till my flight. I'd have to hit the drug store on the way to the surf shop. By the dreariness of what little I'd seen so far of the day, the chances of surfing today were low. At least a trip to the store was something to do after I checked in with Arlowe and checked on the cat.

Shit! The cat. Arlowe was taking her to the pound today. I'd nearly forgotten. I doubted Arlowe would take her before I got there, but I should probably hurry.

After a hasty shower, I threw on some sweats and slinked back into the dorm to put my toiletries away before bounding down the stairs. The cute receptionist gave me a friendly wink.

"It's raining again?" I said, getting a clear view of the weather through the open lobby windows.

"You mean it's *still* raining. It hasn't stopped. Although it seems to be letting up. Get out while you can!"

"Fuck. What is happening with this weather?"

"Florida. If you don't like the weather, just stick around. It changes from one minute to the next."

Unfortunately I wasn't sticking around much longer. Tomorrow was going to be my last chance to surf. "Is it supposed to get better?"

"Who knows. It seems a great mystery even to the weathermen. They get it wrong half the time, even with surfing conditions, which is all I pay much attention to be honest. I figure if there's a hurricane coming, I'll hear. And we're pretty much out of the woods for that. Tomorrow will probably be sunny and flat calm. That's Florida."

Flat calm wasn't ideal for surf either but anything was better than torrential rain. "I hope you're right." At least we had a momentary reprieve now. "I'm going to brave the elements—while I can." I winked with a grin as I turned on my heel. "See you later."

I caught a little twinkle in her eye as she grinned back. "Try to stay dry. I'll be here till five."

Was that a come-on? After my encounter with Jules at the oyster bar, I wasn't so sure. I wasn't so sure about much of anything.

The walk through the light drizzle was almost pleasant in the crisp morning air. The gutter where I'd found the kitten was dry by comparison to the rushing river it had been yesterday. I hoped she hadn't been scared all night in the shop alone. At least she was dry. I smoothed my frizzy curls as I approached the shop. Washing my hair had been a wasted effort.

I swung the door open and bounced in, stopping short when Slim's wide eyes looked up from behind the counter, his lips curling into a grin. "Trinity! I thought you might have left ahead of this dreadful weather."

"You did warn me it might turn south. But I didn't expect days of rain."

Arlowe smiled as he emerged from the back room. "No one expected this storm to stall over the Bahamas—but it did."

"If it's over the Bahamas, why is it so bad here? It must be a big fucking storm."

Arlowe nodded. "It's a big fucking storm that's getting bigger by the minute, strengthening over the warm water."

Slim's brow flattened as he interjected, "They expect it to be a Cat 1 by noon."

"A hurricane?!" I was surprised to hear my voice climb an octave. How were they so relaxed if a hurricane was coming?

"Don't worry, it's still far offshore and heading north. Or it was before it stalled. They don't expect it to hit us, but we're in for a lot more rain."

Surfing was out tomorrow. I slumped onto my elbow on the counter. "There goes my plan." A rainy end to my trip seemed appropriate. But the mention of a Category 1 hurricane nearby reminded me of the cat and kept me from feeling sorry for myself. "Where's the kitty?"

"It's in the box. I put a clean towel in." He waved me back as he turned toward the equipment room. "We need to get a litter box."

"Why? Surely they'll have that at the shelter. Or did you reconsider keeping her?" I blinked hopefully as I lifted the kitten from the box.

Arlowe's brow crinkled. "Maybe it's a him. And, no, I have not reconsidered. But the shelter is closed to new entries during the storm. I called a few minutes ago. So it's staying for another day or two."

"Something is something." I nuzzled into the kitten's velvety neck. "We'll take it."

"Indeed. And as for your plans, this storm might turn them upside down. Slim said that flights are cancelling left and right. You should check your flight. You might not be going anywhere for at least a couple of days either."

I rested the kitten on my shoulder as we headed back into the shop. Keeping her company wouldn't be the worst thing in the world, but I was anxious at the prospect of my travel plans being waylaid. What a fucking hassle. "That wouldn't be horrible. But dealing with a cancelled flight might be."

Slim's ears perked up as he cocked his head. "When's your flight?"

"Day after tomorrow."

A faint wince passed over Slim's face before it softened into a smile. "Oh, I doubt you're going anywhere, darlin'. There's craziness at M-I-A already."

"Great." I balanced the cat against my neck with one hand while I fished my phone from my back pocket with the other. I clicked on the Qantas icon to open the app and went into My Trips on the menu. It took a second for the red letters to register. DELAYED. But the departure time was dashes instead of numbers. At least it didn't say CANCELLED.

"You checking your flight?" Arlowe stared expectantly as I blinked up from my phone.

"Yeah. It says it's delayed but it looks like it hasn't been rescheduled yet." I turned the screen to show him.

He studied the screen as he took the phone from my hand. "You should call later if it's not updated. But you're definitely not leaving when you thought you were."

My heart beat faster but I felt a wave of relief. If the hurricane offshore had me stuck, my parents couldn't be angry. An act of God was certainly beyond my control. "I guess you're right." But I couldn't handle more than a couple more nights in the hostel. Close quarters with dozens of rowdy surfers was already old. I still had a little money leftover. I could spring for an Airbnb. I took my phone back from Arlowe. "In that case, I'm going to look for a private room. Maybe I can find one that will let me bring the cat."

Arlowe's brow raised. "Careful not to get too attached."

I blinked up at him. "I know, but she'll be lonely here in the shop."

"Yeah, you can take it home, Arlowe. That way it won't be lonely," chided Slim as he threw Arlowe a glance that said he'd be happy to get the cat out of the shop.

Arlowe chuckled. "Thanks, but the cat will be fine here." Then his face lit up like he had an idea and his mouth twisted into a grin. "Unless you both want to move into my spare room for a few days."

I chuckled to myself at the irony. Dante offering up a room in his house in Antigua had changed everything. "You have a guest room?"

"I do. Two bedrooms, but you'd have to share a bath with me."

I knew that Americans called the loo a bathroom even if it wasn't where you actually bathe, but it still sounded funny enough to be a good point of ribbing. "I have to share a bath with you to secure the kitty a home? That sounds like blackmail. Or extortion. Or something sinister."

"Coercion?" His playful smile made me grin.

"That's it! Not fair." I cocked my brow. "I won't bathe with you, but keep talking. What do you charge to rent the room?"

His brow crinkled in confusion. "Charge? I wouldn't charge you."

Slim cleared his throat. "I wouldn't let him. Max is family, and by extension, so are you. Arlowe has plenty of space. Take him up on it."

"I suppose you want to get the cat out of the shop." I pulled away to distance the fur ball on my shoulder from Slim. "Has she made your allergies act up yet?"

"Allergies? I'm not allergic to anything. We didn't have allergies when I grew up. Or gluten intolerance." He laughed at his own joke. "But I wouldn't mind getting the cat out of here." He looked apathetic as he eyed the cat.

I giggled but threw Arlowe a narrow-eyed glance before I smiled back at Slim. "I don't know where I got that idea." My gaze flitted back to Arlowe. "But if you'll take us both, I'd be happy to stay at your house." A free private room? Yes, please. An excuse not to go home yet? Hell fucking yes. So long as Arlowe didn't get any ideas.

That's what I told myself, yet there was a fluttering in my stomach when he said, "Nothing would make me happier than to have you both." Dante had said something similar when he invited me and Lena to stay. My thoughts drifted to what had happened later. Whose idea had that been?

Slim's baritone voice snapped me back to reality. "So it's settled. You'll take the cat to Arlowe's."

"It's only for a few days, hopefully it won't be too much trouble."

Arlowe hurried to answer. "It's no trouble at all. Do you want to get your stuff now? I need to run a few errands. I could take you."

"Oh, um, yeah." I hadn't expected to move in this very second, but it was early enough to check out and not pay for the day in the hostel if I could charm the clerk into letting me cut my reservation short without penalty. "That would be amazing."

85

Slim stepped close to Arlowe so he could elbow him in the ribs before putting his arm around his shoulder. "We'll see what you say after a couple of days with this guy."

"Will you stop? She's going to start believing I'm the creep you make me out to be."

Part of me hoped he was, but I didn't think that Arlowe was any kind of creep.

CHAPTER 11

ARLOWE

While Trinity showered, I boiled water for pasta —the only thing in my cupboard for dinner. I still couldn't believe she'd said yes to staying. Monica would be furious if she found out.

Trinity smiled and ran a towel through her damp curls as she stepped around me to get to the fridge. Her jersey shorts clung to her hips while her T-shirt fell loosely from the perky little breasts underneath. An electric jolt surged through me as her butt brushed against mine as she leaned into the fridge. "You want a beer?"

I chuckled. "Sure. And, by all means, make yourself at home."

"Sorry, was that presumptuous?" Trinity grinned as she handed me a beer and tapped the refrigerator door with her foot to close it.

I took a swig from the beer before answering. "Of course not. I mean it. Make yourself at home." I tipped the neck of my bottle toward her. "How was your shower?"

She held the bottle between her hands after taking a long pull. "Heavenly. You don't know the joy of not having to wear thongs in the shower."

I knew she meant flip flops, but the image that her choice of words conjured made me smile. I pretended I was thinking about shower shoes, too, and *not* sexy underwear. "You don't know how long it's been since I've scrubbed that shower."

"Well, it's a million times better than any communal shower I've encountered, and I've seen a few. Bonus that I didn't have to buy shampoo. I should have known you'd have nice hair products." She smirked before taking another drink.

"Are you making fun after enjoying my fancy shampoo and conditioner?"

"Not at all. I'm glad you care so much about your hair. My shampoo seriously finished this morning."

The nice shampoo came from an ex-girlfriend's salon. I didn't give a shit about my hair. But Trinity didn't need to know any of that. "I'm glad you enjoyed. And I hope you like pasta with pesto, because that's all I've got."

"My favorite."

I quirked a skeptical brow. "Yeah? I like to add chicken or shrimp or something, but I need food. Maybe tomorrow we can shop for us." I nodded toward the kitten, chowing down on the canned food Trinity'd picked up on the way home.

Trinity carried her beer to the couch while I dumped the steaming pasta from the strainer back into the pot. "Do you like extra parmesan?" I scooped the green sauce from a jar into the noodles.

She rolled her eyes. "Is that even a question?"

We ate in front of the television while watching the weather channel. The storm was getting stronger. "You made the right call coming here. It may be worse than I thought."

"Definitely the right call. I was so done with the hostel."

I handed Trinity the remote as my phone buzzed on the coffee table. I figured it was Slim calling to tell me we needed to put plywood over the storefront, but it was Monica. I turned the phone face down and let it ring. A few seconds later, she texted. *Hurricane party tomorrow? My place or yours?*

I answered quickly. *Sorry can't talk right now. I'll be tied up at the shop tomorrow.*

She texted back immediately. I read it with the bitchy tone I was sure she intended. *Until when?*

Not sure. I'll let you know.

I grinned when I looked up at the television. Trinity had figured out the remote without assistance was impressive, but that she'd cued up *Morning of the Earth* was astounding. My stomach fluttered as she blinked up at me expectantly. "Have you seen this?"

"Once or twice." I chuckled.

I stopped myself from putting my arm behind her on the sofa, but the heat of her body where our knee were touching skin-to-skin sent a pulse up my leg all the way to my cock. I kept my eyes on the movie but had to conjure up thoughts of golf to try to keep my erection at bay.

The kitten looked minuscule meowing from the spare bedroom doorway as the final credits rolled. Trinity smiled as she cooed, "Did you decide to wake up now that it's my bedtime?" She looked up at me. "I hope she doesn't keep me up all night."

"You can sleep in if you like. I have to get an early start tomorrow. Let's see what this storm does overnight."

"Hopefully it goes away."

"Well, right now it's not going anywhere. That's the problem. Let's see."

"*Vamos a ver.*" Her accent was even sexier when she spoke Spanish.

I winked with a grin. "*Si, señorita.*"

She scooped up the kitten as she stood. "*Buenas noches.* I'll get up early so I can tag along. See you in the morning."

That she was joining me tomorrow sweetened the bitterness of watching her walk away to go to bed alone.

Slim already had two plywood sheets out front when we got to the shop. By now everyone knew that the storm was nearly a hurricane. Most computer models had it drifting east, but a couple of them had us in the middle of its projected path. I patted his back. "Preparing for the worst?"

"That's the best insurance that it won't come anywhere near us." He was right. How many times had we boarded up for nothing? "And if it does, we'll be ready." He grinned at Trinity. "Thanks for coming to help."

"It's the least I can do." She smiled. "Tell me what you need."

Trinity worked as hard as we did under the mist of light rain all morning to get all the windows covered. She stood back and stared at the wood-clad storefront. "Isn't this overkill?"

A tinge of jealousy twisted in my stomach at the ease with which Slim slipped his arm around her shoulder as he answered. "Let's hope so. What did you find out about your flight?"

"It's cancelled. It looks like you're stuck with me until after the storm. Who knows how long it will be before they get it rescheduled. Even then, I may not get on since I booked with miles."

"We're happy to have your help. If you're still around, I'll put you to work when we open back up. You'll be stuck with this guy in the meantime." Slim nodded in my direction. "Did you check on your folks?"

I hesitated, still processing the job offer to Trinity—and the fact that she hadn't responded. "Not yet. I'll go help Dad get the shutters up this afternoon. I have to hit Publix first."

Slim blew out a long breath as he chuckled. "That should be a shit show."

"No kidding. And I need everything."

"You and everyone else. Good luck with that."

He wasn't kidding. South Floridians raid grocery stores like ants in a picnic basket at the first mention of the H word. Publix was teeming with half-crazed patrons. Some shelves were already bare. There wasn't a bottle or a jug of water to be had anywhere. The toilet paper section was barren. Trinity's mouth dropped open at the dozen-or-less loaves of bread sparsely scattered on the shelf.

"Jesus, it's like the apocalypse."

"People hoard. If the bottled water is gone, I bet there's no beer either."

"Priorities. At least that makes sense. But why all the toilet paper?"

I shrugged. "Essentials." Which explained why there was no beer at all. None. I stared at the empty cooler. "Hurricane parties are serious. Hoarding beer might actually make more sense than even water."

"Luckily they're not hoarding pet food."

I glanced at the cans of cat food in the cart. "No beer means I guess it's wine for us. You prefer red or white?"

"Wine is red." She picked up and studied a bottle of Cabernet before adding it to our cart, smiling wryly. "But red makes me sleepy, so white is for lunch. Both?" She moved down the aisle to the white wine selection.

I could drink white, but it wasn't what I liked, so I grabbed two more bottles of the Cabernet before catching up. "I like the way you think."

The meat section was pretty much cleaned out too. I grabbed a lone package of skirt steaks and two packs of chicken breasts. "Skirt steak makes the best fajitas."

"Good thing no one likes fresh veggies as much as they like beer." Trinity picked three colors of bell peppers, some onions, and a slew of other vegetables. "And I love fajitas."

After stocking up on food and booze as best we could, we headed toward my parents' house.

"This is insanity." Trinity turned to stare as we passed a line of cars spilling into the street from a gas station.

"Thank God I filled my tank a couple of days ago."

Trinity shifted nervously in her seat. "Are people worried they may have to evacuate? Are you worried?"

I waved my hand to dismiss her worry. "Nearly no one will evacuate for a Cat 1 or 2. They're worried the gas may run out, so they buy it all up, causing it to run out."

"Lovely." She shook her head at the irony.

My dad was pulling corrugated metal shutters out of the garage when we arrived. Trinity smiled. "He looks ready for help."

"He'd never admit he needs it."

"I can relate to that." So could I.

She looked down at the kitten in the box. "Do you think she'll be okay in the car?"

"It's only sixty-five degrees out, so yeah."

Trinity scratched the cat's head before reluctantly setting her box on the seat. "See you soon."

The rain had abated to a light mist. "Never a dull moment, huh, son?" Dad slipped his leather work glove off his hand and extended it to Trinity as she hopped down from the Jeep. "Arlowe."

Trinity looked surprised. "Oh, another Arlowe? I didn't realize. Nice to meet you. I'm Trinity." I hadn't told her I was a "junior," but why would I?

My father flashed a grin. "And Australian by the sound of it."

Trinity nodded as she shook his hand with a smile. "That's right."

"Trinity was supposed to leave tomorrow. Lucky for me, she's stuck here for another few days." I winked at her, amused by the thought that she was already meeting my folks. Monica would be so pissed.

"I'm not sure how lucky anyone is that the hurricane cancelled my flight, but I plan to make the most of it."

"As soon as we get all these shutters up, it will probably pass a hundred miles offshore." I started into the garage.

Trinity followed behind me. "So I hear. Preparation is a deterrent. Who knew? I usually opt for procrastination."

My father chuckled. I could tell he liked her smart-assed tone as much as I did. "Oh, no, procrastination will make a hurricane bite you in the ass."

I tried not to think about biting Trinity's ass as her blue eyes widened. "Well, we don't want that. So, what can I do to help?"

Dad's smile spread as he handed her a pair of gloves. "You can grab one of those shutters and carry it to the porch."

Trinity went straight to work while my father apologized for giving her the only spare pair of gloves. "Sorry, no more gloves, but you can handle it." He rustled the back of my hair.

I took a deep breath and willed my face to relax from the cringe that threatened. He still treated me like the twelve-year-old who'd do anything for his approval. Just because I could handle it didn't mean I should have to take it. "Yeah, Dad, don't worry about me."

I grabbed a shutter and motioned with my chin for Trinity to follow. She held the shutters in place while I screwed them in with the drill. We made a good team.

Dad noted her efficiency as we put in the last of the screws. "You're not afraid of hard work, are you?"

She grinned as she patted the metal shutter. "No, sir."

"Well, I appreciate your help. Arlowe's not the only one who's lucky you stayed." His kind smile made me a little jealous at how easily he showed gratitude to anyone not named Arlowe. He wiped his hands on his jeans and his smile faded as he turned toward me. "Did Slim get the shop battened down?"

"We *all* got the shop ready for the storm we hope never comes."

He didn't even register my blatant reference that I had done as much of the work as Slim had. "Ah, you put Trinity to work at the shop too?"

There was no use in fishing for an acknowledgement, he wasn't going to bite. That's what I hated about fishing. You do everything you're supposed to and often come up empty-handed. It was a colossal waste of time. I'd rather keep his focus on Trinity, which he seemed to enjoy. "All hands on deck. I'll put her to work for as long as she wants to stay. You should see this girl surf." I wiggled my brows as I glanced her way.

"She might be able to teach you a thing or two." Dad punched my shoulder softly while grinning at Trinity.

It was true, but for some reason it bugged me that he said so. I loved that Trinity interjected. "Hardly. I've already learned a thing or two from him."

"He ought to be good at surfing. It's pretty much all he does. Until he gets a real job." He shot me a look. "You ever hear anything back?"

The question reflexively made me hope no one ever called to follow up on the resumes I'd sent. "Nope, not yet."

"Keep at it. Something will pan out."

I thought to tell him to mind his own business but swallowed it and changed the subject. "Where's mom?"

"She went to Winn-Dixie for groceries, trying to beat the crowd."

Trinity's eyes widened. "It's probably too late for that. Publix was already ravaged."

Dad laughed. "Hysteria."

"Hurricane hysteria." I shrugged before I patted Trinity's shoulder. "We should brave it again. We have groceries and a cat in the Jeep."

Dad took off his baseball cap and rubbed the top of his head. "Cat?"

"Trinity rescued a kitten, which was going to the pound until they shut down for the storm. So we're all stuck together until this thing passes"—I grinned—"hopefully a hundred miles offshore."

He smoothed the wrinkles on his forehead as though it would help abate his concern which seemed far greater than my own. "Hopefully." His face was solemn with the implied *For all our sake*. We always went through the motions when a storm threatened, hoping that our efforts were in vain. More often than not, they were. But the chance that it could hit us had us all worried.

CHAPTER 12

TRINITY

Skirt steak made the best fajitas. Arlowe was right. I savored the scent of the steaming plate he carried in from the grill. It helped that he was as expert on the barbie as Dante was. The meat was cooked to perfection. I made the simple guacamole I'd pretty much lived on for months in Guatemala.

Arlowe smiled across the table as he scooped some onto his second tortilla. "This is delicious. What did you put in the guac?"

"Lime, salt, pepper, onion, garlic, and a little tomato."

"I always buy it pre-made. This is way better."

"Everything is better homemade."

"If you know how to make it." Arlowe winked.

"I don't think it's the guac that makes these fajitas so delicious. The steak is so juicy." I popped the last bite of my first fajita into my mouth.

"I'm glad you like it, but it's both. The combination is magic." His lips curled into a grin before they parted for another big bite.

We were nearly comatose with exhaustion by the time we finished the meal. My body was a satisfied sort of tired from all the day's efforts as I carried our plates into the kitchen. The weatherman's voice from the television drowned out the music. "Hurricane Xavier bears down on south Florida." I stopped stacking the dishes into the sink and craned my neck to listen. That didn't sound good.

I wiped my hands quickly before joining Arlowe on the couch. "It has a name now?" I reached down for the kitten as she came bounding over to attack my ankle.

Arlowe was intent on the map of the projected path on the screen. "It does. And sustained winds of a hundred and three."

The weatherman made it sound like we should all be ready to take shelter when the storm hit in another twelve to eighteen hours. "That's a huge range. What the hell? Can't they predict better than that?" The uncertainty was as annoying as how my voice rose a pitch.

Arlowe glanced up from the TV. "It's moving so slowly it's anyone's guess where it will drift."

I gnawed at my lower lip as I scratched behind the cat's tiny ear. "The forecaster sounds pretty certain that it's coming straight for us."

"Hysteria sells."

"Well it certainly sells a lot of bread and beer. I hope we'll be alright."

"We'll be fine. We have six more bottles of wine." Arlowe grinned and tipped his wine glass toward me.

I stretched my arms up overhead in a yawn. "I warned you. Red wine makes me sleepy." I was more exhausted by the uncertainty than the booze, but I'd take any excuse to escape, if that meant hiding my anxiety. "I'm beat."

"After all that hard labor, I'm not surprised."

"At least we're ready." I hoped I was convincing enough to believe it myself.

"Don't worry, we're ready." Arlowe patted my leg. "I promise." His hand on my thigh made me feel safe. Maybe that's why I felt a pang of loss when he let go. "You'll see. This thing will pass tomorrow and we'll be back to normal before you know it. You'll probably be out of here by the end of the week."

That idea sounded more ominous than the approaching storm.

I woke to my phone buzzing insistently on the nightstand. I squinted to make out the time on the screen above the word DAD. Six a.m. here was 8 p.m. in Sydney. They'd probably been worrying all day. My voice cracked as I answered. "Good morning."

"Sorry, I know you must still be sleeping, but your mother has been harassing me to call you for the past three hours."

"It's okay. Are you there, Mum?" They usually called me on speaker.

"Yes, dear. I'm here, and worried sick." I could picture the concern that must be etched on her brow as she paused. "They say the storm should be hitting Florida in the next few hours. I wanted to be sure you're going to be somewhere safe."

Few hours? Shit! I threw the sheet back and flung my legs over the edge of the bed, but kept my voice steady. "I am, Mum. Don't worry. We're in a concrete building on the second floor. I'll be fine."

I blinked through sleepy eyes to find the power button on the remote and clicked it while my mum pummeled me with questions. Did we have a generator if we lose power? Where would we go if the building flooded? What about refrigeration?

My eyes widened at the blob whose outer edge was already over us on the map on the telly. I whispered so as not to wake Arlowe. "I told you, we're on the second floor. We'll be fine." I hadn't thought about losing power. But I hadn't thought newly-named Xavier would have become a Cat 3 overnight, either. *Fuck!* No wonder they were worried. Still, I had to reassure her. "We have everything we need. And I'm sure they're prepared in case the electricity goes. Don't worry, Mum."

"Of course I'm worried. I was on the phone with the airline all morning. They don't know when you'll get out. Where are you exactly?"

"Exactly? I don't know the address if that's what you mean. But I'm at Arlowe's apartment, like I told you in the text when my flight was delayed. And we're safe here." I doubted that my reassurance eased her worry any more than it did mine.

Dad piped in calmly. "I'm sure you are, but can you get us the address please? It's good to have it under these circumstances."

"Of course. I'll text you with it once Arlowe wakes up. Meanwhile, just relax."

My mother's voice strained with concern. "I'll relax when you're home safe."

As much as I wanted to delay my return, being home with my parents sounded pretty good in the face of a serious storm.

By the time Arlowe got up after eight, I had scrubbed the kitchen spotless. It was a productive nervous habit of mine. I could clean until my fingers bled when I was anxious.

He rubbed the sleep out of the corner of his eyes and smiled as he pushed past me to pour himself a coffee. "Wow, you're up early."

"My parents woke me up at six." I glanced at the map on the telly that I'd muted. "The hurricane is a Cat 3 and coming right for us."

His eyes widened as he watched the weatherman draw green lines on the screen that intersected with Jupiter. "Well, that all changed quickly, didn't it?" He picked up the remote to turn on the sound.

I stopped polishing the already-sparkling granite countertop and went to join him behind the sofa. "No kidding."

We listened to the forecast. Hurricane force winds would make landfall by two but the eye wouldn't pass over us until after five.

"What do we do now?"

"Hunker down and wait for it to pass."

I took my time making us breakfast. Killing time. Going through the motions when your mind is elsewhere, bound in worry. I knew the feeling well from my days in lockdown with Lena and Dante. Holed up in a fortress. Hiding from armed kidnappers wasn't much different to hiding from the hurricane bearing down on us.

I was relieved when Arlowe suggested a movie after I'd done the dishes and scoured the kitchen once more. I chose the movie remake of Charlie's Angels, which was a poor imposter of the original series that had become our inspiration when we were beating the bad guys with Dante and Lena. We were Dante's Angels.

I settled into Arlowe's arm that was stretched along the back of the sofa behind me. Even though my heart beat faster at the most physical closeness we'd ever shared, I felt surprisingly relaxed. After so many nights cuddled up on Dante's couch, every part of me craved to snuggle up to Arlowe—a longing for the familiar security that touch provided on those long Antigua days that had gone by too fast. But I held back on the urge to do more. Getting involved with another man wouldn't cure my loneliness. It would just remind me how much I hate men. But it wasn't memories of Diego that made me lonely. It was Guatemala.

Missing Lena and Dante must've made me more emotional. That, combined with the underlying stress of the storm creeping closer by the minute, made me a borderline wreck when the telly flashed to black as an audible pop sounded outside and the lights went dark. I jumped with a start and Arlowe wrapped his arms around me. Once I realized that the electricity had gone out, I felt silly for reacting the way I did, but I didn't want to pull away.

I lifted my eyes to Arlowe's and met a stare that radiated protection and concern so intensely that I could feel it deep in my belly. My lips were only inches from his cheek but I didn't pull away. "Sorry, that freaked me out for some reason."

I recognized the spark of desire in his burning gaze, holding me still with bated breath like a spotlight. "If that's how you're going to react, you can freak out all you like." His arms tightened around me just long enough to get the message across.

I was literally speechless. All I could do was stare up into those hazel eyes. Overcome by an inconvenient emotion, I ripped my eyes away and tried to take a steadying breath. It turned to a gasp as Arlowe's finger hooked under my chin, turning me back toward him. His lips lowered onto mine and for a glorious second I almost surrendered to his kiss.

But the voices of reason screamed in my head and I pulled away with a pent-up force that surprised us both. Arlowe's hands flew up in apology.

"God, I'm sorry. I didn't mean to do that. Really. I've been trying *not* to do that for days. I was pretty sure I had it under control. I guess not. Sorry."

I felt guilty for his stammering, endearing as it was. And hearing that he'd been fighting back the urge to kiss me made me wish I'd let him. I wanted to tell him that it wasn't that I didn't want it—want him—it was that I didn't trust myself any more than I could trust anyone right now.

By the age of twenty-one, I'd established a distinct pattern of fucking to forget. The last time had landed me in Diego's bed, which had relieved the acute absence of Lena and Dante in my heart. But we all know how that turned out. So when

103

Arlowe's lips found mine, I didn't trust myself to entertain the possibility. The possibility of feeling anything for anyone brought back the searing pain in my chest that radiated into a colossal emptiness in my gut. I took the easiest out I could think of with my racing mind. "I appreciate your honesty, Arlowe. I really do. But I like girls." It wasn't exactly a lie. But it wasn't exactly the truth either.

"You like girls?" He cocked his head while peering through squinted eyes. "You mean you're lesbian?"

"That's what they call it in my country when a girl likes girls."

He stiffened and started to retract his arm but stopped awkwardly. "Oh, wow. I'm sorry. It's none of my business. I didn't mean to pry."

"There's nothing to be sorry for." I rested my hand on his chest.

A deep pink rose to his cheeks. "Let's pretend that never happened."

That fit in perfectly with my plan to pretend that nothing at all was happening with Arlowe—ever. I put on the most innocent face I could muster. "I have no idea what you're talking about."

CHAPTER 13

*Y*ou could have knocked me over with a feather. I hadn't seen that one coming. Of course the one girl that might be the right one was a lesbian. Just my luck.

But there was little choice than to accept it. Annoyance churned in my gut that it kind of turned me on that she liked girls, but I was careful not to let it show. I didn't want Trinity to think that I was mad that she'd rejected me—or worse—because of her sexual orientation. I found the flashlights and candles I had stored in the closet, but the lights came back on when the building's generator kicked on.

"Oh, thank God." Trinity's face relaxed as she petted the kitten on her lap.

"Yeah, at least we have power. But not enough to run the A/C."

"Since we can't open the windows, I guess it's going to be a hot one."

"We don't want hundred mile an hour winds blowing through here when it really hits."

"Isn't it hitting now?" Her chin tilted to listen to the wind whistling outside.

"This is just the beginning." I turned the television back on to track the storm. Sustained winds of 65 mph and the eye was still three hours away.

Trinity's brows scrunched together in worry again. "So we have hours of this ahead of us?"

I decided not to remind her that it would get much worse before it got better. "Yeah, so we'd better find something to pass the time." A board game wouldn't have been my choice activity with her, but considering our options, it seemed like the best suggestion. "Do you play backgammon?"

"Since I was five. I'll kick your arse in backgammon." I loved a challenge, and if Trinity was anything she was that.

"We'll see about that."

"Is it too early for wine?" Trinity shifted on the couch.

"There's no such thing as too early to drink at a hurricane party. Besides, white wine is for daytime."

"Sometimes we think so much alike it's scary."

That was precisely the word I'd use to describe it. "I know what you mean. Arms easily twisted."

"And both eager to twist. I guess we both need a partner in crime."

Her playful grin made something swell in my chest. At least it wasn't my cock. But it might have been worse. "It's certainly more fun that way." I winked. It still felt like we were flirting, which made me think that we never really were.

We polished off a full bottle of white over four games of backgammon. As with everything else, Trinity hadn't overstated her expertise. She'd kicked my ass as promised the first and fourth games, and I'd barely eked out wins in the other two. "Best out of five?"

Trinity eyed the empty wine bottle. "I think we'd better make some dinner, before I open another bottle of wine."

"Making dinner *requires* that we open another bottle of wine. But we have to switch to red for that."

Trinity held her arm out. "Twist my arm."

I pushed her hand up her back gently and nudged her toward the kitchen.

Trinity pulled out every vegetable we'd bought. "Stir fry?"

"I'll make the rice."

After a delicious dinner, we chatted about our favorite Chinese dishes while we loaded the dishwasher. The lights flickered once before they went out again. Trinity gasped and stepped toward me. I took hold of the backs of her arms instead of pulling her into mine like I wanted. "It's okay. The generator probably ran out of fuel. I'm sure they'll have it back on in a few minutes."

I released her to pull my phone out of my pocket. I used light to navigate to the flashlights and candles I'd pulled out earlier. I gave one to Trinity, which she used to track down the kitten, while I lit the last of the candles I'd placed around the room.

I sensed her worry as she sat on the couch, clutching the

kitten into her chest. But I didn't know how to console her, when my instinct was to pull her into my arms. I sat down, not too close, and reached over to pat her knee awkwardly. "Hopefully it will be back on in a flash. Well, maybe not a flash because that could be bad." I was rambling bad jokes. I didn't know what to do—or say—with this woman.

"This isn't so bad."

It wasn't bad at all. "I'm glad I got to be here for this rite of passage—riding out your first hurricane." We held up the last glasses of Cabernet for a toast. If this was all that it was, I'd take it.

Time passed with the easy conversation, so I didn't think about how long it had been since the generator shut off until Trinity paused to check her phone. "I don't have service."

"Neither do I. And it's been over half an hour. It must be more than out of gas."

"Unless they couldn't get gas today." Trinity's eyes were wide with worry.

That we wouldn't have a fuel supply stocked up sounded ridiculous, but also entirely plausible. Our building administrator was less than thorough. "Fuck, I hope not. But at least we'll be sleeping. As soon as the storm passes they'll be working to get the power back on."

"Thankfully, red wine helps me sleep." She yawned and turned on the flashlight. "I'm going to need it with this wind." She craned her neck to listen to the steady howl that still rattled the impact-resistant windows.

"Are you tired?" I didn't want her to go. I didn't want either of us to have to be alone.

"The sooner I get to sleep, the sooner I wake up and it's all over."

I was also eager for the storm to pass, but I hated that it was already over with her before it even began. "Valid point."

She picked up the kitten. "Thanks for everything. See you on the other side."

"Sweet dreams." I wished there was another side, another reality where she might be into me. The last sip of my wine was soured by the irony of it all.

I blew out the candles and breathed in the scent of burnt wicks smoking. Somehow having Trinity in the other room made me feel more lonely than I ever did living alone. I shook my head at my stupidity as I went to brush my teeth. What a fucking fool. Pining over what you can't have is so cliché.

The wind sounded like a freight train. Damn this storm was big. The wind hadn't stopped for eight hours. How many trees had snapped? There was going to be a mess out there tomorrow. I hoped sleep would come soon despite the noise, but the end of the hurricane would be just the beginning of the aftermath.

I hugged a pillow and tried to focus on the low hum of the wind instead of the high-pitched wail accompanying it. I'd just forced my eyes closed when Trinity's voice called out from just inside the doorway, and I nearly jumped out of bed.

Her flashlight cast a pale yellow circle over the rug at the foot of my bed. "Arlowe?"

"Yeah, what's up? Everything okay?"

"Yes. I mean, no. I can't sleep with the noise. And neither can the cat. She's scared. Can we sleep here with you? Or at least try to?"

"Of course you can." I patted the empty side of the bed. "There's another pillow in the top of the closet."

She grinned as she shined her light on the one I was hugging. "You're attached to that one."

"Yeah, a physical therapist told me to sleep with a pillow between my knees." I shoved the pillow down between my legs as I rolled onto my side to face her. It was true. I'd briefly dated one a couple of years ago. But I needed the pillow between us more than I needed it between my knees.

CHAPTER 14

TRINITY

*F*eeling weak wasn't usually in my wheelhouse, but I couldn't bear the sounds of debris hitting the window beside my bed. I'd waited longer than I wanted to go to Arlowe's room. After I'd shot him down with the lesbian lie.

We laid in silence but the heat between us spoke. And suddenly I was aware of how much the temperature in the apartment had risen. I flung the sheet back. "I hope I don't make you too hot." I realized how it sounded after it was too late to take it back.

Arlowe pushed back his side of the sheet, too, then whispered, "Don't worry about me. I'll live. Try to get some sleep."

I wasn't sure if I was disappointed or relieved that he didn't crack a joke at how hot I made him. "Okay. Goodnight."

"Goodnight." I wanted him to call me beautiful and pull me into his arms even though a sheen of sweat coated my skin.

My heart beat so loud in my chest I could hear it over the roar of the wind. Yet somehow, sleep found me.

I woke to silence and rolled over to get my phone. It was almost seven a.m. I blinked at the sleeping kitty beside me before my eyes traveled over Arlowe. I angled the phone to see him better in the blue light of the screen. His chest rose and fell in a steady rhythm. Still fast asleep. I took the cat under my arm to the kitchen. I tried the light despite the display on the microwave being dark. Still no electricity. How was I going to make coffee—or anything? I walked over to the soft halo of light penetrating the edges of the living room window.

I perched on a stool at the breakfast bar to read the three messages my parents had sent. Thankfully the cellular signal was restored. I'd better call them so that they could sleep tonight.

My father answered on the first ring, sounding anxious. "Trinity."

"Were you staring at the phone waiting for me to call?"

"Maybe." I missed the smile I could hear in his voice. "How'd you fare?"

"Fine. The power went out, and then the generator failed. So it's at least 40 degrees in here, but other than that, it was fairly uneventful."

My mother sighed as she spoke. "Thank goodness you're okay. Is there much damage where you are? The pictures we've seen are scary."

"I haven't been out, so I have no idea. All I can see out the window are branches in the street." It was hard to fathom the damage that much wind could over the course of several hours. I shivered at the memory of the freight train that had kept me awake. I wasn't about to share the scarier details with my parents though. "Hopefully it's not too bad. I'll text you later with an update. I just wanted to let you know I'm okay so you can get some rest tonight."

"Were you able to sleep?" My dad should know better than to poke the bear of Mum's worry.

"I did. It wasn't bad at all." I was deliberately short.

He seemed to get the hint. "Good. Take care and keep us posted."

My mum rushed to add, "I'll call the airline as soon as I get up tomorrow to see when we can get you home."

I could picture the soothing look on my father's face. He knew how to calm her like no one else could. "Leave it for a day or two, Trisha. You'll be on hold for hours to get no answers at all. It will be chaos. We can be grateful that Trinity is fine for now and figure out the logistics later."

Thank God we thought alike. I couldn't think about the future when I didn't know what the present was going to look like when we got outside. "I agree. I'll text you later. Love you guys."

"Folks?" Arlowe walked up behind me, placing his hand on my back before he leaned in to kiss my cheek. It was just a friendly peck, but my first instinct was to pull away. It was the wanting him closer that made me want to run. I held still.

"Yeah. They're relieved we're okay, but worried about the damage."

"So am I. Which is why I need coffee." Arlowe went to the pantry.

"The stove's electric. How do we do that?"

He pulled a camp stove, propane canister, and French press from the top shelf of the pantry. "Like this."

He was prepared. That he could give me coffee made him even sexier than the fitted boxer briefs that clung to his firm butt. "I love French press coffee." That's how we made it at Dante's house.

I sniffed the steam coming from the mug Arlowe handed me —heavenly. "The electricity has been out for a while—not a good sign I'd presume."

He gave me a reassuring look. "They may have it a block over, though. It could just be a tree down. It may not be that bad." I liked his optimism, even if I remained skeptical.

After our coffee, we ventured down the stairs to see for ourselves. Someone had already pushed the shutters back from the front door. The day was grey but the rain had passed. Debris—mostly palm fronds and cardboard—littered the sidewalk. I stopped in my tracks when I saw the giant tree uprooted across the street. The roots had come up in an intact disk that was as tall as the the two-story house beside it. The top of the tree had narrowly missed the Jaguar parked in the driveway. "Bloody hell."

"Missed the house and the car. Bloody lucky, I'd say."

He had a point. As we drove through town, seeing others that hadn't been so fortunate, I realized how lucky we'd been. The metal roof of one house was peeled back like a sardine can. A family stood in the yard staring up at the damage. Work crews were out cutting fallen trees and tending to the power lines. Arlowe inched the Jeep up onto a sidewalk to drive around a palm tree they hadn't gotten to yet. "We'll swing by the shop on the way to my parent's house, just to see." To see how bad it was, he meant.

"Have you talked to your parents? How's their house?"

"They've got a mess but no serious damage. Let's hope the shop fared as well."

At first appearance, it had survived unscathed. It took a second for my eyes to adjust to the darkness in the shop before I could make out Slim shaking his head with a mop in his hand. "Tore a hole in the damned roof. It's twenty years old, so not a shock."

Arlowe shined his light around the shop. It didn't look bad, but everything was wet. Everything. "Where should we start?"

Slim shook his head as he leaned into the mop handle. "At your mother's house. Have you talked to them?"

"Yeah, they're good. We can help here first. How's *your* house?"

"Yard's a mess but the house is okay. You guys don't have to stay. Go check on your folks first. You can't see anything in here anyway. Hopefully they'll get the lights back on. It's hotter than hell in here so I sure hope so. Joe's bringing some tires and a tarp in case it rains more."

Arlowe clarified for my benefit. "Joe's his neighbor and best friend."

"He's bringing his two sons. We'll get this water up in no time. We can deal with the rest of it later."

Arlowe looked toward the doorway to the store room. "How bad is it back there?"

"About the same. Go. We'll deal with it later."

Arlowe reluctantly turned to leave. I held the kitten close as I followed, calling over my shoulder to Slim. "Good luck, mate. See you later." I loved that he was willing to take on the work himself so that Arlowe could be there for his family. But they were all family, and that's just what you did.

The senior Arlowe was out clearing palm fronds from the driveway when we pulled up. He walked toward us and smiled. "Xavier was a doozy." He was unusually chipper considering the state of his front yard, scattered with tree limbs and coconuts. I guessed he was just happy that none of them had ripped a hole in his roof.

"It looks like it did a number on us."

"Not so bad. We'll get this cleaned up in no time. The Wilsons' car is under a tree. Lenny went to borrow a chainsaw. We can help free it when he gets back."

Arlowe winced. "Shit. Is their house okay?"

"It got the gutters and part of the garage roof."

Something didn't make sense as I listened. "Why wasn't the car in the garage?"

Arlowe chuckled. "It's probably full of stuff. That's what garages are for—stuff, not cars."

I bit my lip. "Very wet stuff by now, I'd imagine. That's a shame."

In the kitchen, we found Arlowe's mother. She looked up from the gas stove as we walked in. "I'm making pancakes. I hope you're hungry."

"I'm always hungry for your cooking." Arlowe hugged his

mom. "Let me introduce you to Trinity. I'm sure Dad told you she's staying at my place."

"Your father doesn't tell me anything." She wiped her hands on her apron before shaking my hand. "Charlotte. Nice to meet you, Trinity. And who's this?"

"She doesn't have a name. Or he. We're not sure yet. I found her in the gutter before the storm."

"Oh you poor little thing." Charlotte took the kitten from me. "What a precious little creature." She examined the cat. "I believe that calicos are always female."

I gloated at Arlowe. "I thought she was a girl. Lucky for her the shelters were closed."

Charlotte glared at her son. "You are not taking this animal to the shelter."

"You want it, you can have it." Arlowe sounded like he was joking.

"We're looking after her for now." I took the cat back into my arms.

Arlowe smiled at his mum. "Trinity's flight back home to Sydney was cancelled. She's stranded, I suppose. Like the cat."

"I hope you're making them both feel at home."

"I hope so, too. I do my best." Arlowe grinned.

"I know you do. Now set the table."

I admired her six-burner gas range. "Nice that you have gas."

"I prefer it, especially in times like these. Do you like pancakes?"

"Who doesn't like pancakes?"

Charlotte chuckled. "Gluten-free vegans. Or skinny girls. So many young girls are so concerned for their figure they wouldn't dare."

I giggled. "Carbs don't scare me."

"Because you burn them off." Arlowe grinned as he turned to his mum. "She's a hard worker."

"We need a few of those about now." Charlotte's Southern accent reminded me of Lena.

After breakfast Arlowe went down the street with his father to cut the tree off the Wilsons' car. I wanted to join them, but it seemed rude to invite myself and leave Charlotte here alone. "What can I do to help?"

"As soon as I finish these dishes, we're going to get some gloves out of the garage, and the machetes. The backyard is a fallen jungle."

Thank God we weren't relegated to the kitchen. "Machetes? That sounds fun."

Charlotte grinned. "It kind of is."

By the time the men returned, we'd cleared half the yard. I was covered in a thick layer of dust and an itchy coat of sweat. Arlowe was an even darker shade of grey-brown. "Wow, you guys have made some real headway."

I pulled off a glove and pushed my hair back off my forehead with the back of my hand, smiling. "Girl power."

"The best kind, I think you'll agree." Arlowe grinned and rubbed a smudge off my face. "Thanks for your help."

His comment was surely a lesbian reference, producing a

guilty pang in my stomach I tried to ignore. "All hands on deck."

Charlotte smiled as she pulled her fingers from her gloves. "Arlowe's right to be gracious. We appreciate it. And I think we deserve a break."

Arlowe's grin spread. "Do you have any sweet tea made?"

"Of course I do. Pour some for Trinity."

His dad joined us in the kitchen, leaning in to kiss Charlotte's cheek. "You did a fine job in be back yard."

Charlotte nuzzled her cheek into his chin. "How'd it go at the Wilson's"

"It went great once we finally got everyone on task."

Arlowe startled me when shot back, "You mean until you got everyone on task. And by everyone I mean me." His seething undertone chilled the balmy air.

His father waved him off with a strained chuckle. "Are you still worked up over that?"

I averted my gaze, embarrassed and uncomfortable. Charlotte's hand landed on the countertop, her worried eyes darted between the two men. She looked like she was bracing for a fallout.

Arlowe was clearly worked up when he denied it. "No, Dad. I don't bother getting worked up over you anymore. I'm used to the abuse."

"Looks like I awakened Drama Queen Arlowe."

I wrung my fingers together nervously as I lifted my sympathetic gaze but Arlowe's angry eyes were fixed on his father. His jaw clenched and before he spat out in a calm voice that was laced with rage.

"I can never do anything right. Nothing I do is good enough for you. It never has been."

The tightening in my chest must have been my heart aching for Arlowe. His father's expectations had weighed heavier on him than I'd imagined. The hairs on my arm prickled at how cold he sounded as he barked through gritted teeth. "You just can't help yourself. You pick apart every little thing and find the flaws."

His dad threw up his hands. "How else are you supposed to know when you're screwing something up?"

"According to you I screw everything up." Arlowe's voice shook lividly.

Charlotte rubbed his shoulder as she soothed, "No one screwed anything up, dear. Your father gets testy with the heat. We all just need to cool down." She shoved a glass into her husbands hand with a warning glare.

His rigid brow relaxed as his mouth turned up in a soft smile. "You're probably right."

Making excuses for her husband and smoothing thing over came easily for Charlotte. She'd probably had plenty of practice.

Arlowe's gaze finally swung my way. His smile was almost convincing as he nonchalantly changed the subject. "Thanks for getting your hands dirty today."

I studied him curiously for a moment before I followed his lead to pretend like nothing had happened. "You don't have to thank me. It's inspiring to see how the community comes together to help one another. I'm happy to be here to help."

Arlowe grinned after long swig of tea, looking genuinely relaxed. Maybe his mother was right about cooling off. "I keep telling you that I'll put you to work as long as you'll stay."

"I might be staying for a while. Who knows when I'll be able to get a flight out? Meanwhile, use me while I'm here."

"In that case, I'll be hoping for further delays." Arlowe's flirty brow wiggled.

Arlowe's dad was equally calm when he finally spoke. "I wouldn't wish for more complications for you, but we sure do appreciate your help."

I washed down the bitter taste that his free-flowing gratitude produced with a sip of tea. The irony surely wasn't lost on Arlowe that his father could doll out praise when he wanted to. That's what made it sting. But if it did, Arlowe didn't let on.

His eyes creased with a wide grin as he took a plate of cookies from Charlotte's hands. "Thank you. You know oatmeal raisin is my favorite."

She tapped him on the shoulder playfully. "They're not all for you. Share with your friend."

I eyed Arlowe hesitantly as I took a cookie from the plate that Arlowe offered. Their family dynamic was more than a little unsettling, but tensions were high. I hoped for Arlowe's sake that this wasn't their norm. I'd learned the hard way that ignoring your problems doesn't make them go away.

I was sizing Arlowe up—trying to suss out what was really going on in his head—when his phone buzzed in his pocket. He set the plate on the counter before a smile lit his face when he saw the name. "It's Kate." He answered on speaker.

"Hey, Sis. How's it going? I've got you on speaker here with Mom and Dad and a new friend, Trinity."

"Ohhhh, what sort of friend is Trinity?" Kate chided. I liked her already.

"You heard the part where I said that she's here and you're on speaker, right?"

"Of course I did." She laughed. "Lighten up, Arlowe. I've got you on speaker here with Sally, too."

Their dad yelled from across the kitchen. "Sally! How's my favorite grandson?"

"He's your only grandson, Dad. And he's lovely. If he'd only learn to sleep through the night we might all be happier."

Arlowe's mum chimed in with her Southern drawl. "You might be losing sleep for the next twenty years. I can't wait to meet him, and you."

What? Charlotte hadn't met Sally yet? Arlowe had said that he went to Chicago with his Dad. But I hadn't thought about his mum having a step-daughter and a grandson she still didn't know. Wow. That was another weird dynamic.

Sally spoke to her like she was family, though. "Us, too. But enough about us. We're calling to check on *you*. How is it there? They keep showing the same images of the worst damage on the news. It looks awful."

Arlowe's dad walked closer to the phone. "I haven't seen the worst of it firsthand yet, but where we are isn't too bad. The backyard fence is damaged and it'll take a week or two of clean up, but we'll be okay."

Kate chimed in. "That's a relief. I haven't heard how they fared on Paradise Key."

"We still don't have power so I haven't seen the reports from the Keys. But it's two hundred miles south of us, and we got the eye, so it shouldn't be too bad there. You never know though."

Arlowe slapped his father's shoulder with the back of his hand as he shot him a look before consoling Kate. "It's probably fine. Don't worry, I'm sure they'll be ready for your wedding, Sis."

"I hope you're right. It's beyond my control at this point."

"Keep the faith." Arlowe smiled.

My chest swelled with admiration for Arlowe's resilience. His animosity seemed to have dissolved as they went on to chat about the baby and the wedding. Spying on intimate family conversation on speaker was a tad awkward but they made me feel like part of the family.

After the call, Arlowe's dad put us all back to work, giving his son a wide girth. The distraction of the physical labor erased any remaining tension. We were all back on the same team.

A couple of hours of hard work and we had the backyard cleared and the front looking nearly normal except for the giant pile of debris we left on the curb.

After I washed my hands and my face, I went to find the kitten in its box. Charlotte's face lit up like she remembered something. "I have something you might be able to use." She held up a finger to signal she'd be back in a minute, before returning with a canvas pet carrier. "I bought this for my neighbor who was caring for a sick old stray. He didn't make it so she gave it back."

I took the carrier from her hands. "Oh, I'm sorry. But, thank you. This will be more comfortable than the cardboard box, by far."

She smiled at Arlowe. "It'll come in handy when you have to take that precious little thing to the vet soon."

I giggled under my breath as I put the cat into its new carrier. I didn't have to worry about convincing Arlowe to keep her. Lucky for the cat, he didn't seemed to mind nearly much when his mum imposed her will on him.

The air conditioning in the Jeep felt heavenly. Arlowe's eyes hidden behind his Ray-Bans couldn't offer a clue to what he might be thinking for the several silent blocks. It was awkward to bring up his blow-up at his father, but it seemed more awkward not to. "You were pretty miffed with your Dad.

He shrugged. "You can only swallow so much before you choke."

"It's better not to swallow the bitter."

"It's better to ignore my Dad. I do most of the time. Sorry I lost my cool today. I didn't mean to make you uncomfortable.

"Don't worry about me."

"Only if it's a reciprocal agreement."

A grin tugged at the corners of my mouth as I pretended to zip it. If he didn't want to talk about it, I'd just keep my mouth shut and mind my own business.

Back at Arlowe's place, the shower was cold but it might have been the best one I'd ever had. I couldn't see the dirt washing off me in the candlelight, but I imagined the water rolling off was black. I threw on a tank top and some tiny jersey shorts. It was too hot for anything else.

Arlowe had a pot and frypan going on the camp stove. "I had three lobster tails in the freezer, which are nearly thawed and have to be cooked. So it's lobster mac and cheese for dinner."

"Fuck me. Do you have jalapeños?"

"We really do think alike." He grinned, then nodded toward his phone on the counter. "I found my battery, in case you want to charge your phone. Who knows when we'll get power back."

"Good idea." I got my phone from the coffee table. "Oh, Lena called."

"Who's Lena?"

"My friend in Guatemala."

"What kind of friend is Lena?" He mocked his sister's tone as he repeated her question from earlier.

"The best kind." I grinned. "Sorry, I'm just going to let her know I'm okay." I typed a quick text.

I saw your missed call. Flight was cancelled, but all good here. I'll call you soon.

My phone buzzed with a reply as I plugged it into the charger.

Thank God. Call me when you can. Love you.

I will. Love you, too.

I saw the notifications on Arlowe's screen when I plugged my phone in beside his. "Looks like you have three missed calls."

"I'll get to that later. How about you get to opening some wine right now?"

I shot Arlowe a surprised look at him bossing me around. I had to admit I kind of liked it, though. "Another brilliant idea."

Lobster mac and cheese over candlelight was fantastic, but I couldn't have been happier when the power came back on just as we finished. "There will be air conditioning to sleep!"

Arlowe's phone buzzed on the countertop, ringing again. I read off the name. "Monica's calling."

"Ah. Just leave it. I'll get back to her." Arlowe glanced down at the phone as he carried the rest of the dishes to the sink.

He kept talking as we washed dishes, ignoring his phone when it buzzed five times in rapid succession. Then it was ringing again. "Sorry, I better take this." He unplugged his phone and took a deep breath before he answered. "Hey, how ya doin'?"

He walked toward his room to take the call in private. Fair enough. None of my business. He returned a few minutes later looking relieved.

"Monica again?"

"Yeah."

"Everything alright?"

"Oh yeah. She was just checking in."

"What sort of friend is Monica? Is she your girlfriend?" I chided.

He shook his head. "Noooo. Definitely not my girlfriend."

"I figured you'd have at least a couple of those."

Arlowe grinned. "Who says I don't?"

"Touché."

He squeezed in next to me at the sink and started drying dishes from the drainer. "While we're prying, was Lena your girlfriend?"

I bit my lip, unsure how much I should share. "Yeah."

"You met in Antigua? How long were you there?"

"Five months. I only knew Lena the last couple of those though."

"Why did you break up?"

My throat constricted. It was hard to talk about because part of me wished I never left. "The surf guide job in Peru came up, and it was time to move on."

He flung his head to move a blond wave of hair that fell over one eye. His hazel eyes turned serious as they peered into mine. "Can I ask you a personal question? Don't feel obligated to answer."

"Ask me anything." Except whether I wanted him to kiss me right then.

"When did you know you were gay?"

"I knew I liked girls when I was nine. When all the other girls dreamed of kissing their boy crushes, I secretly hoped to smooch Liz Brighton, the high schooler who babysat me sometimes."

"So you've never had a boyfriend?"

I'd had several boyfriends. Up until this point, I was trying not to lie, and hadn't really. I mean, except for the whole being a lesbian part. But there was no way around lying now, except opting to tell the truth. "No, I've had boyfriends."

He looked a little surprised but only for a second. "Ah. And when was your last boyfriend?"

I was a little annoyed at what felt like him prying for details, but that was probably out of guilt for misleading him about my sexual orientation. "Not long ago."

He raised a brow. "That seems unusual for a lesbian."

"I never said I was a lesbian, exactly."

"Did you tell me you were a lesbian to keep me from hitting on you?" He almost laughed. At least he was amused.

"Not intentionally. I didn't know what to say. It's true, I do like girls. After my last boyfriend, I swore off men. So, technically, it's all true."

"Swore off men? Wow, he must've really fucked up."

"It turns out he was married with children, which was news to me. I know how to pick 'em."

Arlowe grimaced. "Ouch. What a dick. I know the feeling. So, prior to swearing off men, you went back and forth between guys and girls?"

"Pretty much. I've probably had more girlfriends than boyfriends. But this past year, I've gotten a lot of dick."

Arlowe's eyes widened briefly before he chuckled. "You talk like a dude."

"Why is crudeness associated with blokes? I blame Max. He taught me to curse like a sailor before I was ten."

"It suits you." Arlowe grinned. "I love it. I'm sure you have no trouble getting laid, wherever you are and with whichever gender you choose."

I shrugged. "I doubt you do either."

"I do alright." He changed the subject quickly. "While we're confessing, where's the bloke who broke your heart?" His attempt at an Aussie accent when he said bloke made me smile.

"Peru."

His eyes widened. "Oh, that recent?"

"Yeah." I started toward the couch, not wanting to say another thing about Diego.

"I'm surprised you didn't go back to Guatemala if you're swearing off men and your girl Lena is still there."

I shifted on the sofa to face him. "It's complicated. She's pregnant and getting married."

"Ah, she found a guy after you left?"

I continued to pussyfoot around the issue. It was hard to explain what I had with Lena and Dante. "Not exactly. We kind of all met at the same time."

Arlowe's brows lifted. "She was fucking both of you?"

I shifted nervously on the couch. I had to just spit it out. "We all were."

"Oh." He blinked a few times. "Like a relationship? Or just a night of fun."

It was definitely a relationship. "We lived together for a couple of months."

I shifted to pull my foot underneath me on the couch as he eyed me in an awkward pause. The crease in his brow relaxed as a smile spread across his lips. "Damn. When I met you a week ago I thought you were young and naive. You've proven otherwise in so many ways every day since." He grinned as he lifted his wine glass to mine. "You're pretty fucking cool, Trinity."

"Thanks, you're pretty fucking cool, too, Arlowe." I wasn't sure if he wanted to kiss me, but I knew I wanted him to. And that was reason enough to throw my arms up and change the subject again. "Thanks to electricity, we'll both be cool all night. Isn't this heavenly?"

Arlowe's gaze meandered from my eyes to my toes and back up like a slow stroll up a stream that failed to quench his thirst along the way. "Heavenly, indeed."

"I'm going to sleep like a baby."

He chuckled. "Wake up crying every few hours?"

I rolled my eyes, remembering Sally's desperation at the lack of sleep and laughed. "Okay, like a bear." I set my glass on the table. "I don't think I can drink any more wine. I think I need sleep." My body ached from the day's work, but I needed to put space between me and that yummy man. He'd been drawing me like a magnet. I knew if I got too close we'd end up stuck together.

I was a little disappointed that he didn't protest, but mostly relieved when he said, "I'm beat, too. See you in the morning."

"We're working at the shop tomorrow?"

"You don't have to. But I do."

"I'm in. I'll do whatever I can for as long as I'm here."

A sideways smile helped light his eyes. "Now only to convince you to stay longer."

It wouldn't take much convincing. A simple suggestion might do it if I ever let myself give in to the temptations my body was begging to explore. Which was precisely why I needed to get home before I started fucking to forget—again. "One day at a time. Tomorrow—the shop."

I caught his clean scent when he leaned in close to scratch the kitten in my arms. "*Hasta mañana.*"

The stubble on his chin tickled as his lips brushed my cheek for a kiss, sending a warm wave down my neck to my chest.

Walking away wasn't easy, so I knew I'd better run.

CHAPTER 15

ARLOWE

*H*ugging the pillow that still smelled like Trinity made me smile when I woke. Then I remembered Monica, on the phone, screaming at me for blowing her off during a hurricane. How could I be so rude and inconsiderate? I didn't have a good answer for that. I didn't give a fuck. She'd said so. Once again, she was right. And then I'd frozen like a deer in headlights and told Trinity that she wasn't my girlfriend. She wasn't, really, not for long. For some reason I felt worse about lying to Trinity than I did for royally pissing off Monica.

The only way I could make this up to Monica would be some serious ass-kissing. But for that, I'd have to care. That's hard to do when you're fresh out of fucks. I had none left to give.

I buried my nose in the pillow for a final long whiff. Trinity. She wasn't actually a lesbian, she'd just lied and said she was. I wasn't sure which was worse, the lie to push me away— ouch—or the very remote possibility of hope of a connection. She was into guys, after all. But, rationally, I knew better than to hope for anything. A reality reinforced by her decision to sleep alone last night. Was she into me? It didn't matter. As soon as her flight was rescheduled, she'd be out of my life forever.

But seeing her in short shorts and a tank top that clung to her perky little tits when I went out to the kitchen made me hope there'd be more to this than just friends. She was stunning as she looked up from the stove with an earnest smile. "Good morning. You like French toast?"

I wanted to wrap my arms around her waist and bury my face in her curls. Instead I went straight to the coffee maker to pour myself a cup. "Good morning. I like pretty much everything."

She winked. "I can relate to that."

Thoughts of her living with another woman and a man, the thoughts I'd gone to sleep with, came rushing back. Part of it was morbid curiosity. I wanted to ask what it was like. How did it work? Did they eat and drink and shower and sleep together or did they take turns and switch it up in pairs? But beyond the curiosity, I was aroused. Intensely aroused. Which felt creepy somehow. Trinity had shared something personal and all I could think about was the sexual dynamics. I hated the stereotype that men think with their dicks, but there was a lot of truth to it.

I wasn't going to be that creep. I liked Trinity too much as a person to risk pushing her away by making another move. I wanted her to feel safe in my home. I'd made that mistake once. I wasn't going there again. "It's better not to be picky."

"Depends. But in the case of food, I agree." She handed me a plate.

I stared at the golden triangles of fried bread. "This looks divine."

"It'd be better if we had some fresh berries."

"That might be a while. I bet the stores are empty. And with the gas shortage all over the state, transport will be fucked up for ages."

"We'll live without berries." Trinity set the plates on the table. "Eat it while it's hot."

After breakfast, Trinity loaded the cat in the carrier while I cleared the table. She seemed more eager than I to dive into the can of worms at the shop. Hopefully, Slim got a lot of the mess cleaned up with the kids yesterday. But we'd have our work cut out for us no matter what.

The shop door was locked. We'd beat Slim there. Yesterday must've tired him out. I took out my keys and let us in. The store looked pretty much normal at first glance. The floors were cleaner than I'd ever seen them. But when I focused on the details, it was apparent that every single thing hanging on a rack or sitting on a shelf had been wet—some still were. Trinity followed me back into the store room. It smelled mustier than usual. Everything was still damp.

Trinity looked around with worried eyes. "Where do we even start?"

"Pick a place. We have to sort through every item in the store. Best case scenario, it can be sold again as new. I'm hoping there will be a lot of those, but it's doubtful by the looks of things. Next are the things with minimal damage that we can probably still sell at a discount. Of the things that can't be sold, we'll sort out what we can use with students or for rentals, and then worst case are the leftovers that we will have to give or throw away."

"Let's hope there aren't many of those."

"On the bright side, you might end up with some cool new gear in exchange for your hard work."

"That would be nice, but not at your expense. Let's see what we can salvage."

"Anything is better than nothing."

Slim didn't make it in until after ten. "Sorry kids. The wife wasn't feeling well. I had to go get her some meds."

"Was the power outage rough on Roxanne?" I knew heat could make her MS flare.

"Yeah, but hopefully she'll be back on track after this shot." He turned to Trinity who looked confused and curious but was polite enough not to ask. "Roxy has multiple sclerosis. And she can't take the meds that worked for her anymore. So when she gets a flare up, we try one thing and then another. Nothing works like those drugs she can't take anymore though. It's rough. Poor bird."

Trinity put down the stack of wetsuits she was carrying to the back to sort on the workbench. "I'm sorry to hear that. I hope your bird is on the mend."

Slim grinned. "I picked up that word from Max. He liked the birds."

Trinity chuckled. "That's Max, alright. And might explain why he's on his third wife."

I showed Slim how we'd started sorting the inventory. He

nodded his appreciation and said, "Perfect. I'll start sorting through what you've already sorted."

I couldn't help but smile. "You like being the auditor after someone else does the work, don't you?"

"Can you blame me?" Slim's palms turned up as he shrugged at the obvious.

"Not even a little. Besides, you did all the grunt work yesterday. This is a cakewalk by comparison."

"Get used to hard work. We've got a couple of weeks ahead of us to get back in business."

I patted him on the back. "Nothing we can't handle, Slim."

"Especially with this one around." Slim squeezed Trinity's shoulder. "I'm going to call Max and thank him for sending you our way."

"He'd probably like that." Trinity picked up her abandoned bundle of wetsuits and headed to the back room.

We got so absorbed in our tasks that we barely spoke other than to address Trinity's occasional question about the condition of a product or package. It was my growling stomach that alerted me that we'd been at it for hours. "Has anyone thought about how we're going to eat?"

Slim looked up. "Good point. Everything's closed."

"We can go back to Arlowe's for a bite," Trinity volunteered. "I can whip something up."

Thank God. I was so hungry I couldn't think of anything but food. "There's chicken in the fridge that thawed in the freezer."

Slim chuckled. "I bet there's a lot of that today. Probably more barbecues than the Fourth of July."

I nodded. "Somebody has all the beer. I hope they bust it out for that."

Trinity shook her head. "We don't have time for a barbie if we're going to get more work done this afternoon. I'll make quesadillas, that'll be much quicker."

Slim glanced my way. "If it's not too much trouble, sounds like a plan."

I had to admire her take-charge attitude. "No trouble at all. Especially if Trinity's cooking. And quicker sounds good. I'm starving."

We munched on some bread and olives while Trinity made lunch. The snacks saved me from gnawing my arm off. By the time I got the quesadilla it wouldn't have mattered if it tasted like cardboard. But it was delicious. "Trinity's signature guacamole does the trick."

She looked pleased with the compliment. "It's basically mashed avocado."

Slim licked his lips. "Whatever it is, it's delicious. Thanks for feeding me. I forget to eat when I have a lot on my mind."

Trinity grinned. "Slim for a reason."

Her wit made her even cuter than the messy curls and pretty little face. Her energy was infectious. She made the shit ton of work ahead of us almost pleasant. Slim saw it, too. "That's pretty good."

Her pretty little mouth curled in a smile. "I try. Only smart people seem to get me, though. It's a problem." I could relate.

Slim scooped guacamole onto his quesadilla. "I doubt you have to try much at being sharp. But you're about the hardest worker I've ever seen."

Trinity brushed off his compliment. "I'm not doing anything more than you are. I just do what I'm told."

"If that's so, I'll tell you to stick around and help us get the shop up and running again. We'll put you on payroll—under the table of course—if you do."

I was again surprised by his proposition, pleasantly surprised. I resisted the urge to jump in. I didn't want my comments to sway her decision—meaning I didn't want to fuck it up. I kept my mouth shut until Trinity blinked up at me with those blue eyes waiting for me to weigh in.

"Your flight's on hold. You could hang out a little longer, help us out, and go home with more dollars in your pocket."

I held my breath while she contemplated the offer. That she was even considering it at all gave me hope. Again, hope.

She seemed to be doing some calculations. Finally she nodded. "I can hang around another couple of weeks to help."

I tried to hide my sigh of relief. Even if we stayed in the friend zone, having her around was better than the alternative. And if Slim was so smitten with her, he might even convince her to stay. She'd be my ideal replacement in the shop. But that was hoping for a miracle.

CHAPTER 16

TRINITY

*a*fter a week of back-breaking hard work, the shop was finally coming together. Unfortunately they'd lost over half their inventory. And insurance didn't cover the indoor repairs. When Slim handed me a wad of cash, I tried to refuse, but he insisted. "You've earned a hell of a lot more than this."

"I know, but the business is suffering. And you've both been so kind, giving me a place to stay and keeping me in food and booze, I don't really need the money."

Slim shoved the bills between my palms. "You're going back to college aren't you?"

I almost winced, not wanting to admit it. "Yeah."

"You'll need it then. Shut up and take it." Slim squeezed his hands around mine. There was no arguing with him. But it didn't feel right. We'd bonded over sweaty labor and take-out lunches. They'd taken me in and made me feel like family. You didn't let family pay you to help them out of a jam. It's just what you do—take care of your own. I reluctantly put the money in my pocket.

I looked up at Arlowe. "I'm buying dinner tonight then."

He started to protest but swallowed his words when I held up my hand. "I'm in the mood for a curry."

"Then a curry you shall have." Arlowe grabbed his keys. "Shall we?"

I left two twenties on the table and showered while Arlowe ordered Thai delivery. I took my time shaving my legs and slathering myself in lotion. I felt like a new person when I emerged in the little shorts and tank that had become my favorite pajamas.

Arlowe brought me a glass of wine and sat beside me. "Feel better?"

"I feel fabulous."

"I feel like I've been hit by a Mack truck."

I laughed. "Well, me too. But doesn't it feel *good*? There's nothing like being sore and feeling like you really deserve to relax with a glass of wine."

"You deserve that, and a medal." He tapped the rim of my glass with his. "You've been a lifesaver, woman."

I loved that he called me *woman*. "Stop it. I'm just helping out like anyone would."

"For real. I don't know what we'd have done without you. You might not know it, but you've kept Slim on task. He listens to you. That has helped him more than you can imagine. And, by proxy, it's helped me. He doesn't complain nearly as much when you're around."

I finished my sip of wine. "That's sweet. But he trusts you implicitly—that's obvious."

"Oh yeah, he trusts me. But he questions everything. Sometimes I think he still sees me as the kid he taught to surf."

"I know that feeling. Max is like Slim. I'll always be ten in his mind. But he's family. Like Slim."

"Probably why I ended up addicted to surfing. Slim adopted me. I was the son he never had. And unlike my own dad, he used to praise everything I did. That didn't last as long as I'd have liked." Arlowe's chuckle was interrupted by a knock at the door.

I got up to grab some plates and spotted the money I'd left on the table. Arlowe was already closing the door with the bag of food in his hands. "I left explicit instructions to use this to pay."

He grinned, happy that he'd gotten away with paying for another meal. "Next time."

We dug into the food like we hadn't eaten all day. The food went down fast. Coconut curries were my favourite. "I'd love to go to Thailand."

"Surfing Phuket?"

"And diving, maybe. I have to learn first."

"You grew up on the largest reef in the world and never learned to scuba?"

"Nope, I was too fascinated with the top of the water. I'd love to try it, though."

"The Keys are nice for that. You hang around long enough, we'll get you certified."

"If I hang around too much longer my parents might disown me. But who knows?" I wasn't sure what I was going back for anymore, other than their expectations. Being free from those had been nice. I'd invented and reinvented myself on the road. I wasn't the same person who'd left Australia a year-and-a-half ago. And even *that* Trinity wanted to be elsewhere. Going home felt like going backward.

Arlowe said, "What I know is that it's supposed to be perfect surfing tomorrow. Diving can wait. It's about time we catch a wave after all this hard work."

"I can't wait." I could relate to Arlowe's enthusiasm. It had been too much work and no play.

Arlowe cleared the table while I snuggled the kitten on the sofa.

"She needs a name. She's more than a Kitty."

"I call her Pussy in my head half the time, but that's probably inappropriate."

I giggled. "Well, she is a pussy, but it's not a very flattering name."

"How about Felix?"

"According to your mum, she's a girl. What do you think of Lola?" I held the cat out and gave her another look over. She didn't look like a Lola.

Arlowe apparently agreed. "Since we now know she's a calico, how about Kali?"

"That could work, but it doesn't fit her."

"What do you think of Kai?"

"Hawaiian for *ocean*. I love it. She looks like a Kai." I kissed the tip of the kitten's nose. If he'd named her, he couldn't possibly get rid of her when I left. "Thank you for taking her in. I know it wasn't in your plan."

"Life is what happens while you're busy making other plans." Arlowe squinted like he doubted his recollection of the quote. "Or something like that."

My heart warmed that he loved that quote as much as I did. "I'd say Lennon was spot on. I'm glad you've embraced another pussy in your life."

"When you put it like that…it's a no-brainer. But the best part is sharing a pussy with you."

I almost choked on my wine. "Is that a line? If it is, you might want to work on it."

"It was a joke, but I wouldn't mind."

I bit my lip, trying to ignore my heart pounding in my chest. A threesome with Arlowe would be divine. "Is that so?"

"I mean, I like the idea."

I rubbed my lips together and squinted at him, trying to act nonchalant. "You've thought a lot about this?"

"No." He shook his head and stammered. "I mean, yes. I haven't stopped thinking about it since you told me about your friends in Guatemala." He looked like he'd gotten a secret off his chest.

His nervousness made him even cuter. I bit my lip before I replied. "Hmm. Have you ever done it?"

He grinned. "Not yet."

"So it's a fantasy—having two women?"

He chuckled nervously. "It's more like a dream come true."

"For sex, it's amazing. For life, it's complicated."

His eyes widened. "I can imagine. One relationship is complicated. But three relationships, four really. That's nuts."

"It's a little crazy. But crazy is fun, for a while at least."

"I'm good at fun for a while." He tilted his head with a sheepish grin.

"I bet you are." I licked my lips before pressing them together to keep myself from inviting him for a round of fun. He was tempting me beyond the limits of my restraint.

I was so lost in his stare that I barely felt him slipping the wineglass from my hand. My gaze followed the glass to the table, but turned up to meet eyes that were asking. He moved like he already knew the answer. His hand slid under my curls to the nape of my neck to pull me close as his lips covered mine.

I stiffened for the briefest of moments, during which all the fear of trusting another man came rushing back. But the silkiness of his lips sliding over mine and the musky scent of aftershave flooded my senses. My body craved his touch like a junkie needs his fix. I'd gone three weeks with no sex, no touch. That may not be that long for the average person, but I'm used to having a lot more sex than the average person. I was entering full-blown withdrawal.

I'd already gotten a little horny over the bartender and the hostel receptionist. And Arlowe, too, which I hadn't wanted to admit. So when those lips swallowed me in a slow and

146

sultry kiss, I let them. My weight sank into his arms and I became putty in his hands. His touch left a tingling trail in its wake as one hand slid up my back and the fingers of the other buried into my curls. His tongue explored my mouth—intent on reaching every part of it. In that frenzy of desire, the fear that my heart might not bear another blow fell away. I wasn't thinking with my heart, or my mind for that matter. It was my body screaming for more that made surrendering to him the only option.

Arlowe's hands released their hold on me but his lips never left mine as he gently moved the kitten—at risk of being squished between us—to the sofa behind him. He pulled me tight, squeezing the breath from my chest. Warmth spread from deep in my core. I wanted his hands on every part of me at once. My palms ran over the contours of his muscular back while his hands slid down to lift my tank top up over my breasts.

The tip of his tongue traced his upper lip while he stared at my chest. "I've been thinking about those since the first time I saw you in a bikini."

I fought the urge to cover myself. "They're not much."

He cupped my boobs and massaged softly. "They're perfect."

Our mouths crashed in a hungry exchange as we pulled at one another's clothes. Arlowe pushed my shorts to the floor, leaving me naked. He pulled back to take in the sight of me once more. My eyes shifted to the growing bulge in his boxer briefs. The teal and white waistband set off his tan. He was the all-American surfer hunk—with an impressive package from what I could see. He had a perfect body, but his smile when he caught me checking him out was the sexiest thing about him.

He pulled me back into a kiss but I quickly broke free to kiss down his neck. I paused to look up from his chest. "There's something I've been thinking about since that first day surfing, too."

"Oh yeah? What's that." His wispy words made me smile as I kissed my way down his chest. His hips shifted when I reached the white elastic stretched over the tip of his hard cock. When I stroked him through the silky fabric, the excitement between my thighs skyrocketed. His hardness throbbed beneath my tender touch. He helped to push his underwear down, freeing a gorgeous specimen of a cock.

I'd been satisfied by sex with Diego, so I never saw him as lacking in that department. But there was no comparison. Arlowe's cock was a class above. As was he.

My fingers wrapped around his shaft, solid as pipe. I *needed* that inside me, but first I wanted to taste him from root to stem. I licked up to the head and circled it with the tip of my tongue. His gasp when I took him into my mouth made me even wetter. I swallowed him slowly, deeper with each pass until he groaned as I buried my nose in the delicious trail of hair that bisected his toned abs.

Deep down, I've known that I wasn't a lesbian since the first cock I ever sucked—I loved it. My affinity for the penis made it clear that my attraction to boobs didn't make me gay. I loved kissing and touching women. But I also loved sucking dick. It was especially pleasurable when it was as perfect as Arlowe's. I devoured him. I couldn't get enough. But after several minutes of pushing the limits of my deep throat capabilities, his fingers snaked into my hair and gently pulled me up.

His chest was heaving with excited breath. "I have some condoms in the bedroom."

"Let's go to the bedroom then." I slinked off him to stand and offered him a hand up. Arlowe's fingers laced through mine and squeezed before he led me to the bedroom.

My heart beat faster when we reached the bed. Arlowe took me by the shoulders and sat me on the edge. He stepped closer and I leaned in, reaching to taste him again. He stopped me and grinned as I looked up, confused. "My turn." My legs fell open as he lowered to his knees. The backs of his fingers trailed up my thigh, kiss after kiss following in their wake. My fingers worked into his blond waves of hair as his tongue found my folds. He kissed my pussy like it was kissing him back.

I bit my lip and moaned when his teeth raked over my swollen clit. Once he'd found the spot, he teased and prodded at it relentlessly.

His eyes opened when I started to moan and his hand moved to my breast, rubbing and squeezing before rolling my nipple between his fingertips. The louder my moans, the harder he pinched until I was gasping between a string of "Oh fucks."

He didn't need to learn my body. It felt like he'd always known it. He recognized the coming wave for what it was and latched on tight, determined to ride it all the way, until I was crashing violently against his face.

My fists relaxed in his hair as I gasped for breath. All the while the aftershock of the orgasm pulsed through me. I bit my lip, watching as Arlowe's lips moved to kiss my inner thigh while I caught my breath. It was hard to believe this was our first time. No one had ever turned me on so much.

He planted a foot and stood, stepping in so close his shins pressed into the edge of the bed as he stared down on me like I was his prize. I ached to feel his cock that stood tall as he leaned to take a condom from the nightstand drawer. He pushed my shoulders down onto the bed and slipped his hands under my knees to yank my hips nearly off the bed. I stared up, craving him.

He bent his knees and pulled me onto him. I groaned another "Oh fuck" as he stretched me open to fill me.My fingers curled around the bedcover as I hooked my ankles behind his back, pulling him deeper with every thrust. He slid easily in and out of my wetness, pushing so deep that I groaned. There was more of him than I could take, which made me want it all.

His pace slowed as he leaned over, his chest close to mine as his hands slipped beneath my shoulders.

"Hold on," he whispered.

I complied, wrapping my arms around his neck, my legs already coiled around his waist. I held on tight as he stood. He growled into my ear as he throbbed inside me, "God you feel so fucking good."

He felt better than any man I'd ever known. With our sweaty chests pressed together, wrapped in his arms as his lips found mine, I hoped he'd never let me go. He cupped my ass, lifting and lowering my hips up and down his length. The friction of his happy trail on my clit sparked an electric storm in my core as I clenched around him. He found my deepest parts—no short board on this ride. The wave built from deep within and crested into a perfect barrel.

I rode him until the wave crashed over me. I howled several more "Oh fucks" that vibrated through my chest into

Arlowe's. I was still coming when he lowered my feet to the floor. He smiled into my eyes and I stared back, wondering how he'd done that to me again so easily. He spun me around, one hand moving between my legs while the other guided him back into me from behind.

I stepped a foot up onto the bed to let him in deeper. His fingers slid over my clit faster and faster as he pumped harder and harder. His other hand moved over my sweaty breast to my throat as he growled, "You're fucking amazing." I could hear his wave cresting in his voice. When he went over the edge, my orgasm came back full force. Our moans intertwined like our steaming limbs. His heavy breath on my ear sent shivers up and down my spine.

We trembled silently for several seconds as we caught our breath. Arlowe finally slid out of me and went to the loo. I stood beside the bed, the reality of what I'd just done hitting me like a ton of bricks. My body still teemed with the pleasure he'd given me, but my mind went nuts. I hadn't thought about the aftermath of sex with Arlowe. It was just sex, I told myself. It had been a while and I was horny, but my roommate was probably the worst choice of friendly fucks I could have made. He'd made it clear that he had a thing for me. And I'd liked his flirty way more than I wanted to admit. I was playing with fire and sure to get burned one way or another. This had been a mistake. I should have known better. I *did* know better, but I did it anyway.

I hurried out to collect my clothes from the living room floor. Arlowe came out as I pulled my tank top over my head. He grinned but suspicion slanted his eyes. "Leaving so soon?"

I tried to smile but I could tell my face wasn't showing it. "Not leaving, just getting dressed."

He stepped closer and pulled me toward him with a hand around my waist. "Hey." He waited for my eyes to lift to his. "You alright?"

"Yeah, I'm good." But my averted eyes betrayed me.

He pushed my hair back from my face, his fingers lingering on my cheek. "You don't seem good. You seem…weird."

"Not the first time I've heard that." I laughed but I felt like I might burst into tears.

Arlowe took my hands and pulled me to sit beside him on the sofa. "What's going on, Trinity?"

I wanted to open up and tell him I might not be ready for this but the walls around my heart were already cemented in place. "Nothing. Why does it have to be weird?"

Arlowe's eyes narrowed as he studied my face. "Do you regret what just happened? Because I don't. Did I do something wrong?"

"No, you did everything right." And *that* was the problem.

"Then come here." He pulled me into his arms and kissed my temple. "Let's go to bed."

Part of me wanted to run, but most of me needed to be in his arms. I took a deep breath and nodded. "Okay."

He scooped up Kai and kissed her head, too, before handing her to me. "Don't forget your pussy."

I snickered and followed him to the bedroom. It didn't have to be weird. He wasn't the relationship kind of guy. Surely he wouldn't expect anything from me. We both knew what we were getting into. It was just for fun.

I snuggled the kitten while Arlowe spooned me. "I wish I could keep her."

He pulled me tight and kissed my hair. "I know the feeling."

CHAPTER 17

ARLOWE

*T*he sweet scent of sandalwood tickled my nose, but when I blinked my eyes open I realized it was the dark curls where my face was buried. Waking up with Trinity in my arms beat the hell out of hugging my pillow. I resisted the temptation to hug her tighter and held still to relish the rise and fall of her breath. The rest of me woke up even while I was trying to let her sleep. My body responded to her proximity like she was a power source. I took a deep breath and tried the golf-thoughts trick to stop my surging erection, but it was too late. I was rock-hard and throbbing, even while imagining Tiger Woods putting for a birdie on the eighteenth hole in the Majors.

Not wanting to wake her, I scooted my hips back so my cock wouldn't press into the fabric covering her perfect little ass. But my shifting must've woken her anyway, because her hips moved back, seeking me out. I tried one more time to hide my excitement but her round butt found it. She groaned softly as she swiveled her hips and pressed herself harder onto me.

Trinity lifted her head to speak through the mound of curls riding her shoulder. "Mmm. Well, good morning." I felt like a high schooler trying to hide his hard-on in the locker room. The secret was already out. When she turned to face me, her smile set me at ease. "Hi."

"Good morning, beautiful." I started to make an excuse for my morning wood, but I couldn't speak when her hand honed in on it.

"I love that you're so glad to see me."

I wanted to tell her she had no idea how glad I was that she'd calmed down after her little freak-out and come to bed with me last night, but I was afraid I might scare her off. Downplaying my excitement wasn't easy with my body screaming for her. There was no sign of hesitation now, though, as her fingers wrapped around my length. Her eyes sparkled with her naughty smile. I took her face in my hands and pulled her mouth to mine while she squeezed me in her fist. Our lips and tongues moved in a slow, slippery rhythm. "You're such a good kisser."

Her blue eyes sparkled in the morning light. "So are you. I could tell you'd be good at all of it as soon as you kissed me last night."

Trinity's mischievous grin made me grow even harder in her hand as she pushed up to her elbow, rolling me onto my back before flinging a leg across my hips to straddle me. Her pelvis pressed into my hardness as her lips moved over mine. I worked her tank top up her back and she seemed reluctant to pull away but broke the kiss to let me undress her. She wiggled her hips to work them out of her shorts.

I lifted my head to admire the narrow brown strip of hair

above her slit rubbing against me while I reached for a condom from the nightstand drawer.

She raised up to let me roll it on before I guided myself into her waiting wetness. I groaned as she slid onto me. She felt like a pocket custom made to my contours.

My hips swiveled, pushing deeper the wetter she got. The heat and the friction between us increased the friction between us as she kissed me hard and pressed harder onto me. Her lips left mine when she sat up, her fingers curling in my chest hair as she rode me. My hands lingered on her hips, but she didn't need a guide. She knew exactly how to make herself come on my cock.

She kissed me hard and pressed harder onto me, increasing the friction between us.

Her gaze locked onto mine while her hips moved intently. An almost frightened look in her eyes worried me at first, but her moans told me she was okay. I grinned and dug my fingertips into the sides of her hips. "Yeah, come on that cock, baby girl." Her eyes lit up like blue flames and her lips twisted into a smile as she moved harder and faster, moans cresting. She seemed to like that.

And *that* turned me on even more than the sight of her taut stomach and tits bouncing as she took herself to orgasm. Her desperate moans were making mine come quicker than I'd hoped. As she trembled over me, I struggled to hold it back. Even Tiger Woods couldn't help me. I'd wanted it to last, but her moans only intensified as I pulled down on her hips and came with her.

Her gasps for air masked my own as our bodies shuddered in aftershock bliss. She finally opened her eyes. "That was fun."

I chuckled. "Maybe even more fun than surfing."

Her smile relaxed and her brow crinkled as she looked toward her phone on the nightstand. "What time is it?"

I reached for her phone. "Quarter of eight."

"We need to get moving if we want to hit the tide right. *Vámonos.*" She raised up on her knees, sliding off of me, and stepped off the bed without further ceremony.

The abrupt ending to sex was as humorous as it was curious. She stood over me, waving with a backward hand to coax me up. If I weren't looking at her flawless naked body, I'd wonder if she wasn't really a dude.

She had her priorities straight. First came surfing. Sex was a close second. If there was a way to make both happen, even better. We were definitely on the same wavelength. I grinned as I took her hand and let her help me up.

She was in and almost out of the shower by the time I got the condom off and took a leak. My dick was still charged with the memory of her clamping down around me while we both came. The warm water flowing over it reminded me of the only time I'd ever done Ecstasy. Supercharged senses. Trinity was as good as the best drug I'd ever tried. I'd never done the drug again because I could see how someone could get addicted to that kind of fun. Trinity might be just as dangerous.

She was already dressed when I wandered out, still in an ecstatic fog. I hurried to pull on shorts and grabbed my keys as she shoved a piece of toast slathered with strawberry jam into my hand. "We can share this coffee. You only have one to-go cup." She held up the stainless steel cup and gathered two more slices of toast in a paper towel between her fingers.

Patting my back, she nudged me toward the front door. She was certainly efficient.

It was a good thing we didn't dawdle. By the time we grabbed the boards from the shop and got to the inlet, it was two minutes after low tide. We rushed down to the beach and stopped only briefly to leave our towels on the sand. I looked out into the climbing sun and regarded the waves, which were cresting in just the right spot. Conditions were perfect.

I still felt like I was in that post-ecstasy heightened state of being when I spotted a promising swell approaching. Trinity was fifty yards ahead of me and had already turned to kick like hell into position. It seemed like time slowed down when the pull of the wave stalled and then lifted me. I jumped to my feet, which seemed to bond with the board, sensing the forces and adjusting with continuous subtle changes. I looked up to the massive lip forming over me, pulling my rail to hug the wall of the barrel. The cold blow of the ocean depths raring behind me chilled my neck as the darkness closed in. Hugging that wall, carving on the edge, harnessing its force to stay one step ahead, thwarting its attempt to swallow you whole—that's the thrill of surfing. And when you blow out of it on the other side like a geyser into the sunshine, it's like you cheated death and went straight to heaven.

I hadn't had this much fun surfing since the early days, when I'd finally mastered the skills. It helped that a gorgeous Aussie was pushing me to do better than my best.

I already knew she was a badass, but Trinity's prowess on the board somehow surprised me once again. She had to know how awesome she was, but she didn't show it. She just did it.

My arms ached from paddling back out to one wave after

another. Trinity didn't appear even faintly fatigued after we'd shredded hardcore for a couple of hours nonstop. With a lull between waves, she hopped off her board and kicked over to mine. She propped up on her elbows to kiss me. "This is so bloody fun! Thank you, Arlowe. You sure know how to show a girl a good time."

"You're the first girl I've ever had this much fun with. Surfing and sex makes for the perfect morning."

She kissed me again, pulling away with a smile. "Really? You've never boned a surfer chick?"

"I didn't say that. But none as good as you." I didn't mean just the surfing, but I didn't want to say more.

My growling stomach was a good excuse to change the subject. "I feel like a burger after all that."

Trinity grinned. "I'd say we deserve some greasy goodness for lunch. I'm famished. Where's good?"

"Moe's is the best. You ready?"

"Not really, but we need to eat."

It seemed to take forever, but when I finally sunk my teeth into the juicy burger, it was worth the wait. They say hunger is the best seasoning. Hunger fueled by surfing and sex might have made the most bland of burgers delicious, but the warm fluid that ran down my hands and dripped onto the plate attested to the flavor.

I was still in a euphoric daze when we strolled back into the shop. Trinity kissed Slim on the cheek and smiled as she handed him the sandwich she'd thought to order for him. "We brought you lunch."

"Aww. You two are looking after the old man."

She grinned. "It's the least we can do when you're holding down the fort while we piss off surfing."

"You know I don't mind."

I was glad to hear he wasn't miffed. "It's supposed to be good again tomorrow. And maybe Thursday too. You sure you don't mind single-handing the morning shift?"

"You have to rip when the waves are running. We're almost finished here. I've got what's left under control. You guys enjoy." He winked at Trinity as he lifted his sandwich for a bite. "After all this work, you deserve to get it while the gettin's good."

She slipped her hand behind his back and gave him a hug. "Thanks, Slim. You know I like to earn my keep. So put me to work."

"You can start with the sunglasses display. You're better at making things pretty than either of us will ever be."

Trinity carried a box of sunglasses over to the empty display. "Leave the pretty stuff to the pretty one."

I was happy for their comfortable way. Slim looked at her with the same paternal love he had for me. She was part of the family.

Trinity enthusiastically rifled through the fridge when we got home. "I'll just throw something together."

How she had energy to even think about cooking dinner was beyond me. After surfing all morning and working all afternoon, the couch was calling, but if she was going to cook, I could find the energy to help. Shouldn't be hard—her tireless nature was infectious. I took a bottle of wine from the rack over the fridge and reached around Trinity for the corkscrew.

Her hips pushed back into me and she smiled over her shoulder. "You read my mind."

I pulled out my phone to put music on. "What would you like to hear?"

Trinity took a long pull of wine, then wiped her lips. "I like everything. Surprise me."

When Prince's "Kiss" started through the sound system, she started jumping up and down. She really was an Energizer Bunny. I grinned. "Good choice?"

"I love this song. It's one of the last songs I played in Antigua."

"You play this song? I'd love to hear that."

"I haven't since Antigua. I've barely played at all since then."

"Yeah I noticed your guitar has been in the closet. I wondered why you lug it around the world and don't play it, but I figured that was your business."

"I played every day before I got to Peru. Between leading groups and traveling back and forth to Cuzco, I got out of the habit."

"I love Cuzco, but the altitude is rough." I'd done the Machu Picchu trek with a few friends in college and puked the entire first twenty-four hours despite gnawing on bitter coca leaves. "Why were you based in the mountains when your trips were on the coast?"

"Stupidity." I knew the answer and regretted asking when I saw the pained look in her eyes. But her smile quickly returned. "I'd be happy to play for you, though I might be a bit rusty."

"I doubt you've lost it." Everything she did, she did well. But not only well. She did everything with an ease and grace that you can't teach. I bet the guitar was no different. "What else do you like to play?"

"All sorts. I've been obsessed with John Mayer lately. Maybe I'll work on a few of his once I'm finally settled."

"Hey, remember that Lennon quote? 'Life is what happens while you're busy making plans.' There's no time like the present to start doing what you love to do."

Trinity grinned as her hand fell onto my chest. "You preach to my soul." Her tiptoed kiss took me by surprise.

I let my eyes close as her lips brushed mine. I wanted inside that soul.

I put on Mayer's *Born and Raised* album, hoping that would ensure Trinity sang for me. It was a bonus to see her dance while she cooked. She was by far the sexiest and most entertaining chef I'd ever seen. And she'd finally relaxed. There was no sign of the anxiety that took hold of her last night. Like it was just a bad dream when she'd turned cold after the most amazing sex of my life. But she'd come around, and full circle now, it seemed. Hopefully that meant she was over it. But deep down, I knew that a panic response like that had to come from something.

Was it just Diego or something more? I wished I could have a few minutes alone with Diego. He deserved an ass kicking for the damage he'd done to this beautiful soul.

She was strong yet fragile. She didn't need protection from Diego. He'd already come and gone. It wasn't Diego who might break her heart. With my track record, I'd second-guess shacking up with me, too. I wasn't sure I deserved it, but she'd decided to stay. For now.

She bumped my hips and handed me a plate while she sang. I ran my hand down her back before I picked up the wine bottle. I couldn't pass up a minute of this. I might not ever find it again.

She might only be here another week, but if she'd spend it in my bed, I'd take it. It might be crazy that I liked her more than any woman I'd ever known, but I'd be crazy not to take every second that I could spend with her. She might not be the only one risking a broken heart.

When Trinity pulled out her guitar, nothing could have prepared me for the soulful voice bottled up inside that pixie frame. Fuck. She was good. Of course she was. But fuck.

The ballads flowed straight from her heart. Her voice captured the rawness of her heartache, but her strength shone through. This woman never ceased to amaze me.

I kicked my feet up on the table for the serenade. I could feel in her gaze that she felt something, too. But the question was, when would her walls go back up?

After a few songs, I raised my glass as she paused, "You're really good."

"Thanks. I love it. Thank you for reminding me. And thanks for listening."

I wanted to say I'd listen for years if she'd keep singing, but I felt like a moron for even thinking something that sappy. I didn't want to scare her off. "Are you ready for bed?" I was beat, but I'd stay up if she wanted to play more.

"Yeah, I'm knackered." She slid her guitar into the canvas case on the floor.

"I'm glad to see that even your limitless energy needs a recharge." I was even more glad when she pulled me by the hand toward my room. There was no question where she was sleeping tonight.

When I plugged in my phone, I saw a string of missed texts. Luckily none from Monica. She must be seething. Or maybe she was getting over it. I hoped so. I felt like a dick for not contacting her, but a week without talking to her just made me more sure… There was nothing there. There never had been.

I clicked on a message from an unknown number.

Please check your email. We'd like to schedule an interview.

I started to open my email app when Trinity stepped behind me, her arms snaking up my chest while she kissed my back. "I think we need a shower. We've haven't done that yet." One hand slid down over my cock. Her libido was as astounding as the rest of her.

I forgot about the email—and everything else—as I turned and wrapped my arms around her waist. I grinned as I teased her. "I thought you were tired?"

"A shower with you is just the recharge I need. Then sleep."

I loved her confidence to ask for what she wanted almost as much I loved that she wanted me.

CHAPTER 18

TRINITY

*T*hree days in a row of surfing and sex had recharged me, alright. It was all I'd needed to erase the stress of the storm, not to mention the burden I'd shouldered from Peru. My sorrow had been a heavy package that Arlowe had helped transform into a horny release. Shower sex, sofa sex, kitchen counter sex. We hadn't made it to every surface of his flat, but it wouldn't be long at this rate.

For nearly two weeks I'd been floating through a nirvana of no plan. My parents had asked if I was ready to rebook, but they backed off when I responded with a simple, "Not yet." I didn't want to think about the future, or anything else.

But now that the shop was ready to reopen, my excuse for staying was running out. I didn't want to think about leaving, but staying wasn't an option. I'd been able to let loose and enjoy Arlowe because I knew I was leaving. There was no risk of attachment. No risk that I'd start imagining a life together and plotting how I could stay and make it happen. I'd made that mistake once and wouldn't make it again.

It was what it was with Arlowe—a fling. A really really fun fling. I couldn't help but want it to last a little longer. If there was more fun to be had, I wanted to have it.

I got dressed after a quick shower and found Arlowe ready with a fresh mug of coffee and a smile. We had a big day at the shop ahead, putting the finishing touches to open tomorrow. He kissed me softly. "Good morning, beautiful. I made us some eggs."

My stomach fluttered every time he called me that. "I need protein after all that surfing."

Arlowe smiled over his shoulder as he carried our plates to the table. "I gotta say, my body is grateful that the waves suck today. Good timing, too. Now we can finally finish the shop."

I took my seat and paused before digging into the steaming pile of scrambled eggs. "Yeah I felt a tad guilty taking you away when Slim needed you the most, but damn it's been good."

Arlowe wiped his mouth with the back of his hand as he chewed. "Slim understands more than anyone else."

"I know he does. That's why he's so cool."

The shop looked ready, but we still had a full day ahead of compiling a new inventory. Small wonder Arlowe hated this part. It was tedious—and he was terrible at it. He didn't have the patience. While he bickered with Slim, I got it done. Literally. It was nearly finished when we took a break for a late lunch.

Slim acknowledged my efforts with a jab at Arlowe. "*Someone* stayed on task all morning instead of bitching every chance they got."

Arlowe rolled his eyes. "I agree. Trinity is way better at inventory than I am." He turned to me with a grin. "Please, take that job. I'll gladly never do inventory again."

"Well at least you know you have a solid start," I said. My way of deflecting. "It shouldn't be hard to keep up with now."

"If you'd stay, it wouldn't be an issue at all."

I chuckled. 'You know I can't do that."

The corner of Slim's lip drew to the side as he squinted skeptically. "You sure about that? Because it would be nice to have you around. Especially if this one gets a *job*." He said it with a hint of disgust.

"Yeah, I'm not sure why he'd do that." I eyed Arlowe, wondering if he'd told Slim about the interview he had coming up. "You've got a pretty good job already."

"I do, but you know I have my reasons."

His reasons didn't make much sense to me, but it was none of my business. "You have to do what feels right."

"We'll see. I'm just exploring possibilities. But Slim's right, you'd be an ideal replacement."

I didn't want to be his replacement. I didn't want to assist him in making a huge mistake. And I couldn't anyway. "That's flattering, really. But you know I have my reasons, too."

"Right...uni." Arlowe raised a brow. "What if you went back to school here?"

"That's impossible. And isn't uni crazy expensive here?"

Arlowe shook his head. "State schools in Florida are great, and affordable. My dad's best friend is an immigration lawyer. He says he can help you get a student visa, pro bono of course. You could try it for a semester."

Wow, he'd really thought this through. I blinked at Arlowe as I processed what he'd said. "My parents are already annoyed. Mum is badgering me to book my ticket. I probably can't stretch it too much longer." It wasn't exactly true, but I was sure it would be soon enough.

The truth was, I didn't want to leave. And that scared me. Arlowe's carefully devised plan sounded perfect. My hedonistic side wanted to stay and soak up every minute of our magic. But that he was plotting for a future freaked me the fuck out.

Slim chimed in. "I'd make you manager and we can pay you pretty well. Despite how it may seem, the business does pretty well. We'd work around your class schedule, of course. And make sure you get some good surfing when it's pumping. I bet you'd be a great instructor."

"I'm told I'm pretty good." It sounded like a dreamy way to pass a few months, but how could I keep it casual with Arlowe? We already lived together—a first for me. Which was fine for a few weeks. But doing that for much longer would be a relationship. And I definitely wasn't ready to even think about that.

Leaving felt all wrong, but staying didn't feel right. It felt scary.

Lena would tell me to stay. But she didn't understand how broken my trust was. No one did.

Still, I had the nagging feeling that this was an opportunity I shouldn't pass up. I wasn't sure about anything anymore, and feeling put on the spot had my anxiety soaring. I had to divert. "That is a lot to think about, and I will. Thank you for the offer." I smiled at Slim before turning to Arlowe. "And for the research. You must've put a lot of effort into that homework."

Arlowe shrugged. "Nah. Just a phone call."

I didn't believe him for a second, which was sweet. But that didn't mean I could trust this to last. "Well, thank you anyway. I'll think about it. All of it."

So much for not thinking about the future.

CHAPTER 19

ARLOWE

*M*y phone buzzed in my pocket as we pulled into my parking spot. I slipped it out and then right back in. Monica had broken her silence. But she was the last person I wanted to hear from right now.

Trinity hadn't said yes. She hadn't said no either. I didn't want her to "think on it." I wanted her to stay. The thought of losing her made me nauseous.

It was a big decision, but I suspected that her hesitation had as much to do with her broken heart as it did her parents. Jumping in with both feet was easy when the days were numbered. But now that there was a longer-term offer on the table, I was afraid I'd fucked it up by sleeping with her. I'd say that I wouldn't trade the past few days of sensational sex for anything, but—mind-blowing as it was—I might trade it for having Trinity around for longer, even if that meant returning to the Friend Zone.

She didn't bring up the job offer while we made dinner, but I needed to let her know that there was no pressure. I didn't want to be the reason she might leave.

I patted the sofa beside me and she slinked into the spot under my arm that seemed made for her. "It's surprising how much I love having you here." I felt like a sap and wanted to take it back as soon as I said it.

She eyed me with a curious grin. "Why's that?"

Why had I said that? was a better question. I stammered to recover. "I haven't lived with anyone since college. And I've never lived with a girl." I was rambling in the wrong direction. I took a deep breath to stop myself from saying anything even more stupid.

But Trinity's smile was relaxed as she chided. "Really? Commitment issues?"

"Maybe. Or maybe I never found anyone worth committing to." Jesus. I couldn't stop myself. I was trying to tell her it was okay to take a step back but what kept coming out was how different she was than all the other girls. The truth was like that. It had a way of coming out. That's how I ruined most relationships. Which was probably what I was doing again this time with the hole I was digging. I had to get back on track.

"But that's why I brought it up. I don't want you to feel pressured to live here if you decide to stay. I can help you find something if you'd rather get your own place."

"You're already kicking me out?" She slapped my knee and giggled.

I pulled her in close to my side. "Not at all. I don't want you to go. You are more than welcome here." I wanted to tell her that nothing would make me happier than her staying in my house, in my bed, but I knew better. I wasn't the only one with commitment issues. And understandably so, at least in her case. "I'm having a blast with you. But that was true before all this." I motioned between us. *Before us.* "This doesn't have to be part of the package. I have no expectations." That much was true. But I had desires and she was the subject of every last one.

"Thank you for saying so. And for being considerate. It means a lot. I'm having a blast with you, too. It's surprising." Trinity smirked and slapped her knees as she jumped up to start across the room. "You ready for a backgammon rematch?"

With her ability to change the subject, I couldn't get a read on which way she was leaning, but she seemed her usual peppy self. And she beat me four games in a row.

I wasn't sure if it was good or bad that this situation was weighing heavier on me than it was her. It was definitely good that she was still her usual amorous self. Her hand slid up my inner thigh to my groin. "You up for another game or shall we call it a night?"

Her fingers brushed my cock as she squeezed my leg, sending a surge up into my chest. Her sexual energy was astounding and what it did to me was unprecedented. I'd never been this into a woman. Ever.

I held her with a determined stare. "I think my odds of winning are higher in bed."

The way she bit her lip made me grow in my shorts when she said, "I'd say they're about a hundred percent."

I pulled her up by the wrist as I stood and led her into the bedroom. I stopped beside the bed and held her hands in mine. "You know, a lesser man might have a hard time losing so many times in a row to his lady." I tried not to shudder visibly at my choice of words. As much as I wanted to claim her, now was not the time to share that urge.

"Lucky for me, there's nothing lesser about you." Her palm rubbed my half-chubby through my shorts, erasing the unease.

It's always nice when a woman loves your cock, but when a woman you thought was a lesbian seems to worship it—that means something. Which might explain why it responded like a ready soldier anytime she showed it the slightest attention. The head pushed up into the waistband of my board shorts while her fingers squeezed the shaft.

When she pulled the tie to loosen my shorts, the head peeked out like a beacon that beckoned to her lips. Her mouth lowered over it as she sat on the side of the bed, her tongue flicking the tip while she stared up at me with those deep blue eyes that made me yearn—sending my cock dancing at the edges of her mouth. She clawed to push my shorts below my hips so that she could swallow more of me.

She took me deeper and deeper until her nose touched my belly. The surge of passion she stirred in me took my breath. I wanted to let loose all over her face, and picturing that almost made it happen. But I steadied her with a hand on her shoulder and arched my back to slide myself out of her mouth.

Blue eyes sparkled with satisfaction as she stood. Pulling me by the cock, she passed it behind her back like a baton to the other hand as she spun around and pressed her butt back, shifting so that my pulsing shaft slid in and out of the cleft between her firm cheeks through her thin shorts. She pleaded over her shoulder, "I *need* you inside me."

Just like I needed her to open up and let me in.

I grabbed her by the hips and turned her to face me, my hand trailing up her side then over her chest, to hook beneath her chin. "I want to see your face."

She looked away, suddenly bashful, but she had to know how goddamn gorgeous she was. My lips lowered to hers as I guided her back to the pillow. I slid her shorts over her hips before I fumbled for the nightstand drawer. She looked like a kid waiting for the new toy to be assembled on Christmas morning as I unrolled a condom. She sighed when I finally slipped inside.

Each of my slow thrusts took me deeper, and she winced slightly as I reached her limit. But her hands on my ass urged me on as her hips moved to meet me. She wanted more. She wanted it all—even if she couldn't quite take it yet. I didn't want to hurt her, but she seemed to take great pleasure in the pain, which turned me on more than I could have imagined.

I held back, relishing the feel of her tight walls around me. Her pussy was so wet her lips smacked as I slid in and out.

"See what you do to me." She grinned, her gorgeous tanned skin flush with arousal. "I love that sound." Her hips lifted and swirled, faster and faster despite my efforts to keep a steady pace. Her command came out in a desperate sigh. "Harder."

If I fucked her any harder, I wasn't going to last. I didn't want this to end too soon, any of it.

Her nails dug into my flesh, insistent as she pulled me deeper. I pressed to her limit and stayed, throbbing inside her as I shifted to one side so that I could wrap my fingers around her wrist.

Her eyes locked on mine with a seductive playfulness that made the urge to come worse. I stared back with a look of warning as I pushed her arm up over her head, pinning her wrist to the bed. She inhaled sharply and a smile spread across her lips as I pushed her other arm up and held her still.

I slid in and out of her with slow strokes, only stopping when the swivel of her hips tried to speed up my measured rhythm. Her quizzical look turned to a smile and she moved her hips in slow circles. She'd gotten the message. I pressed her hands hard into the pillow overhead, wishing that holding her like that might keep her from leaving.

Trinity's moans sounded more like pleas with every thrust. The throbbing tingle in my cock intensified when her eyes glazed with intoxicating desire.

She'd taken me back to the brink, but my edge moved further away as I pushed into her. Expanding the boundaries of my restraint took my pleasure to a new plane.

Trinity gasped as I filled her with my girth, her eyes so wide I could see clear into her soul as she clenched around me. Our bodies moved in sync while the our heavy breath echoed through the room. It was just us in that moment, and for that moment it seemed like we might last.

My heart pounded in my chest. I'd never wanted anything more than I wanted this to last. Not the sex. Well, that, too. But it was *us* that I wanted to carry on. Her penetrating stare told me that she felt the same.

Locked in her loving gaze, an unfamiliar warmth swelled in

my chest and I had an overwhelming urge to say "I love you." I didn't, of course. That would have been suicide. But that the thought had even crossed my mind threw me for a loop. I'd only said it to two girls in my life and I'm not sure I'd really meant it either time. I know I didn't. Not like this.

Her fingers clawed at the pillowcase and her hips lifted to press her clit onto me as her moans strung together into a shrill call. "God, yes. Yes. Yes. Yes!"

She was on the edge and I wanted to be there with her. Her sweet pussy pulsed around me as I pressed harder and faster. She held my gaze, calling through gasps, "Yes, babe, come with me. Come with me."

I stared deep into her eyes and groaned as the roaring wave spread through me. My desire poured into her in a warm gush and my heart followed. In that moment, I'd give her anything. Everything. A tear formed in the corner of her eye as she shuddered, gasping. But then something recognizable —fear—flashed through her eyes and she looked away.

Brick by brick, the wall went up. My grip on her wrists relaxed before I trailed a hand down her cheek to turn her chin up. "You okay, beautiful?"

When her eyes returned to mine, there was no fear, but there was no love either. "I'm better than okay."

And I knew she was lying. There was nothing to think over. She'd already made her decision.

CHAPTER 20

TRINITY

*S*lim's eyes lit up as he looked up over his wire-rimmed glasses from behind the counter, while I struggled to simultaneously manage the front door and Kai's carrier. "Good morning."

I put Kai on the ground behind the counter. She'd slept through the tussle. "It must be a great morning after the stellar re-opening yesterday."

"Yeah, it sure was gangbusters all day. I was exhausted last night. Did you guys rest well?"

Did Arlowe bending me over the dining table before we could get the plates down count as relaxing? "We did."

The day had been so busy we'd barely had time to catch our breath. There'd been no mention of his job offer. I hoped we'd make it another day without making it awkward. I couldn't talk about it when I wasn't sure what I thought about it.

After all the great days of surfing and seeing everything

come together at the shop, not to mention getting along with Arlowe like best friends—and the best of lovers—I was on a high I didn't want to come down from. I was leaning heavily toward staying.

After we chatted about the first day back in business for several minutes, Slim looked around toward the front door. "Where the hell is Arlowe? I thought he'd be in right behind you."

"Oh, he didn't tell you? He dropped me on his way to help his dad repair their backyard fence."

"Arlowe's a better son than he is a business partner. His father might not agree, but it wouldn't be the first time we see things opposite."

It wouldn't surprise me if they'd butted heads. I could only imagine what Slim had seen of their dynamic over the years, if what I saw after the storm was any indication. My heart stung for Arlowe at the thought. "Seems like his dad has a stubborn streak."

"They both do. Where do you think he got it from?" Slim chuckled. "That apple fell directly from the tree. And he's been trying to get out of the shadow for as long as I've known him." I was tempted to agree, but refrained. Talking about Arlowe behind his back felt wrong, even if it was the truth. Slim huffed, rolling his eyes as he shook his head. "But they have a pretty good relationship, all in all. They're a nice family—a lot nicer than most."

Slim's assessment matched mine to a tee but I decided to stay on the high road and focus on the positive. "They were so kind to me when we went over to clean up after the storm."

Slim grinned. "I bet they loved you."

I shrugged as I rearranged the sunglasses display. "I suppose."

Slim's brows raised over the rims of his glasses. "If there's anything Arlowe's father admires, it's work ethic. I'm sure yours knocked his socks off."

"They were both extremely grateful for my help, which seemed silly since everyone was helping everyone."

"It's what we do in times of crisis. The rest of the time we bitch and complain and mostly hate each other. Welcome to Florida."

I laughed. "America is known for its Every Man for Himself mentality, but that's probably true the world over."

"That might be one designation we actually rank number one in. Something to be proud of?" Slim shook his head. "But we're not all bad."

"On the contrary. I think you're mostly good."

Slim's warm smile reminded me of Max and what a teddy bear he could be under his gruff facade. "That's probably true the world over. Thankfully."

Goosebumps tickled up my arm. "That reminds me of *The Diary of Anne Frank*. Did you ever read that?"

His head tilted as he eyed me with surprise. "I did. And I know exactly the part you're referencing. Didn't she say something like 'In spite of everything…'?"

I chimed in to recite the rest of the quote with him: "*I believe people are really good at heart.*"

Slim smiled, as pleased as I was at the little moment we'd shared. "True or not, it's better to think like Anne."

Boy, was he right. "Agreed. I know too many pessimists who call themselves realists."

"The self-fulfilling prophecy. Their reality is as shitty as they expect it to be."

"It's literally what we make of it, so much of the time, because we make it. We are the creators of our own destiny."

Slim stared at me for a second before his lips turned up in a smile. "You're wise beyond your years."

I smiled. "Thanks, I guess. I think I was born with that philosophy though."

"We probably all are." Slim grinned before the loud chime of his phone on the counter distracted him. He glanced down at the screen. "Much as I'd love to philosophize all morning, I need to run a couple of errands and check in on Roxy."

"Right. How's she managing the flare up?"

Slim shrugged but his tired eyes said it all. "Managing." He forced a smile. "Will you be okay here for an hour or so on your own?"

"Of course. No worries, mate. Take your time."

"I'll hurry back. I'd hate for you to get swamped all alone." He grabbed his keys and headed for the door.

"I'll be fine."

If anyone was good at heart, it was Slim. His devotion to Roxy despite their many struggles gave me faith in true love.

I tallied up yesterday's sales and was updating the inventory when the bell on the door chimed. I looked up, halfway expecting Arlowe since I was doing the task he loathed the most. Instead my eyes landed on a smartly dressed woman with dark brown hair that looked like it had been professionally straightened this morning. She looked so startled to see me that I thought she might be afraid I would steal the pink Prada purse clutched between her fists at her chest as she approached the counter. She looked over my shoulder toward the storeroom. "Hi. Where's Arlowe?"

"Oh, he's not here. Is there something I can help you with?" I heard the doubt in my voice. She didn't look like a customer herself, but maybe she was shopping for her boyfriend. I shuddered at my presumption. Maybe not all surfer chicks looked like surfer chicks. "Are you looking for anything in particular?"

"Yes, Arlowe. Where is he?"

I blinked and took a deep breath. It was not my place to share his whereabouts, least of all with someone who was clearly agitated. "He'll be in shortly. I can tell him you stopped by if you like."

She eyed me before responding. "Who are you?"

I blinked as I took a slow breath, trying not to show my discomfort. "I'm Trinity. And you are…?"

"Monica. Arlowe's girlfriend."

I was relieved when the cat's meow gave me an excuse to look away as I answered. "Oh. Sorry. I'm new. I didn't realize he had a girlfriend."

I leaned over and lifted Kai to my chest. The commotion must have woken her. Or maybe she'd heard the shrill shrieks of crippling anxiety in my head. Monica was his girlfriend. That cocksucker.

She eyed the cat before looking up with an accusing glare. "How long have you been here?"

I held the cat to my chest like a shield that might protect me from the inquisition. "A few weeks now."

"And you're here from Australia?" She sized me up from head to toe.

I petted Kai's back to calm my nerves. "That's right. Just passing through."

"Well, isn't that a coincidence?" She looked as disgusted with the cat as she was with me. "Are you the one who found the cat?"

"That would be me." Had he told her about me, or just the cat? I didn't want to ask.

"The reason he was late for our last date. And the reason he's ghosted me ever since, I imagine." She glowered before looking up to the ceiling like it might have the answer as she tapped her foot.

"I don't know anything about that. I saved the cat from being washed down the gutter and brought her here. Arlowe was going to take her to the shelter the next day, but they closed when the storm was coming."

Her lips twisted in a scowl. "Did he take you in like a stray, too?"

She was a woman scorned. I should know better than to engage, but I had to defend myself. I hadn't done anything wrong. He was the dog. "Excuse me?"

"I've spent the past two weeks wondering what went wrong. Everything was going so well between us. Then, poof, it wasn't." Her fingers released the pink Prada clutch that was tucked under her elbows long enough to signal the elusive explosion of *poof*. "Now I know."

I didn't want to defend a lying cheat. But I didn't want to be involved. "I'm sure it's nothing like you think."

"You're right about that. I thought he was a nice guy." Her voice quivered before she pressed her lips together and drew in a long breath through her nose. "Do me a favor, don't mention that I stopped by. Just forget this ever happened. I intend to."

I did my best to feign a smile but I was sure it failed. "No worries."

She glared like she hoped her dirty look might send me straight back to Australia. "If you think he's a nice guy, you should worry." She turned on her matching pink pumps and made a beeline for the door.

I stared after her long after the jingle of the bell on the handle had silenced. I knew exactly how Monica felt. I'd been as composed as she was just now when I discovered Diego's deception. I felt for her. But my heart was fracturing in my chest—again—for being so stupid as to even consider letting a man in.

I had to pull myself together when an actual customer came in asking for lessons. I took his number and told him Slim would call him to schedule. I wanted to cry but tourists kept trickling in. The distraction made me hold myself together.

Slim returned looking disheveled, carrying a bag of sandwiches. As much as I wanted to ply him with questions to determine the extent of Arlowe's betrayal, it was inappropriate on every level. And there was no need to confirm that Arlowe was a colossal disappointment. I felt it to my core. But Slim didn't need to know that I was gutted.

I unwrapped the sub he'd handed me. I could only stomach a few bites.

Slim eyed the sandwich as I crumpled it back into its paper wrapper before giving me a concerned once-over. "Not like you to not eat."

"Yeah, sorry, my stomach's not feeling so great. I just didn't think about it."

"If you need to scoot, I got this."

If I had a key, I would have gone home and packed my bags hours ago. "Thanks, but I'm sure Arlowe will be here any minute."

Slim grinned as the door jingled. "Speak of the devil."

He could say that again.

"Take this girl home. She doesn't feel well. And you left her here all day while mending fences with your father."

Arlowe flashed the pearly grin that had made me fall for him. "We got the fence fixed. Sorry it took so long." He stepped in behind me and rested a hand on my waist. "You okay?"

I didn't look back. I couldn't look him in the eye. "Just a weird stomach. I can't eat. Which has made me a little weak."

"Oh shit, really? I'm sorry, Trin. I hope you haven't been feeling like this all day. I feel terrible leaving you here to work when you're sick."

"I'm not sick, really. There must be something I can't stomach, though. I'll be alright. But a lie down would be nice about now." He had no idea that he was what had taken my appetite, and I planned to keep it that way. There was no point in discussing it. I wouldn't believe anything that came from his mouth.

"Even when you're sick, your accent is cute." Arlowe grinned as he squeezed my waist.

I rolled my eyes and tried to fake a smile, but I truly wanted to vomit all down his front. "Thanks."

Luckily Arlowe didn't expect much conversation from my side on the short ride home. He was just finishing a brief synopsis of what they'd had to do to secure the fence when he unlocked the apartment and swung the door open for me.

I'd never gotten a key. I didn't need it. We'd been together 24/7. And yet somehow he had a whole other life that I knew nothing about.

"What can I get you?"

I walked in ahead of him. "I just need to rest."

"Of course. Lie down. I'll make some food and see if you're up for it in a while."

I tried to smile, but it didn't work. I knew I looked as miserable as I felt. "Thanks, but food is the last thing on my mind. I just need a good sleep." I carried Kai in her carrier to the room that was supposed to be mine before I'd started sharing his.

I fell back onto the bed and stared up at the ceiling. I wished I could cry, let it all out. But I couldn't feel enough to conjure tears. I just felt numb.

I was the biggest moron on the planet. If I ever thought about trusting another man, I hoped someone would shoot me in the head.

CHAPTER 21

ARLOWE

*M*aybe she was being considerate or maybe she just felt like being alone, but I didn't like sleeping without Trinity one bit. It had only been a week that she'd shared my bed, but I'd gotten used to having her at my side.

I hoped that she was feeling better. I wandered out into the kitchen in hopes that she would be up making breakfast. The lights were all off and the guest room door was closed. If she was still sleeping after nearly twelve hours, she might be sick. I thought to go check on her but decided to give her a few more minutes and set the coffee maker to brew.

Traffic to Miami might be a bitch. I needed to get moving. Showing up late for an interview would make it unlikely to be successful, but I didn't really care if I got the job. I'd agreed to the interview for practice more than anything. And it was not good practice to show up late.

I barely recognized myself in the bathroom mirror. I hadn't worn khakis and a button down since my annual obligatory church visit on Easter. No way in hell I'd dress like this every day. But there was no way in hell I'd take a job where I had to be in an office every day either. A suit would be more appropriate for an interview, but I'd given those away when I left Boston.

I heard the faint sounds of music coming from behind Trinity's closed door while I put bread in the toaster. I walked over and knocked softly, turning my ear to listen. The music stopped. "Come in."

Trinity sat cross-legged on the bed with her guitar on her lap and Kai curled up at her feet. She tried to return my smile but it looked strained. "How are you feeling?"

"Better."

I studied her face but couldn't decide if she was mad or just felt crappy. "I'm making toast. Do you want some?"

She shook her head. "I'll grab something before I head to the shop."

"You don't have to go in today. Slim will manage. Just rest."

She avoided looking me in the eye. "I'll be fine. I planned to go in around ten."

I worried she was freaking out again. "Don't feel obligated." I meant about anything, not just work today.

"I don't. Thanks."

Even in a long-sleeved button down I felt the chill in the air. "There's coffee."

She glanced up before quickly averting her gaze. "I'm alright for now."

If she was turning down coffee, there was something wrong. "You sure you're alright?"

"I'm sure. Good luck on your interview. You certainly look the part." Finally the hint of a smile broke her stoic expression.

I glanced down at the outfit. "It feels like a costume. So weird."

"Right? A little different than board shorts and thongs."

"True. But if I'm working from home I'll still be in board shorts and flip flops."

Her expression didn't give me a hint at what was going on in her head. "Good luck. I hope it works out, if that's what you want."

She'd only known me a few weeks, but she knew me well enough to know that I didn't know what I wanted. Right then, I just wanted her to be normal. But I had to get going. "I've got to run. Don't rush and if you change your mind, just let Slim know. He will understand."

Her smile didn't make it to her eyes. "Thanks. Drive safe."

It didn't feel right leaving like that. I wanted to tell her to get up and give me a kiss or tell me what the hell was going on. Instead I just smiled like an idiot. "Feel better."

I took my toast and coffee to go. Sitting in traffic gave me time to ponder Trinity's strange demeanor. I understood when she wasn't feeling well yesterday, but this seemed like more than a stomach bug. Had Slim told her something yesterday to turn her sour? He wouldn't sabotage me intentionally. He wanted Trinity to stay nearly as much as I did. All I could figure was that she'd been thinking about what to do and was leaning toward leaving. That would explain her distance. But it didn't explain her personality change. She was not acting like the Trinity I knew. But what did I know?

I had to put that out of my head for now. If I was making the effort to show up for this interview, I needed to get my head in it. I reviewed what I knew of the company. BioLogic had become a major player in healthcare software solutions. But they had major corporate competition. I didn't know how they were still alive amongst the giant conglomerates. Somehow they'd managed to maintain their foothold.

I took the elevator up to the nineteenth floor and gave the receptionist my name.

"I'll let Ms. Malone know you're here."

I sat in one of the leather armchairs. They looked expensive —a good sign that the company might be able to afford me.

A slender blonde older woman appeared a minute later, welcoming me with a warm smile.

"You must be Arlowe."

I stood and shook her hand. "Guilty."

"Melanie. Nice to meet you." She wore a fitted skirt and heels that made her nearly my height. She must be 5'10".

"Very nice to meet you, too, Melanie."

"You're early. I like it."

"It's a long haul from Jupiter. I wanted to leave plenty of time for traffic." I realized how informal I sounded. I didn't know how to do this anymore.

"Miami is horrible."

"We already agree on something." Thirty seconds in and I was already insulting the city where the job was located. Three more minutes and the interview would be over at this rate.

But Melanie chuckled as she took her seat behind her desk and motioned for me to sit across from her. She might be a well-preserved fifty. She was attractive, not that I was attracted to her. There was something about her, though, that intrigued.

"I'm sure you did your homework, but let me tell you a little about BioLogic." She proceeded with her elevator-pitch synopsis of the company's accolades.

"It's quite impressive you've managed to stay relevant among the competition. IBM and GE? Who knew they had Healthcare divisions?"

"They've kept us on our toes. But we do things differently. That competition has made us work harder to define our niche, but we've been quite successful at doing so." She leaned across the desk, lowering her voice like she was sharing a secret. "One of those two tried to buy us out five years ago, but we like our niche."

Without knowing the details of the offer I couldn't say whether it was a mistake for them, but I liked that they hadn't sold out. "Break out or go down fighting."

There wasn't a hint of hesitation in her answer. "We're going nowhere but up. That's why we're adding a project manager to our team."

I loved her confidence. "So it's not a replacement position?"

She shook her head. "No, it's an expansion. Let's talk about your time in Boston. Looks like Anderson snatched you up right out of college." She pulled my resume to the top of the pile of papers on her desk.

"That's correct. I started in coding. After two years, they put me through a project management certification course and promoted me."

"And you were managing some big projects that last year. Your professional experience is impressive, but it looks like you've been out of the game for a while."

"I consider buying into a business that had been on a steady decline, and turning it around, professional experience. And more impressive on every level than my two years in corporate project management."

Her head tilted as she studied me. "And yet you're looking to return to the corporate world?"

I grinned. "For the right opportunity."

She folded her hands across the file on her desk. "What does that look like for you?"

"Work from home. Flexible schedule. Autonomy. Clear performance expectations. And a salary that would make it worth hiring a manager to replace me." That's all.

She was quiet for a few seconds. "But why? Why come back now?"

"I worked hard for my degrees, and I'm good at what I do. Seems a shame to let that all go to waste." It probably sounded cocky, but it was the truth.

The corners of her mouth curled. "You took the words right out of my mouth."

I tilted my head as I weighed her comment. She hadn't been put off by cockiness. "Thank you."

Her palms flattened onto the desk as she leaned forward. "I'll be straight with you. Of the twenty-seven resumes we received, you were my top pick for the position, in part because of your varied experience. And the guts to leave when you were on your way up to do something different. I did something similar. Eight years into my career I bought a catamaran instead of a house and quit my job to charter my boat in the Bahamas for five years."

"Oh yeah?" I knew there was something about her. "So why did you come back?"

"It was time for something different. And with BioLogic, I felt I could make a difference. I still believe that."

"How so?"

"I've fought—and trust me when I say that it's been a fight—to stay true to our mission. Of course we need to be profitable to stay in business, but our mission is to make healthcare work better."

She was too seasoned and knowledgeable to be naive, but she sounded more like an idealistic new grad than a VP. Every company needed a VP like her. "That's admirable indeed."

"If you're committed to coming back, I still think you're the right man for the job."

Wait. Was she offering me the job? I tried not to look surprised but I could feel it written all over my face. "You do?"

She smiled but had a serious look in her eyes. "I do. If you're committed."

There it was again. I couldn't escape it. Commitment was unavoidable. I'd been accused of being incapable of it enough times to make me ready to rebel. "For the right opportunity, I'm committed."

"Then it's just a matter of details. I'll have Elaine draw up an offer and have it for you by the end of the day. I can say that we're able to compensate on the level that you finished at Anderson, plus about twenty percent. And working remote is not an issue. You'd just have to come to the office once every couple of weeks for meetings. Flexibility and autonomy are not issues. I hire people I trust to do their jobs, then I let them."

I blinked through wide eyes. "What a concept."

"With the right people, it works."

Her warm smile made me want her as my boss. "It certainly should. I like your style." I grinned.

"I like yours, too." She looked me over again and smiled. "I bet you don't even own a suit."

"You'd win that bet."

She chuckled as she shook her head. "I'm betting on you, Arlowe. You'll have the formal offer by five. Look it over and get back to me with any questions."

I was flattered. "Thanks so much for your confidence. I'll be in touch very soon."

"I hope so." She pushed my resume into the file folder. "It's been a pleasure." She stood and came around the desk to walk me to the door.

I unbuttoned the cuffs of my shirt and rolled them up to my elbows on the elevator. I hadn't expected to walk out of here with a job offer, least of all for the perfect job. I nodded to a man in a suit when the doors opened in the parking garage. My hands rubbed my face as I sank back into the seat of the Jeep. Fuck.

Heading back into the mayhem of Miami traffic was a welcome distraction from the decision on the table. But once I was heading north on I-95, my mind was free to race. It was an opportunity I shouldn't pass up. Trinity staying to take the helm at the shop would be ideal.

By the way she was acting, it was better not to get my hopes up. I couldn't blame her. I'd probably fucked it up hitting on her after knowing she was jaded. I hadn't planned on falling for Trinity. Everything about her said that she had fallen right with me until yesterday. She'd gone back into panic mode. I should have known better.

It figured that the first woman I'd ever really connected with was emotionally unavailable. I'd been that guy enough times to deserve to be on the receiving end. Karma was a bitch.

Five minutes of thinking about Trinity and I didn't even remember the job offer. It wasn't even a factor in my wanting to convince her to stay. This wasn't about work. Losing a job opportunity was nothing compared to losing her.

CHAPTER 22

TRINITY

*a*fter hours of tossing and turning last night, I wondered if what Monica said was true. Were they happy before me? Maybe they'd had a shot at something real before I was in the picture.

It wasn't an excuse for his deceit. I could never get over that. I couldn't trust him, or anyone. And my being around was fucking things up for us both. It was time to go.

I didn't mention anything to Slim. I couldn't tell him before I told Arlowe that I was heading home. Which made for an excruciating day. He seemed to be avoiding the subject—to give me space I presumed. They were fine without me before. They'd be fine without me after I left.

Fortunately, a steady stream of customers kept us busy all morning to keep us both busy.

Slim came from the back room as I finished a sale. He waited for the customer to get to the door. "You forgot to feed me again. It's after two. How about Chinese?"

I hadn't eaten a thing all day, but the thought of food made my nose wrinkle. I needed sustenance though. "Sure."

Slim called me out of the back room when the food arrived. I opened the styrofoam container he set in front of me, staring into the mound of Vegetable Lo Mein. It was my favorite but I didn't know if I could stomach it. I wound some noodles into a wad on the end of my chopsticks and shoved it in my mouth.

Slim scarfed down three more bites while I tried to chew my first. He smiled up while scooping another load onto his chopsticks. "It sounds like Max has done well for himself."

"I suppose he has. Despite three marriages and a kid with the first two, he still has the life he wanted." I took another bite that went down a little easier.

"I'd suspect that Max never wanted family life."

"He certainly doesn't seem suited for it." I could relate.

"I'm not sure I am either. When Roxanne discovered that she couldn't have kids she worried I'd leave her. But I was worried she'd leave me if we did."

I chuckled as I pushed my food around in the container. "Why's that?"

"I'm a marginally decent husband. I don't know how Roxy puts up with me sometimes. But I doubt I'd be a good dad."

"I think you're selling yourself short. I see how you are with Arlowe. You're like a father to him."

"That's different. It's part time and shared duty. His dad had to do the real work. I just taught him to surf."

"I'd say you taught him a lot more than that." Respect like what Arlowe had for Slim was earned.

"I hope so. How about you? Do you want kids?"

I couldn't imagine being responsible for another person. But more than that, I couldn't imagine finding someone I'd want to make a family with. God knows I didn't know how to pick them. The only decent guy I'd ever been with was making a family with Lena. "I don't think so."

"You're still young. You have *years* to think about that. Enjoy, kid. They pass in a flash."

"I'm doing my best."

"I'd say you're doing a damn good job. I did a lot of wandering, but not like you have already."

"I'm lucky I could travel like I have. It's been the best time of my life. I lived in Australia for twenty years but I grew up in the Americas in the past year-and-a-half."

"You really are wise beyond your years."

I would laugh out loud were it not so depressing how unwise I felt. Slim didn't know that I'd left Guatemala with a big hole in my heart and that it had shattered into a million pieces in Peru. And somehow I let another man work his way into the pile of rubble that remained, only to have him to pulverize the last of it. That was not wise. "I don't know about that."

"I do. But stay humble."

I grinned. "I try."

The jingle of the bell on the door gave me a jolt. I must have been shell-shocked because I half expected Monica when I looked up, but Arlowe was grinning as he strolled across the shop. I looked down to try to hide the redness that rose to my cheeks.

"Did you hold the fort down without me?"

I looked down half-disgusted at my food before I closed the container and shoved it into the plastic bag while Slim answered.

"We managed. It's easy with this one here."

"I'm glad to hear it."

I tried to smile but it felt foreign on my face. "How'd it go?"

Arlowe stared at me for a second before he spoke. "Very well. They loved me. Let's see how it is on paper, but it seems like they offered me the perfect job."

Wow. I hadn't expected that. But Arlowe's charm was even brighter than his intellect, and he was wicked smart. Of course they'd loved him. He was easy to love.

"That's great, if that's what you really want."

Arlowe studied my face. My fake smile and faraway eyes would give me away. His smile faded before his gaze shifted to Slim, who was already protesting.

"Well. I think it's terrible. But I agree with Trinity, if that's what you want then you should go for it." Slim glanced toward me. "I hope to hell you're staying if he goes. I'm going to need you."

I steadied my hands on the counter and hoped my voice wouldn't fail me when I lifted my eyes to Slim's. "Actually, I wanted to talk to you both about that." I took a deep breath to muster the courage to spill the beans. "I really appreciate the opportunity. As much as I love it here, and I adore this shop, after a year and a half, I think it's time to go home." I had to consciously relax the wince that twisted my mouth and squinted my eyes. I couldn't bring myself to look at Arlowe.

Slim said, "I see," but he pushed his glasses up onto his nose like it might help him see better. "Kiddo, you have to do what you have to do. You both do. I was young once. I remember not wanting to stay anyplace too long. There's a big world out there." His eyes swung toward Arlowe. "But if you're leaving, you better find me someone as good as Trinity."

When I finally turned my sights to Arlowe, he looked like he'd been punched in the gut. His wide eyes were full of questions as he blinked at me while answering Slim. "Finding someone as good as Trinity is damn near impossible. But someone half as good can do the job. I'm proof of that."

His compliment made me want to cry. And to slap him. I'd wanted to slap him since I found out he had a girlfriend. I didn't want to cry, and slapping him was out of the question, so I looked away.

Slim patted me on the back. "He's right about that. All of it."

"I hope you'll find someone who can do a better job than either of us." We had a way of fucking things up. Surely someone could do better than we could.

Slim chuckled. "You sure we can't persuade you to stay?"

"I'm afraid not. I spoke to my parents this morning. They're trying to rebook my ticket now. I'm heading back."

Arlowe's voice strained. "When?"

"I'm waiting to hear. It shouldn't be too long though."

The hurt in his eyes opened the gates to all the hurt in my heart. He nodded as he rubbed his lips together. "It won't be long enough."

CHAPTER 23

ARLOWE

*W*ith the top off the Jeep it was hard to talk, but I could tell Trinity was relieved to not have to engage on the way home.

I wasn't surprised when she went into her room and closed the door. She'd barely spoken a word after breaking the news. I guess there was nothing left to say. But there was so much left unsaid. The wall was up, fully erect. I might never be again after what she'd done to me.

My head was pounding with a splitting headache. I'd only had toast all day. I doubted that hunger was the cause. It was more likely the bombshell that she was leaving exploding in my brain. But I needed to eat. I rummaged through the fridge and pulled out the provolone. Grilled cheese. *Ugh.* I loved how she called them 'toasties.' I didn't feel the least bit hungry, but I set the frying pan on the stove. Surely Trinity needed to eat too. By the looks of her leftovers from lunch, she hadn't made a dent. But I didn't want to bother her after she'd run off so quickly. I'd bothered her too much already. That's why we were here. Or why she was there and I was here. Soon, *there* would be the other side of the world. She would be there, and I would be here. Unless I could convince her to stay.

But since I was pretty sure that I was why she was leaving, I didn't have an angle. She'd be perfect for the job at the shop. But we were in too deep to pretend this could be a business transaction. I was the moron that had fucked it up with her. She wasn't ready for a man in her life. It seemed ridiculous to suggest that we could be just friends now and maybe she would reconsider. We were much more than that. There was no turning back, but if moving forward took her away from me, I didn't want to go there. I had to do something, if only I knew what.

Faint guitar sounds came from behind her closed door as I washed my plate. Would I ever hear her sing again?

I'd gone to bed alone 99.7% of all the nights of my life and somehow, now, it felt like a cruel punishment. I didn't want to get used to not having Trinity beside me. How I'd gotten so used to having her next to me was what had me perplexed. I'd enjoyed the company of many women but with Trinity it was different. It was fireworks. It was hot and heavy and thoughtless and fearless. It was perfect. It was fucking perfect.

And she was leaving. Soon. How were we not talking about this?

I brushed my teeth and swallowed three Tylenol. If I could get rid of this fucking headache I might be able to think of something.

~

Clanging in the kitchen woke me. In my sleepy daze, I hoped Trinity was making breakfast and things would somehow magically be back to normal. Maybe it was all a bad dream.

I swished mouthwash before I wandered out to the kitchen. She was fully dressed in jeans and a T-shirt with a jacket tied around her waist. "You're up bright and early."

She barely looked up from the single egg she was frying. "My parents called at six thirty."

I swallowed hard to try to clear the lump that formed in my throat. "Oh yeah? What's the news?"

She glanced up for the briefest second. "They booked my ticket."

My fingers curled into my sweaty palms as all the blood drained from my face. "For when?"

"Saturday at 6 a.m."

The bad dream just became my worst nightmare. It was settled. In seventy-two hours she'd be on a plane. At least we had that. "Wow. So soon?"

"Not as soon as they had hoped but Qantas is booked." She flipped the egg onto a buttered slice of toast and carried it around to the breakfast bar.

"You have three more days. We should do something fun."

"I'm actually heading down to Miami this morning." She took a bite of her breakfast like it was no big deal that she was leaving immediately.

My cheek literally burned, so strong was the slap in the face. "Miami? Why?"

"My flight is so early I'd have to be down there Sunday

anyway. And I want to see the Art Deco district and South Beach before I go. Who knows when I'll be back? I don't want to miss it." Her focus turned back to her breakfast and she took another big bite.

I was going to be missing her in about five minutes by the looks of things. I already did.

I stared at her, dumbfounded, but her eyes returned to the half eaten egg on toast in her hand. Why would she be in such a hurry to leave? Maybe it was her protective mechanism—shutting down.

"Let me show you around down there then. I know a few cool spots you won't find in the guidebooks."

"Thanks, but I'm good."

She couldn't have been colder without telling me to fuck off. "Are you okay? You seem pissed off. Have I done something to upset you?"

She was still chewing when she answered. "It's just time to move on. There's no sense in prolonging the inevitable."

"It doesn't have to be inevitable." I felt like my crying was inevitable at that point.

"It is. I've got to go, so I might as well go now."

Her calm resolve scared the hell out of me. I had to try to reason with her. "The only thing truly inevitable in life is death. Every day above ground is prolonging the inevitable." The crushing pain in my chest made her leaving feel like the death of me. "Life, by definition, is prolonging the inevitable." I reached for her hand but she jerked it away like I was a hot stove.

My heart pounded in my chest. My world was spinning out

of control. This couldn't be happening. "So that's it? It's over?" I resented the desperation in my voice.

Her cold stare froze me. "It was over when it started, Arlowe. What did you expect?"

Her words stung. Even if we had an expiration date from the start, why did she have to go now? It wouldn't be any easier to say goodbye later, but I wanted every second I could have with her. "I didn't expect anything. But I don't want you to go like this. Stay. Or let's go to Miami together. We still have three days."

She shook her head with her icy reply. "It's better like this."

What was better about not spending her last few days together? She wanted to be alone. That was that. "Well at least let me drive you down."

"It's okay, I already booked a Greyhound. It leaves in an hour so I have to get going."

I blinked at her in disbelief. This couldn't be happening. "Greyhound? Don't be ridiculous. Let me take you."

"It's fine. I'm used to buses."

"Come on, Trinity. If you won't let me drive you, at least let me call you an Uber."

She was distant and full of contempt. "The bus isn't that bad. Have you ever even been on one?"

The truth was I hadn't. "Not a Greyhound. But there's a reason for that. Please, let me do this for you." I was ready to beg and plead to keep her from leaving right then.

"You don't need to do anything for me, Arlowe. I'm good."

She was stubborn. And she could deny it all she wanted, but

she was pissed. She washed her plate quickly and went into her room without a word. She came out holding Kai, her backpack on her back and guitar slung over her shoulder. "Please tell Slim I'm sorry I couldn't say goodbye." She kissed the kitten and nuzzled it with her nose. She whispered a tender goodbye, clearly intended for Kai. "I'm going to miss you." She looked up with sad eyes. "Promise me you'll take care of her. Please don't give her away."

That cat would be all I had of Trinity. I could never give her away. "I promise." I took Kai when Trinity pushed her into my hands with teary eyes, but it was Trinity I wanted in my arms. That wasn't going to happen. She was out the door as fast as she could scoot.

Slim was nearly as surprised as I was at the news that Trinity was already gone. He eyed Kai in her carrier. "That means you can get rid of the cat now?"

I looked at the kitten through the mesh screen. "I've gotten kind of attached to her. I think I'll keep her."

He huffed out a chuckle. "Looked like you got pretty attached to Trinity, too. Maybe the cat will stick around longer."

He knew how to pour salt in a wound. "Let's hope so."

"How you doing with that?"

I focused to keep my voice steady as I felt myself on the verge of falling apart. "Nothing I can do about it. She made up her mind. She's so stubborn she wouldn't even let me call her an Uber after she refused to let me take her to Miami."

Slim shook his head. "When a headstrong woman sets her mind to something, you don't have a chance."

I drew in a deep breath. "She's headstrong alright."

Slim's glasses lifted when he wrinkled his nose as his brows came together like he'd remembered something. "Did you pay her? We owe her a wad of cash."

Fuck, I hadn't even thought of it. "No. Honestly, I was so shocked that she was leaving that it didn't cross my mind. But you're right. How much do you think we owe her?"

His head tilted while he calculated. "At least a grand, probably more."

I pulled out my phone and sent her $1500 by Paypal. "There, she's paid." If she accepts it. Knowing her, she wouldn't.

"Have you thought about what you're going to do about this perfect job offer now that your perfect replacement is out of here?"

It hadn't entered my mind. It seemed utterly unimportant now. "I have to think about it."

Slim's voice took an uncharacteristic soothing tone. "Take your time." He patted my back. "I'm sorry about Trinity. I know you really liked her. I can see why."

His unexpected empathy stirred the sick feeling I had in my gut. "Yeah. Life has an ironic sense of humor. When I finally meet a girl I really like…"

His sarcasm returned full force. "After all the hearts you've broken, maybe you're due one yourself."

More salt in the wound. But he was right. I deserved it.

I'd been dating the wrong women on purpose. It was my

defense mechanism. I didn't have to think about committing when there was no possibility of it ever working out. But it was different with Trinity. We had potential. She could be the right one, but she was still all wrong. I'd fallen for an impossible woman. I knew from the start. She was too young. And leaving. It was never going anywhere. But I fell for her anyway.

My phone buzzed in my pocket while I looked through the new inventory spreadsheet Trinity had compiled. Monica. I turned the phone face down on the counter and left it to ring. Now I knew how she must feel—chasing an impossible idea and not wanting to let it go.

Slim kept to himself the rest of the morning but by lunchtime I was done trying to act okay. There was no need for us both to be there. "Why don't you grab lunch for your lovely wife? If I need you I'll call, but I'm sure I can handle it."

"You sure? Roxy would love that. So would I, to be honest."

"Go. She needs you. I'm good here." I was far from good, but I'd rather be alone.

It was dark out when I left the shop but I could picture the sun lighting up the golden streaks in Trinity's windswept curls. Kai meowed up at me from her case in the seat where Trinity should be.

The air in my apartment was stale. I set Kai's carrier on the table and pulled her out, lifting her to my nose. "It's just me and you, kid. I bet she's missing you right now."

Trinity had accepted the money with a terse *Got it, thanks.* Then, nothing.

I cracked open a beer and tossed the bottle cap into the trash. The metal ding echoed through the hollow silence of the room. The house was as empty as I felt.

I slumped onto the couch and swung my feet up on the coffee table as I pulled out my phone. Still nothing. I texted again to ask if she'd made it to Miami.

I looked over my shoulder to find Kai when I heard her squeaky meow from next to the closed guest room door. She looked up at me, expectant. Not understanding why Trinity was gone. I got up to get her. "I know how you feel."

I snuggled her on my chest as I laid on the couch. I pulled up *Morning of the Earth* on Netflix and took a long swig of beer. There was something addictive about salt in a wound.

CHAPTER 24

*T*rinity

What should be an hour-and-a-half drive took nearly four hours on the bus. Arlowe was right. It sucked. I would have taken him up on the offer of a ride if the thought of an hour-and-a-half in the car with him didn't make me nauseous. I couldn't stomach him.

The Uber from the terminal to my shitty hotel in Miami Beach was expensive but worth it. Public transport in Florida wasn't easy. Nothing had been easy lately.

I laid back onto the lumpy pillow and stared up at yellow stains on the ceiling. It was a private room but it was in worse condition than most hostels. Three nights of the hard mattress and threadbare sheets was hardly appealing. And sixty blocks north of South Beach was not an ideal location. I'd booked the room in an angry hurry. I didn't care where I was going, I just had to get away. But I hadn't expected it to be this bad. The musty smell of carpet—probably older than me—made my nose wrinkle. I was tempted to move to a nicer place after I'd gotten the money from Arlowe, but something wouldn't let me.

The practical part of me knew I'd barely be in the room. The masochistic part of me thought the miserable space was an appropriate setting for these last dreadful days that I was stuck in the US.

It was true that I'd wanted to see Miami, but that's not why I'd left Jupiter. I needed to be as far away from Arlowe as possible until the plane finally took me away. I was more angry with myself for letting him into my heart than I was with him for being a lying bastard. I didn't deserve a nicer room. Stupidity deserves squalor.

I walked out to buy a sandwich and a packet of crisps in a convenience store down the block. The sky was streaked with pinks and yellows. It was probably a gorgeous sunset. Normally I'd be in search of a rooftop to enjoy it with a cocktail. But enjoying anything seemed impossible at the moment. The elderly man behind the desk grunted up from the show he was watching on his phone. "Good evening."

His smile forced me out of self-pity as I walked past with my plastic bag of pathetic dinner. "Good evening to you, sir."

I stopped when he called after me. "You have big plans for tomorrow?"

I turned, my smile feeling more natural now. "Just wandering around Wynwood."

"Don't miss the graffiti. I mean, you can't miss it. But pay attention. It's good." His eyes twinkled.

His appreciation for street art was a pleasant surprise. "Thanks. That's one of the reasons I want to go." And thank you, stranger, for reminding me of the good things.

"If you're going to be here Saturday you should go to Wynwood then. It's the Art Walk."

"My plane leaves at six o'clock that morning so I'm afraid I'll miss it." I'd love to see it, but thank God I'd be gone.

My phone dinged with another text from Arlowe while I sat cross-legged on my bed, chewing the dry sandwich. I muttered, "Piss off," and tossed my phone to the foot of the bed. It might have been bitchy to not answer, but I didn't want to engage in any conversation. I didn't owe him the peace of mind of knowing that I was here safe and sound. I needed a clean break in order to put the pieces of myself together.

CHAPTER 25

ARLOWE

A full day had passed with no word from Trinity. She was more than capable of taking care of herself. I was sure she was fine. But it seemed pretty shitty that she didn't at least respond. Not that I was one to talk. I'd ignored two calls and five texts from Monica in the same timeframe.

It was infuriating, but there was nothing I could do. Trinity was gone and I had to move on. I cursed myself for letting her tie me into knots. I couldn't help her unload her emotional baggage if she wouldn't let me.

I swung by my parents' on the way to work to pick up some homemade cookies Mom had texted me a photo of. She didn't know yet that Trinity was gone but she'd made my favorite comfort sweet—oatmeal raisin cookies. Mom served me an omelette, despite my protests that I was in a hurry and not hungry. Dad joined me at the table while I tried to eat.

I washed down my food with a swig of OJ. I might as well spit it out. "Trinity left yesterday to spend a couple of nights in Miami before her flight."

My father's expression was uncharacteristically sympathetic. "Oh, that's a shame. I thought she might hang around."

"Yeah, me, too." I tried to force another bite of omelette but gave up and left the fork on the plate. "I had an interview at BioLogic down in Miami. They offered me a job."

My mother sat beside me. "Are you going to take it?"

"I'm not sure. It seems like exactly what I was looking for. I'm still thinking about it." I went on to describe the offer.

My father didn't mince words. "It sounds like you'd be a fool not to take it."

I was a fool to do anything that wasn't his idea. My first instinct was to rebel. The thing was—I'd pretty much reached the same conclusion myself. "I don't know, maybe I'm a fool to have applied. But it is a great opportunity. I'm very tempted. Logistically, it's complicated with the shop until we find a manager."

My mother reached over to cover my hand with hers. "Take all the time you need. If this one doesn't work out, something else will."

She was right. I could wait, and something else might come along, but it wasn't likely to be this good. I'd squandered too many opportunities already. Trinity would be on her way back to Australia before I knew it. If I didn't take this job, another one like it might not come along. "Thanks, Mom. But I think it's time to try something different."

My father grinned. "Landing a job like that is an accomplishment, Son. If you take it, I don't think you'll regret it."

He had no idea how much I regretted already.

Slim barked when I finally got to the shop. "It's almost eleven, where the hell have you been?"

I looked around the empty shop. "I took my time. Did you need me? You know you can text me. Those things called phones are magic little boxes."

Slim rolled his eyes. "The Smith rep stopped by. You always deal with them."."

"Again, you could have called. But you're perfectly capable of ordering sunglasses, Slim. I'm afraid you're going to have to get used to doing at least some of the stuff I've always done."

His eyes narrowed. "Why's that?"

I wasn't sure how I was going to tell him, but it came out easy once I'd decided. "Because I'm going to take the job." I waited for his reaction but there was only a pensive stare. "Don't worry, I'll find you the help you need. In the meantime, I'll work double duty. But you're going to have to pick up the slack."

Slim pressed his lips together and nodded. "Alright then. We'll figure something out."

I'd expected a protest, or some sort of bitching. But Slim was chill. I hurried to affirm his resolve. "Trinity left everything so organized it won't be hard to manage."

He nodded. "She left us in good shape."

She'd left me in shambles but I had to pull myself together and get on with my life.

Guilt got the better of me when Monica called again later that afternoon. I could empathize with how shitty it felt to be ghosted. I needed to flip the karmic scale. As much as I didn't want to, answering the phone was a good start.

"Hey Monica."

"Hey? After you ignore me for over two weeks?"

I bit my tongue and suppressed my initial reaction to defend myself. "Yeah, sorry about that. I've been swamped at the shop."

"I thought your new helper would have things under control."

The hairs on my forearms stood up. What was she talking about? I tried to chuckle but it came out dry and forced. "I could use a new helper. It's just me and Slim. Fortunately business has been good since we finally re-opened."

The line was silent for a second before Monica responded. "Where's Trinity?"

My throat tightened. How the fuck did she know that name? I looked into the back room at Slim adjusting the fins on a board. Had he failed to mention talking to Monica? "She's gone. How do you know Trinity?"

"She didn't tell you?"—she huffed—"I'm surprised. I asked her not to but I figured she'd run right to you with the news."

"What news?"

"That I met her in the shop a couple of days ago. I went looking for you after you'd ghosted me for days."

Fuck. She'd met Trinity? Fuck. "No, she didn't tell me. But she's gone."

"Gone where?"

It was none of her business but I'd brought it up. "Back home, to Australia."

"You must be heartbroken." Her words seethed sarcasm but she was spot on. How the fuck was she always reading my mind?

I tried to blow off the comment. "What are you talking about?"

"I'm talking about how you disappeared off the face of the earth when everything was going well. Coincidentally, that happened when Trinity arrived."

It sounded like they'd had quite the lengthy conversation. My mind raced. "What did you say to Trinity exactly?"

Monica sounded more annoyed by the minute. "I told her the truth. That we were happy before she came around."

I sat back on the stool as the words sunk in. I'd flat out denied that Monica was my girlfriend when Trinity had asked me. Hearing Monica's delusional interpretation of our relationship must have stabbed her right through the heart. Especially after what Diego had done to her. Now it all made sense. No wonder she hated my guts.

I could see why Monica was pissed, too. I'd been a dick. But she was acting like we were in a relationship. That had to stop. "That's not the truth, Monica. We were barely dating."

I was expecting a shout but she was calm in her reply. "It's good to know how you see it."

The sting of rejection in her voice tugged at my conscience. I knew it all too well. "I'm sorry, Monica. On our last date I realized I didn't really have the same feelings for you that you had for me. I should have told you then, but I didn't really understand until later. Still, I should have told you."

The line was silent for a long moment. "So you're *not* fucking Trinity?"

"No, I'm not." It was true, I wasn't. But it still felt like a lie. After where half-truths had landed me with Trinity, I owed it to myself—and Monica—to be forthright. "Not anymore," I amended, then held my breath, waiting for the fallout.

"So you *were* fucking her?"

"We had a thing, barely." It felt like more than that, but according to Trinity it was nothing. "But it had nothing to do with her, Monica."

"Right. Go fuck yourself, asshole."

I stared at the black screen after she hung up. She was right. I was an asshole. I deserved it. All of it.

I waited until I was home to call Trinity. I had to explain. I hadn't been truthful, but I couldn't let her think I was a lying cheat.

CHAPTER 26

TRINITY

*T*he splendid street art was as lost on me as the perfect afternoon weather in Wynwood. The beauty of art is in the eye of the beholder, and mine was clouded with melancholy. Even a gelato couldn't lift my spirits. It had melted to a sloppy soup before I could finish it. I didn't even bother with dinner.

I slumped back onto my lumpy pillow. I hadn't told Lena that I was leaving. I didn't want to talk about it, but she'd be hurt if I didn't call to say goodbye.

She answered on the third ring. "Hey you! I was just thinking about you!"

Hearing the smile in her voice muted my sadness for a moment. "I was thinking about you, too. How's everything?"

"Great! Fortunately I'm feeling more normal now. This baby moves a lot, though."

"That must be a good sign. I can't imagine the feeling though."

"Yeah, it's crazy. It feels like an alien flipping around in there. So weird. But how are *you*? It's been a couple of weeks. How's the aftermath of the hurricane?"

"Pretty much back to normal here. And I finally got my flight rebooked."

"Oh yeah? When are you heading back?"

I resented the tremble in my voice. "Saturday morning." Only two more sleeps and I'd be on the plane but it felt like an impossible wait.

"Oh, wow. So soon?"

I bit my lip, reluctant to go into any details. "I've run out of reasons to stay."

"It didn't pan out with the surf shop guy you were hanging around for?"

"No." I tried to hold back the tears but they rushed out with my words. "Turns out he has a girlfriend."

Lena tried to comfort me after I spilled the whole ugly story. "Oh. I'm sorry, Trin. Where are you? Are you alone?" Lena's voice rose an octave with worry.

I sucked in a deep breath as I wiped the tear from my cheek. "I'll be alright. I'm in Miami already." A beep on my phone interrupted me. My heart jumped into my throat when I saw Arlowe's name on the screen. "Fuck. He's calling me right now."

"Are you going to answer?"

I could picture her sweet face which made me wish she was there to hug me. "No fucking way." I hit the red X to decline his call.

"Good. Fuck that guy."

"I'd say 'Fuck them all,' but that hasn't worked out so well for me." I laughed but the tears still streamed down my face.

"These guys don't deserve you. You deserve far better."

I twisted my hair around my finger. "I don't know about that." Maybe I was getting exactly what I deserved for being such a fool.

"Nonsense. Don't let this get you down, beautiful. As much as I wish you were coming here instead, I'm glad you'll be home soon."

I let out a sigh. "Me, too. I'm so ready for this to be over. I just want to get home and never think about another man."

"That's a little extreme but I can see why you feel that way right now. Give yourself some time. You'll find the right person when the time is right."

I choked back the tears. "I don't know if I'm cut out for that anyway."

"You don't have to worry about any of that right now, sweetie. Just try to enjoy your last day in the States tomorrow."

I took a deep breath. "I'll do my best. I'm heading down to South Beach."

"That sounds lovely. A day at the beach will do you some good."

"I think so, too." Hoped so was more like it. If anything could make me feel better, it was the ocean.

"Good, get some rest."

"I will. Tell Dante hi and rub your baby belly from Aunt Trin." I wished I was snuggled on the couch between them.

"I love you. Call if you need anything, anytime."

"Thanks. I love you, too." If anyone could do anything to make me feel better, I'd let them. But I had to wade through the heartache to get to the other side. It was my cross to bear.

Maybe a day at the beach was what I needed, but what I wanted was a drink. I'd be tempted to go out and drown my sorrows in vodka tonics if I didn't have to see people.

Two more sleeps in this musty bed and I'd be home.

A decent night's sleep was better for my outlook than half a bottle of vodka would've been. Even the dingy grout between the tiles as I showered looked better than it did yesterday.

I threw a sundress over a bikini and shoved my travel towel and a bottle of sunscreen into a rucksack. The elderly man smiled from the reception desk on my way out. "Still with us?"

"Yes, sir. One more day. My flight leaves early tomorrow." Saying it made me smile.

"That's right. You're going to miss the Art Walk tomorrow. Did you make it to Wynwood yesterday?"

"I did. The graffiti was as impressive as you described. Thank you for that. Any recommendations for South Beach?"

He chuckled as he shook his head. "Stay away from it."

My head tilted with a curious grin. "Yeah? Why's that?"

"Hordes of people. But you're young, you probably like that."

"Sometimes." Now wasn't really one of those times, but I couldn't miss South Beach.

"Have fun, sweetheart."

His genuine smile reminded me of my grandfather, whom I'd barely spoken to in a year-and-a-half. "Thank you. I hope you have a lovely day as well."

"Every day above ground is a good one."

The hairs on my arms stood, recalling Arlowe's use of the same phrase. When he'd said that life—by definition—was prolonging the inevitable, it'd tugged at my philosophical heartstrings. But when the old man'd said it, I realized I'd been wasting the last precious days of my trip—moping. A smile as warm as the feeling in my belly spread across my lips. "Thanks, I needed that."

By the time I got to the coffeeshop down the street I'd decided I was finished feeling sorry for myself. I wolfed down a breakfast sandwich under an umbrella at an outdoor table. I could finally taste food. I decided against gluttony when I was tempted to order another. The sun was already strong. I leaned my head back out of the shade to feel it on my face. Brighter times were ahead.

I walked to the corner to wait for my Uber. As I tracked the car on the screen, another call from Arlowe came in. "You're not going to ruin my day," I said to myself as I hit the red X as fast as I could, but my phone trembled in my hands. I climbed into the back of the SUV that stopped at the curb.

The phone vibrated in my hands five minutes later. "For fuck's sake." I thought I'd muttered under my breath as I punched the decline button, but the driver eyed me in the rear view mirror.

"Something wrong?"

Reading the text that came through immediately thereafter delayed my response.

Trinity, I need to talk to you. Call me ASAP, please.

My heart raced with a mixture of sadness and rage. I typed the word *Stop* but erased it. Fuck him. I clicked on his contact info and scrolled down to the red option at the bottom of the list. It felt better to block him.

"Nope, not anymore." I smiled up at the driver as I slipped my phone into my bag.

I slipped the driver a five dollar bill and kicked off my thongs when I got to the edge of the sidewalk. I looked up and down the crowded beach. The old man wasn't kidding about hordes of people. "Blimey."

The warm sand on my toes soothed my cold heart as I scanned the crowed beach. I finally spotted an open patch near the shore to spread my towel. After I'd slathered sunscreen over all my exposed bits, I stretched out, propped on my elbows so I could people-watch as I looked out into the calm crystal blue sea. Muscle-bound men and women jogged past at the water's edge. Surrounded by beautiful women in the teeniest bikinis I'd ever seen was a bit shocking after so long in Latin America. If I'd worn a suit like that in Peru, I'd have had to beat men back with a stick. I certainly didn't mind seeing so much skin, though. They could be naked for all I cared. A pretty blonde who reminded me of Lena caught my eye and grinned. Things were looking up.

After half an hour of sizing up the passersby, I was broiling. I waded into the clear water, stopping when an unexpected chill hit the top of my thighs. The water had cooled at least a few degrees in the past week. Everything had.

I dove in head first to get over the shock all at once. That was the only way I was going to get over what I'd been through in the past month. Head first. I swam out until it was just over my head to tread water where I could still see my rucksack on my towel in the sand. The last thing I needed was to lose my wallet the day before my flight.

A couple wrestling on a blanket a few meters from my stuff made me smile. The muscular bloke flipped the girl off him, clambering to his feet and threw her over his shoulder. Her squeals as he ran into the water with her drew smiles from all around. She kicked and screamed in false protest. She was clearly enjoying every second of it as he lifted her high into the air before falling over with her into the clear depths. Their laughter when they surfaced produced a jealous pang in my gut. When he shook the water out of his blond hair and her dark curls streamed down her back as he pulled her into a kiss, I realized why they were so beautiful to me. They looked like us. And they acted like we did last week.

Us. I couldn't stomach watching the couple frolicking in the water. I could imagine how she felt all too well. The breeze was warm but chilled my skin as I walked back to my towel.

Soaking up the Vitamin D was soothing but my mind kept wandering, along with my eyes, back to the couple, back to Arlowe.

I pulled my phone out of my bag, halfway hoped to see a missed call or text from Arlowe, even though I knew it wasn't possible. The irony was nauseating. I'd been hoping for the impossible from the minute I let my guard down with him. He couldn't get to me through my phone, but he'd already wormed his way back into my mind.

I laid back on my towel and watched the happy couple jog back to their blanket. I closed my eyes to try to forget but was flooded with memories of that first day alone on the beach with Arlowe. I'd seen him drinking me in that day, his eyes thirsty as I pulled another beer out of the cooler for him. I had sworn off men a few days prior but I'd stuck my ass up higher when I bent over, so he'd have a better view. He'd been a perfect gentleman, though. Which had of course made me want him.

Why did Arlowe have to be like Diego? Was that my lesson? They're all like Diego.

Everything happens for a reason. Arlowe showing me his true colors when he did kept me from making a huge mistake. At least I could be grateful for that.

The cool breeze on my face tickled my eyes open. I must have fallen asleep. The sky had turned dark grey and the air smelled of imminent rain. A storm was moving in from the water, but the sky was bright to the west. There might still be time to seek shelter before the thunderheads made landfall. I called an Uber on my phone before stuffing it with my towel into my bag. Clutching my shoes and dress to my chest, I hurried up the beach,

I set my rucksack at my feet to pull my sundress over my head as I waited on the curb for a red Toyota Corolla. I checked my phone again as I slipped my feet into my thongs. Three minutes until the car arrived. I looked back at the black cloud closing in. I might have that long before it drenched me.

I was so focused on the sky I hadn't noticed the couple from the beach approaching until they were right beside me on the sidewalk. Was it evil that part of me loved that the weather was ruining their lovely afternoon? I heard her complain, "Eighteen minutes? How can it be eighteen minutes?" The petite brunette who reminded me of me looked at the phone in her dreamy boyfriend's hand. "And twenty two dollars? It's twelve blocks. Fuck that, we'll walk. We'll be soaked by then anyway."

We had more than brown curly hair in common. The cute guy could only shrug in the face of that logic. I felt bad for wishing foul weather upon their bliss and called after her as they started to walk away, "You guys heading north?" It was an obvious assumption since they'd turned to walk that way. She stumbled into him as she stopped short to look back over her shoulder. I smiled. "I have an Uber coming now. I'm sure he won't mind dropping you on the way."

Her confused face softened in gratitude. "That would be amazing. We're just twelve blocks up on Ocean Drive."

"Perfect. Here's Edwin now."

The driver spoke in a thick Spanish accent through the tinted back passenger side window that lowered as he rolled to a stop. My first instinct was to answer him in Spanish but I wasn't sure if he'd be offended. I leaned into the window. "Hi, yes. That's me. I wonder if it'd be possible to drop my friends at their hotel on the way. It's just up the street."

He looked at the couple behind me before his gaze returned, confused. I knew that look. He had no idea what I was asking. "Mejor en español?"

Relief instantly spread across his face. "*Si, por favor.*"

After I spouted off the request in Spanish, adding that of course they would tip him separately, Edwin smiled and nodded. "*Claro que si.*"

I waved them over as I slid into the back seat. "Come on."

Within fifteen seconds, the rain was upon us as the Corolla inched out into traffic.

"Thank you so much. You're a lifesaver." The cute guy reached his hand across his girlfriend. "I'm Clay. We can't thank you enough."

His southern drawl made me think of Lena, which was far better than associating him with Arlowe when I took his hand. "It's nothing. I'm happy to help."

His girlfriend's hand grazed my knee before landing for a squeeze. "You saved us from getting drenched. That's something. We really appreciate it."

"Please. It's no big deal. Just give him a tip and everyone's happy."

"Of course. You should let us buy you a drink." She glanced at Clay with a smile.

I looked down at her hand on my knee. *Were they hitting on me?* I didn't know anything anymore. But my pattern of running straight to another bed was obvious if only to me. I was hoping they were hitting on me so I might have a chance to fuck them to forget. Not because I was horny or because I wanted anything at all with them. Attention was an analgesic. That's what fucking to forget was all about. Unfortunately that strategy had brought me nothing but grief.

"Oh, thank you. That's very kind. But I have to get back up to my hotel. It's miles away."

He smiled. "You sure? Your Spanish is amazing. Where'd you learn that?"

"Mexico, Guatemala, and Peru."

Her eyes brightened with excitement. "Awesome. And now…?"

"Back home to Australia."

"We're going back to Georgia Sunday. Not quite the same."

I smiled and focused on keeping my hands to myself. "Home is home."

Edwin stopped in front of their retro-looking hotel. Clay reached for the door handle but paused as his girlfriend turned with a grin. "You have a safe trip. And thanks for your help."

"It was my pleasure. I'm just sorry the rain ruined your lovely day at the beach."

"If it hadn't rained, we wouldn't have met you. The storms are what keeps life interesting." She winked before she slid out of the back seat.

The universe was giving me one good perspective after another today. I needed it when a big fat calico cat cowered under the awning outside my shitty hotel. She rubbed against my leg when I showed her my hand. I scratched along her jaw. "You could be Kai's mum." Highly unlikely considering the distance, but still. Did everything have to remind me of the things I missed?

I wouldn't miss this shitty hotel. I pulled out my travel

clothes and stripped down while the shower heated, laying my damp clothes over the noisy A/C vent. When my phone dinged from across the room, for a brief instant I thought it might be Arlowe again. Thank God I hadn't let him suck me into his drama. A sweet text from Danielle made me smile.

Hey Trinity, Just wanted to see how's life back home. I've been thinking about you.

I haven't made it back yet. Long story—hurricane—but I'm flying home early tomorrow.

Oh! Were you stuck in the hurricane?????

Yep!

All good now?

Yep! REALLY looking forward to getting home. At least the second part was true. All was not good , but it would all be better when I finally got home.

Call me when you get home. I might have some work for you if you're interested.

We'd talked about how I could help with sales several times while I worked for them but I hadn't thought about doing it from home. Their compensation had always been generous, and online work wouldn't interfere with uni. *Ohhhh, that sounds great! I'll call you in a couple of days."*

Ok but take your time. Enjoy your family and your friends. You've been away a while and you've been through a lot. Call me when you're settled in. Safe travels.

Her empathy touched me. I was self-reliant and dealt with things as they came, but I needed a support system. It would be good to be home.

As I plugged my phone into the charger, I realized the room was fogged up. Apparently I'd let the shower warm long enough to run through the hot water tank.

The tepid shower reminded me of the one I'd had at Arlowe's by candlelight when the power was still out after the storm. The night that Arlowe tried to kiss me and I told him I was lesbian. I giggled at the memory but my amusement was soon replaced by melancholy. I loved him as much as I hated him.

A tear rolled down my cheek as I leaned my head back to rinse my hair. The weak lukewarm stream couldn't wash away the ache. But the satisfaction of packing my bag afterward made me grateful I was going home. Everything would be better when I got home to people I could love *and* trust.

I settled onto the firm mattress and set my alarm for 2:45 a.m. When I thought of the fat calico outside, I longed to snuggle Kai as the rain lashed down. I already missed her.

I stared up at the water-stained ceiling, remembering a quote from a famous nineteenth century poem I'd learned in high school, the name of which and its author escaped me.

'Tis better to have loved and lost than to never have loved at all. Whoever he was, he had more faith than I did. Loving at all was my folly.

CHAPTER 27

ARLOWE

*O*nce I knew that Monica had gotten to Trinity, and Trinity had rejected my call last night, I hadn't been able to sleep. I tried to sleep in but that didn't work either. Kai nearly tripped me as I shuffled out to the kitchen to make coffee.

"Careful, little one. You wouldn't fare well under my hundred and eighty pounds."

She meowed in response. "Hungry?" At least one of us had an appetite. I popped open a can of soft food. My nose wrinkled at the pungent fishy odor. "This stuff is disgusting. I can't wait till you're big enough for dry food." I needed to Google that. I needed to find a vet first to determine how old she was.

"Let's call your mommy again." I rolled my eyes at myself. I was having a conversation with a cat. I held my breath while the call connected. Straight to voicemail on the first ring. If her phone was off, it wouldn't have rung at all. She wasn't even pretending that she missed the call. She rejected it. The message was loud and clear.

I took a cup of coffee over to the couch. Trinity had every reason to hate me, but I couldn't stand the thought of her leaving without a chance to explain. I called again. Straight to voicemail on the first ring again. "Godammit, Kai, your mommy is as stubborn as they come." I was tempted to call repeatedly until she finally answered but that was moving into weirdo stalker territory. I'd known a few girls like that.

If she wasn't going to answer my calls, maybe she'd reply to a text.

Trinity, I need to talk to you. Call me ASAP, please.

The message went from *Delivered* to *Read*. That was good news, at least. After staring at the screen for at least three minutes, hoping to see the dots that she was typing a reply, I tossed my phone onto the counter. There was no hope.

I paced the floors trying to think of a way to reach her. I'd drive to Miami Beach to tell her myself if I had any idea where she was staying. I adjusted the water cooler, wanting to knock it over as anger boiled up inside me. What the fuck was I going to do? There was nothing to do but wait. I pounded the side of my fist into the marble countertop and let out a growl. Fuck that hurt. I shook my hand. *Idiot.*

Kai meowed up at me with frightened eyes. I winced, both from the throbbing in my knuckles and the guilty feeling of scaring the cat. "Let's get out of here before I destroyed something."

Luckily a shipment of merchandise had come in at the shop.

I spent the morning entering it into Trinity's nice new inventory system which kept my mind off her for the most part.

Of course Slim brought her up while we ate subs he'd brought in for lunch. I could always count on him to twist the knife. "Have you talked to Trinity?"

"No. She hasn't answered my calls or texts."

"Ouch. That surprises me. I mean, I get why she's going home. But what'd you do to piss her off so badly she won't talk to you?"

I didn't like talking about women with Slim, or anyone. It was nobody's business but my own and everyone seemed to have an opinion that was geared toward getting me into a relationship. No one seemed to understand that a relationship was the last thing I wanted. At least, that was true before Trinity.

I took a deep breath and leveled serious eyes on his. "I fucked up."

He stared quizzically. "That's not surprising. What'd you do?"

"Thanks. Well, apparently Monica came in while Trinity was here on her own." I recounted the details as Monica had presented them.

Slim stroked his silver goatee. "So Trinity thinks you were cheating on your girlfriend?"

I sighed. "I can only assume that's the case since she won't answer my calls."

He rolled his eyes. "Way to go, dumbass. You cost us our best manager candidate."

It had cost me a lot more than that. "I know. It seemed like she might stay, but then everything changed. I guess it all makes sense now." Even the part where she doesn't ever want to speak to me again.

Slim shrugged. "It's too late to do anything about it now. You're better off just to let it go."

"It gets worse. Trinity noticed me ignoring Monica's calls during the hurricane and asked if she was my girlfriend. I said no. Little did I know then that Trinity was fresh from a bad breakup in Peru. Unbeknownst to her, the asshole was married with children."

Slim's eyes narrowed as he shook his head in disappointment. "And she thinks you did pretty much the same? I'd say you're pretty well fucked."

My cheeks warmed with the anger that boiled up in my chest. "But it's not the same! Monica is *not* my girlfriend."

He huffed and rolled his eyes. "I guess Monica didn't get that memo."

My heart pounded, making it hard to speak. When I did, I felt like a fool. "I know. It was stupid. But I've never cheated on a girl. That's not who I am. I need Trinity to know that."

Slim shook his head. "She probably wouldn't believe you anyway. Even if she did, it wouldn't make her stay."

I didn't want to accept his grim assessment. "But it might make her feel better to know that she didn't end up in the same situation twice."

Slim almost chuckled, but he held back. "I'd say it's more about making yourself feel better. But all you can do is keep trying to call her. Maybe she'll cave and hear you out."

I started to walk into the back room for privacy but realized it was probably pointless. She wasn't going to answer anyway. Nope. First ring again. I left a message this time. "Trinity, I really need to talk to you. I know Monica came to the shop. It's not what you think. It's not like she said. Please let me explain."

Slim shrugged when I hung up. "That's all you can do."

I wanted to scream and punch something again. A steady flow of customers made me keep my cool all afternoon, but I was a bundle of nerves by closing time. I pulled out my phone. My heart skipped a beat when I misread a text notification from Toby as Trinity. My stomach churned when I realized it was my buddy instead. I clicked on the message.

Heading to the raw bar. Wanna get a beer?

A tequila sounded better. *Sure. Be there in 10.*

I tried Trinity once more before leaving, knowing she wouldn't pick up. There was no point in another voicemail. She probably wouldn't listen to it anyway. But she had read the last text.

I know you talked to Monica. I promise it is not what you think. I can explain. Please give me a chance.

The message appeared to send but it didn't say Delivered. That was weird.

I thought about taking Kai home first but I hated to leave her alone. She'd been with us 24/7 since the storm. And she was still so little.

Toby met me with a wide grin after I patted him on the back with my free hand. "Where the hell have you been?" He peered into the pet carrier. "Rescuing cats, by the looks of things."

"Not my doing, but I'm stuck with it now." I saddled up on the barstool beside Toby and set Kai's carrier on the opposite stool.

"What's your poison tonight?" I looked up to meet Jules' smiling eyes when she spotted Kai as she cooed. "Aww what do you have there?"

"Long story. I'll have a shot of Corralejo and a Negro Modelo, please."

Toby slapped my back. "Oh damn. It's a tequila kinda night!" He grinned and glanced at Jules. "Get me one, too, on his tab."

I rolled my eyes and nodded.

"How've you been, bro? Been surfing? I haven't seen you out there."

"I went a couple times last week. Other than that I've been balls to the wall cleaning up the mess at the shop."

"Yeah? Did the storm get you guys?"

"Pretty bad. Mainly roof damage, but a lot of water came in. At least it was rain and not the ocean, but it was a mess."

"All good now?"

"All good." Nothing was good but the shop was back together.

Jules set the shots down then popped open my bottle.

I winked as I took the beer. "Pour yourself one, too." Misery loves company.

We clinked the three shot glasses together over the bar. Toby crowed, "Cheers, muthafuckas!"

Jules smiled after she finished the shot. "Damn that's good."

"Want another?"

Her narrow eyes were curious and concerned. "Not just yet. Do you?"

I waved with a backward hand. "Keep 'em coming."

She grabbed the tall blue bottle and filled my glass. "What's the story with the new pussy?" She looked to be on the verge of laughing at her own joke.

"This Aussie girl found her in the gutter, then took off."

Jules' eyes widened. "Aussie girl? I met a cute little firecracker from Australia a few weeks back. What was her name...?"

I swallowed a swig of beer. "Trinity?"

"Yes! Trinity! How could I forget? I really liked her."

"Yeah, me too." I threw back the shot.

"But she left weeks ago, right?"

"Nope. She stuck around a while longer."

Jules' brow slanted. "Did she stick around for you?"

"I thought so, but I guess not." I waved for her to fill my glass again.

Toby seemed serious for perhaps the first time ever. "Hence, tequila? I take it you're not celebrating this time. I'm sorry, brother. You seem kinda broken up over it."

Jules piped in as she poured my shot. "I bet you are! Trinity was a catch."

As if I didn't know. "Yeah, the worst part is that I totally fucked it up without knowing why. And now she won't answer my calls." As I slammed the third shot, I wondered if she'd read the text. I pulled my phone out of my pocket. It still didn't say Delivered.

"Hmm. This is weird. It looks like my last text went through but it doesn't say it was delivered or read."

Jules waved for me to hand over my phone. "You can turn off Read notifications but it will always say Delivered. Unless you're blocked."

"Blocked?" Surely she hadn't. I felt like someone had pulled my plug and all the life was leaking slowly from me.

"Send it again and see what happens."

The same thing happened. "But it rings when I call." I rang her on speaker.

When Trinity's greeting started, Jules hit the red button. "It rings once when you're blocked. You're blocked."

"I can't be blocked. It still lets me leave messages."

"You can leave messages but they don't go to her voicemail. They just go into cyberspace."

"So she can't listen to them?"

"Nope."

"Fuck. If she blocked me before the messages I left trying to explain, she won't even know." My beer tumbled in my hand.

Toby winced. "Explain what? What'd you do?"

I took a deep breath. The tequila was starting to take effect, which made me want another. I took another swig of beer instead then told the short version of the long story.

Jules leaned onto her elbows. "Wow. She found out you lied about having a girlfriend from your girlfriend. That's pretty harsh."

"But Monica wasn't my girlfriend. And I'd already decided not to see her anymore when I hooked up with Trinity."

Jules didn't even try to mask her disdain. "Here's a tip for next time—tell Monica that. Oh, and maybe Trinity, too. Especially if she asks."

My head hung. "I know, I get it. I told you I fucked up."

Toby's hand landed on my shoulder and squeezed. "Well, there's not much you can do about it now. She's on the other side of the world."

"Actually, she's somewhere in Miami Beach. Her flight's early tomorrow." That's when it occurred to me. I didn't know where she was right now, but I knew where she'd be tomorrow morning. She was flying Qantas at 6 o'clock. I picked up my phone and Googled the Qantas schedule. There was a 6:02 departure to L.A.

"Would it be psycho to show up at the airport tomorrow?"

Jules poured herself another shot. "Yes, it would. But it would also be incredibly romantic."

"Really? It feels desperate but I don't know what else to do. I can't let her leave without trying."

Jules pursed her lips. "Exactly. That's the romantic part, dumbass."

Toby was in excited agreement. "You should do it, man! That's the stuff chick flicks are made of."

It seemed crazy, but with their encouragement, crazy seemed like a good idea. "Her flight's at six, so she'll have to be there by, what, four?"

Jules cleared the empty shot glasses. "I'd say 3:30 to be safe. Three in your case to be sure to catch her outside."

"She won't think I'm a maniac?"

Jules sipped the rest of her shot. "She might. She might not speak to you. But you never know till you try. That fact that you're trying so hard will get you major points. Trust me."

Theoretically I had time to sleep off the tequila—if I could sleep at all.

I nodded off a couple of times before my alarm sounded at 1:30. I splashed cold water on my face in the kitchen sink while the coffee brewed. I was groggy and pretty sure I still had a buzz. Kai meowed up at me. "You wanna go, little one? Maybe you can convince her I'm not an asshole." That was a tall order for such a small creature. Her chances were better than mine though. By the time I got Kai in her carrier the coffee was ready. I filled a travel mug and grabbed Kai to hit the road. *Here goes nothing.*

The tequila was wearing off, or the coffee was doing its job, but luckily I felt wide awake when traffic on I-95 went from cruising along at eighty to a standstill. Four lanes of continuous tail lights stretched ahead. I opened the maps app. Twenty-eight minutes of traffic. Fuck.

I scanned through every radio station on the dial hoping to catch a traffic report. It was way too early for that. What were all these cars doing out at 2:30 a.m.? The app now read thirty-four minutes for the delay. Ten minutes had passed and it had gone up by six. Not good. I could finally see the source of the congestion on the map, several miles up ahead. Major accident. No surprise but that was the worst possible cause for the delay. That could take hours to clear.

"Why isn't this rerouting me?" I asked no one in particular but Kai responded to the sound of my voice with a squeaky meow from her carrier. I moved the map around. There was no way around it, that's why. And we hadn't moved an inch in at least five minutes. "Kai, I think we're fucked."

People up ahead were out of their vehicles looking around. That was a bad sign. I drummed my fingers on the steering wheel. We weren't going to make it if we were stuck here much longer.

Ambulances and firetrucks blared sirens as they passed in the emergency lane. Maybe that was a better sign. It was still another fifteen minutes before we started to inch forward. The GPS now registered another 27 minutes of traffic and a 3:59 arrival time. I might still catch her outside but there would be no time to park.

I put on Pearl Jam, hoping a singalong would distract me, but it only made me think of Trinity. I'd barely gotten to know her musician side. We were just getting started. And every minute that I sat barely moving was a minute closer to never seeing her again.

By the time the traffic actually started moving, the GPS predicted a 4:47 arrival time. With any luck she'd be running late and still in line to check in. But luck didn't seem to be on my side.

After we started to gain speed, the traffic thinned out enough for me to swerve in and out to pass. By the time traffic was flowing at the speed limit, I was passing at eighty in the emergency lane. I reached over to push Kai's satchel further back in the passenger seat. "Hold on, little one." It seemed impossible that we'd catch her, but this was our only chance.

How I didn't get arrested is beyond me. It was a miracle. I needed another one when I squealed up to the curb at MIA. I parked under the Qantas logo sign on the Departures level and turned on my hazard lights. I grabbed the handles of the pet carrier. "Here goes nothing, kid." I jogged into the entrance and scanned the line at the Qantas counter. She wasn't there. I looked in both directions before spotting a sign for the security checkpoint. Maybe she was stuck in that line. I clutched the cat bag tight to my chest and ran as fast as I could.

The agent checking boarding passes sized me up when I stood off to the side looking for Trinity in the line ahead.

"Can I help you?" She was a stocky black woman who clearly did not want to be fucked with.

"Sorry, I'm looking for someone."

She eyed the pet carrier I forgot I'd been hugging. "If you don't have a boarding pass, I need you to step aside, sir."

I must look suspicious, painting for breath with a bag in my arms. I had seen every face in the line. None were Trinity. She was probably already at the gate.

"No problem. I'll be right back."

I sprinted back to the Qantas ticket counter. An agent was calling for anyone on the LA flight. "Final call for check-in for flight 3130 to Los Angeles."

I waved my arm. The agent came and led me to the front of the long line. "Did you print your boarding pass?"

"No, I need a ticket. Can I buy one?"

"You don't have a ticket?" She looked at me like I was an idiot but then seemed to take pity and yanked me to a counter.

"He needs a ticket for 3130," she said to an older black man, who definitely had a what-the-fuck look before he shook his head and started typing.

"Do you have any luggage?" he asked.

"No. Just this." I set Kai's carrier on the counter.

"Papers?" He waved his hand for me to hand them over if I was in a hurry.

"Papers?"

His look now said *Seriously?* "The cat needs papers to travel. A release signed by a veterinarian."

Fuck. Of course. "Well, here's the thing. I wasn't planning on taking the cat on a flight. I'm still not. I just need a boarding pass to catch a woman at the gate before she gets on that plane."

"I'm sorry, sir, but all pets must have proper documentation to be ticketed." He glanced at the agent who'd brought me over with a *Can you believe this guy?* look.

"Can you sell me the ticket without the cat?"

His brow slanted suspiciously. "What are you going to do with the cat?"

"I can leave it in the car. Or I can leave it here with you. I'll be back before the plane takes off."

He shook his head. "You can't leave it here, and you can't leave it in the car."

Oh yes I could. It wasn't even hot out. "I'll leave it with someone. I'll be right back." I pulled my drivers license and my credit card out of my wallet and left them on the counter. "Can you please prepare the ticket? One way. Fully refundable, if possible."

His head tilted as he held up a finger in warning. "Don't you go dump that cat." He called me closer with a finger. "All this to win back a girl?"

My lips pressed together as I took a deep breath. It was crazy. But I was crazy for her. "Yes, sir." He looked up at the other agent who had a sweet smile on her lips as she touched her chest. He rolled his eyes and whispered gruffly, "I tell you what I'm going to do. I'm going to give you a ticket to take the cat with you to the gate. But if you try to get on that plane, I'll lose my job."

"I won't. I promise. Thank you."

"If anyone asks, you lost the papers for the cat somewhere between here and there."

"Got it." I took the boarding pass. "Thank you so much."

The other agent beamed as she cupped my elbow in her palm. "I'll take you to the front of the line."

She waited while the agent checked my boarding pass then led me to the lane reserved for employees. The pilots and flight attendants waiting moved aside as she pushed her way to the front. I don't know why anyone ever showed up early for a flight, if this was how they treated you when you arrived late.

She patted my shoulder when the TSA agent called me over. "You're on your own from here. Good luck."

I was going to need it. I had to remove Kai from her bag to run it through the X-ray. I shoved her back into the carrier as carefully and as quickly as possible after we were cleared. I blew past the travelers leisurely strolling through the terminal with roller bags in tow, hugging Kai tight to my chest as I sprinted to the gate.

The long line of passengers was a good sign. I scanned the crowd for Trinity's curls. I'd almost given up when I spotted a ponytail that could be hers near the front of the line.

When I got closer, I was sure it was her. How was it possible to feel relieved and scared to death at the same time?

I touched her shoulder. When those baby blues met mine, I forgot my name.

CHAPTER 28

TRINITY

*W*hen I felt a hand on my shoulder, I thought someone was trying to get past me in the boarding queue. I stepped aside as I looked back and had to do a double take. It couldn't be, but it was.

"Arlowe, what are you doing here?"

His blond hair was stuck to his sweat-drenched forehead as he strained a smile. "Hi."

"Hi? What the fuck, Arlowe? You can't just show up when I'm boarding a plane."

His smile faded and a pained look darkened his hazel eyes. "Trinity, I fucked up big time. But it's not what you think. I came to explain."

How could he know what I was thinking? Fuck him. "Don't waste your breath," I huffed.

"Please, just hear me out." His voice trembled as he held my gaze. "I know you talked to Monica. But she's not my girlfriend. She never was."

I turned to face the front of the line and kept a cool voice. "She tells it differently. But it doesn't really matter."

Arlowe's voice grew anxious. "Of course it matters. I wouldn't be here if it didn't. Listen, Monica and I had a few dates before you came. It was nothing."

He wasn't going to take no for an answer. I rounded on him, finally meeting his eyes, which were wide with desperation. It didn't matter—I didn't want to hear his excuses. How can you believe a liar? "It wasn't nothing. But there's no point in discussing it now. You can go home with a clear conscience. I don't care if you were cheating on your girlfriend, Arlowe. I just want to go home. You should do the same."

Arlowe somehow managed to shout in a whispering tone. "She's not my girlfriend, goddammit. I should have made that clear instead of ignoring her. That was a dick move. But I didn't cheat on her, and I didn't mean to lie to you." His expression morphed to a momentary shock and he averted his gaze, down to the bag he held in his death grip. He loosened his arms and held the bag by its handle. The pet carrier.

Kai meowed.

I looked up, shock etched across my face. What the fuck was he thinking? "You brought the cat?" I unzipped the end flap and pulled her to my chest. "You're lucky you didn't kill her. I didn't even see her there."

"I thought we both deserved a chance to say goodbye." The quiver in his voice echoed in my fluttering stomach.

"Or, you know I'm a sucker for her." Kai purred like a motorboat when I kissed the top of her head.

Arlowe shrugged with an innocent smile as we approached the front of the line.

The woman scanning boarding passes eyed Kai. "You'll have to put the cat in the bag before boarding, honey."

"Oh, the cat's out of the bag all right." I tried to hand over Kai to him but Arlowe raised a hand to stop me.

"Please, Trinity, give me five minutes." The tears in the rims of his eyes made me feel like crying, too.

I looked up to the attendant who nodded. I didn't want to hear him out, but I needed to. "I don't think I have that long. What else do you need to say?"

Arlowe pulled me by the elbow off to the side. His hazel eyes stared deep into mine, begging for understanding. "I need to say that I've never felt compelled to drive to the airport in the middle of the night to tell anybody anything ever. I've never cared that much what anyone thought about me. But it's not really what you think about *me* that eats me up." He took a breath probably meant to steady his shaky voice but it cracked as he continued. "It's what you think about you, and what you were—what you are—to me. I need you to *know* that I wasn't cheating on Monica, because I can't have you believing that you were just some side piece. That was never the case."

His words melted my heart but I didn't let it show in my icy reply. "Thanks for that. I'll keep it in mind." I couldn't let him back in, and I had a plane to catch.

He refused to take Kai again when I tried to hand her to him. "Trinity, you were more to me after our first kiss than Monica could ever be." My heart raced in my chest as I met his pleading gaze. "I'd already decided not to see her again after our last date. I think it was the fifth time we went out. You'd been here a couple of days already and we'd had that lovely day at the beach that tested all my willpower. I was trying not to like you. Not because of Monica, though. It was because I knew I might *really* like you if I let myself. And you were passing through for just long enough to make my resolve crumble."

I'd felt that too. All of it. Why had he gone and fucked it up? "That doesn't explain why you lied to me." The pain of the broken trust rushed back into my chest. I had to look away to keep from crying.

"I know. I'm sorry. It's no excuse, but in my mind, it wasn't a lie. She wasn't my girlfriend, had never been, and I'd already stopped seeing her at least a week before." His fingers hooked under my chin to coax my gaze back to his. "But I wasn't truthful, either. I'm sorry." His lower lip trembled a he paused. I handled that really badly, with you and with Monica." His hand rested on mine as I cuddled Kai. "I'm really sorry."

His sincerity tugged at my heart but it was too little, too late. My voice was as shaky as my resolve. "Thanks for the apology, but it doesn't change anything now."

"I know, but after what Diego did to you, I didn't want you believing the universe was conspiring against you by landing you with another lying cheat."

One of the things I'd loved about him was how he could tap directly into my feelings. It was also the thing that scared me the most. My lower lip started to tremble, but I took a deep breath to hold back the tears. "I was going to stay, Arlowe. I'd decided to give it a go and not let my fear of a broken heart keep me from doing what felt right."

He blinked through tears welling up in his surprised eyes. "You felt that I was right?"

The realization in his eyes that I'd felt the same crushed me. We'd been in love and hadn't admitted it—not to ourselves nor to one another. I was too sad to cry. "Yeah, I did. For a minute. But it's all water under the bridge now. I've got a plane to catch." My shoulders slumped. I was deflated.

His hands shook as he squeezed my elbows hard, his voice quivering. "There will be other planes. Please don't leave like this."

My stomach knotted. "Arlowe, I *have* to go."

"Then I'll go with you."

He was determined, I had to give him that. "Don't be ridiculous."

He dropped to a knee and beckoned for my hand. I let him take it. I felt my resolve starting to crumble as he looked up into my eyes. "If you thought even for a minute that this was worth a shot, then please don't go."

The three airline employees had gathered nearby to blatantly eavesdrop.

"Get up. They think you're proposing."

The whites of his hazel eyes were pink as he stared up in earnest. "I'm proposing that you stay here and give us a chance."

My head spun as I looked around at the few other passengers watching us. "Get up. This is crazy."

"I might be crazy, but when I'm with you, I'm a better man." He took a deep breath and pressed his lips together. He was choked up and it made me want to cry, too. His voice trembled as much as his hands when he could finally speak. "I've never met a woman like you, and I've never felt this way. Screwing us up was my biggest fuck-up ever. Give me a chance to at least try to make it right."

Butterflies swarmed in my stomach. My heart told me that he deserved another chance. But could I trust him with my heart? "I don't know if I can."

"I know you feel the same. I can see it in your eyes, and feel it in your touch. You can't move to the other side of the world right now."

I'd tried not to let love in, but it had been there growing for so long it had taken root. There was no denying it. Arlowe might break my heart if I stayed, but leaving was sure to.

I stood speechless while my thoughts raced.

The attendant called over. "Honey, we've got to close the gate. Are you coming with us?"

I hugged Kai tight and squeezed Arlowe's hand. I couldn't walk away from them. I couldn't walk away from love. I chuckled through tears. "My parents are going to bloody murder me."

His hands squeezed mine as he blinked up at me, a smile spreading across his lips. "You'll stay?"

I sniffled as I nodded. "I can't leave. You already have my heart."

Arlowe stood and pulled me into his arms. "I'll take good care of it."

I believed him. "I trust you." That might have been the hardest thing I'd ever said, but it was the truth.

"You just made me the happiest man alive."

I rolled my shoulders forward to protect Kai as he pulled me to his lips. I felt my knees giving way as I melted into his embrace. God he was a good kisser.

My eyes fluttered open at the applause. A man in a cowboy hat whistled through his fingers while the airline employees clapped. My cheeks flamed but my heart was just as warm.

Arlowe chuckled before he whispered onto my lips. "Should we get out of here?"

I glanced at the gawking crowd before I turned back to his adoring gaze. "Yes, please."

Arlowe slung my guitar over his shoulder and slipped his arm around my waist as we walked through the terminal. I paused to read the signs near the exit. "Which parking garage are you in?"

Arlowe stopped, his hand covering his mouth as his eyes widened. "Oh fuck."

"Don't worry, we'll find it."

"Or we won't. I'm sure it's been towed by now. I got stuck in traffic and got here so late there was no time to park. I left it out front."

I drew in a deep breath. "Oh fuck."

"Let's go see if it's still there. A tow bill is a small price to pay to keep you."

The Jeep was still there all right, and surrounded by four cop cars and a firetruck. I looked from the flashing blue and red lights to Arlowe's worried eyes. "This might cost you more than a tow bill."

"Whatever it costs, it's worth it." Arlowe took a deep breath and approached the nearest police officer.

She held up a hand to stop him. "Sir, you need to stand back."

"I'm sorry. This is my car."

She looked at him like he was an idiot. "Leaving a vehicle unattended is a serious offense. What the hell were you thinking?"

"I wasn't thinking. I had to stop this woman from leaving."

My eyes pleaded for mercy on him when the officer glanced my way. She rolled her eyes, shaking her head. "Looks like it worked. I hope it was worth it. Come with me." She led Arlowe to speak to another officer. I gnawed at my nails, watching from afar as they checked his ID and registration while a German Shepherd sniffed around the Jeep. I couldn't hear what he said but the officer's angry face said enough. Arlowe kept his mouth shut and nodded, probably a good strategy. He looked calm when he finally spoke, but I couldn't read in his expression how badly it might be going. At least they weren't putting him in the back of a police car— yet. I held up the pet carrier to peek in at Kai. "I hope he can talk his way out of this."

A few minutes later, the firetruck and two of the police cars left, surely a good sign. The officer handed Arlowe a clipboard and a pen. I breathed a sigh of relief when Arlowe smiled and patted the officer on the shoulder after receiving a citation.

His eyes widened as he approached. "Phew, that was close."

I grimaced. "Yeah?"

"Yeah. I thought I was going to jail."

"How'd you talk him out of that?"

He stepped closer, trailing his fingers down my arm. "Well, when he threatened to arrest me, I told him I understood he had to do what he had to do. But I was just doing what I had to do to keep from losing the love of my life."

My heart swelled in my chest. I hadn't gotten on the plane for the same reason.

He grinned. "Lucky for me, he's a romantic. But I'd have gone to jail if that's what it took. I kind of liked the idea. You've got to admit it would be a dramatic display of devotion."

I shook my head and giggled. "You're insane."

"Crazy for you, baby." His fingers slid behind my waist as he lowered his lips to mine. "Let's go home."

I'd been dying to get home, but I was already there. He was home.

CHAPTER 29

ARLOWE

*a*s I unlocked the door, I held up my hand. "Wait here."

I set her backpack and guitar inside. Trinity peered curiously through narrow eyes when I took Kai's carrier from her hands. I left the cat with the luggage and returned with a grin. "I want to do this right."

She squealed as slipped one hand under the shoulder and the other under her thighs to scoop her up into my arms. "What are you doing?"

I smiled into her blue eyes as I carried her through the living room. "Treating you like a princess, like you deserve."

Trinity's brow slanted but her blue eyes sparkled with contentment as she giggled. "You're treating me like a bride. Just to be clear—I didn't agree to marry you."

"You're here now. That's enough for me." I lowered her softly to the bed. "And now"—I hooked my fingers into the waistband of her yoga pants—"I'm going to show you just how much I appreciate that."

She smiled into my eyes. "I like the sound of that."

I loved the sound of her voice, and every other thing about her. I held her gaze as I pulled her yoga pants down over her hips and tossed them to the floor. "You're so fucking beautiful."

I bit my lip as I spread her legs, my fingers brushing over her perfect little landing strip. "All of you."

Hers was the most beautiful pussy I'd ever seen. From the moment I'd laid eyes on it, I wanted to make it mine. I kissed it like it was a privilege, because it was.

My nose buried in her mound as my teeth raked over her clit, my tongue exploring her folds. Trinity moaned, her hips moving in a circular motion to press herself harder against my mouth. She tasted like honey and smelled like rain.

I groaned as I licked her, sliding two fingers into her silky wetness. She clenched around my fingers as I stroked her clit with quick flits of my tongue. I shook my head to increase the friction, sucking her with an unquenchable thirst. Her nails dug into my scalp as her head lifted to stare with wide eyes. Her moans climbed to the rafters.

I was a slave to her seduction, but I intended to master her by giving her everything she could ever want. I pressed my forearm over her pelvis to hold her hips firm as she writhed under my tongue. She teetered on the edge of ecstasy until she finally succumbed to my attack, her thighs clamping against my ears as her walls clenched and pulsed around my fingers, her scream so loud I was certain the neighbors could hear through my open bedroom window.

Her eyes were glazed over when her head fell back. "Oh my God, Arlowe. Fuck. You're amazing." She sat up, breathing hard as she slipped her T-shirt over her head. "I need to feel you."

I pushed up to my knees, scrambling out of my shirt and shorts as her ivory legs spread once more.

She rested back onto the pillow as I climbed over her. I rubbed the head of my cock around her opening, and she gasped as it passed over her swollen clit. Her pleading eyes ignited a chain reaction that spread through every nerve ending in my body. If my dick got any harder, it might burst.

"When I thought I'd lost you, it felt like my heart had been ripped from my chest, leaving a hole that no one could fill. I've never felt that way about a woman, ever." I teased her pussy until I couldn't resist. Unprotected sex might be irresponsible but I didn't want any barrier to our connection. I needed to feel her, too. All of her.

Trinity gasped as I filled her. "Neither have I," she managed, then added, "About a woman or a man." She giggled and gasped again as I slid out slowly. She gripped me from the inside to hold me there, then crossed her feet behind my ass. "I wanted to go home to get away from the fact that I *needed* you."

"Well, you have me. All of me." Knowing she liked it, I pushed into her deepest point and held still, relishing the rush of her tight grip. As my length moved in and out of her, I somehow managed to hold back the overwhelming urge to come, but my willpower stopped there. My words came gushing forth an untethered string. "You're fucking amazing. Fucking you is amazing. But loving you, that's even better."

"Loving you is the scariest thing I've ever done." Her words trailed in a sigh, a flash of fear igniting in her eyes.

I lowered my weight onto her chest, pushing her dark curls from her face and holding her cheeks firm. Our lips nearly touched as I spoke. "Don't be scared, baby girl. I'll take care of you."

"Fuck. Don't ever stop calling me that."

I wavered between wanting to take it slow and savor every second of her, and wanting to ravage her ferociously. Her hips moved in an insistent rhythm fueled by the want in her eyes. She wanted more. She always wanted more. I could relate. I couldn't get enough of her either.

"I won't ever stop any of this if you'll let me. And if that's what you like, I will make you my baby girl." I growled as I pressed into her, "I will take you every single day."

She pleaded with a sigh. "God, yes, please."

My fingers snaked into her curls and tightened into fists. She sensed the shift in my energy, clutching me tight. Emboldened, I growled, "I will take this pussy and do whatever I want with it, and you'll let me. Because it's mine." I rammed myself deeper into her with a pounding thrust. "Isn't that right, baby girl?" I'd never talked to a woman that way. I'd never felt comfortable enough to. Trinity brought out the animalistic dominance I'd always suppressed.

She moaned and then whined a reluctant, "Yes." Not only did she accept that side of me, she craved it. Her feet locked to pull me deeper as her hips lifted to meet my thrusts. Her tightness pulsed around me as my pace quickened. When I could feel her close to coming, I pulled out and slapped my shaft onto her clit hard and fast. The deliciously wet slapping sound mixed with her moans. When she'd ridden the wave to the crest, I pushed deep inside, feverishly pounding her as I commanded, "Come on that cock, baby girl. Come on that cock."

Her eyes released the last hint of restraint, holding my gaze as she groaned, "God yes, I love coming on your cock. I love the way you fuck me." Her eyes closed as she howled a long moan.

I waited almost too late to pull out, barely sliding my cock up over her clit before I released onto her belly.

The deep blue of her eyes pulled me in as my body shuddered with the aftershock of orgasm. "I fucking love you, Trinity."

She smiled up into my eyes, panting. "I love you, too." Her grin twisted with mischief. "Especially now that I know you can be a Dom."

I chuckled as my lips brushed over hers. We both paused and turned our ears to listen for the faint squeaking sound coming from the other room. Trinity's face twisted in alarm. "Crikey, we left the cat in the bag!"

Kai was still in her carrier, but the proverbial cat was already out of the bag.

CHAPTER 30

TRINITY

*T*rinity

My mother hadn't spoken to me in the three days since I'd failed to board the plane. That was fine by me. She needed time to calm down. Dad had been more understanding, although he was far from happy about the last-minute change of plans. Mum had gone absolutely mental, though. It was no secret where my fiery side came from.

They'd had me on speakerphone when I explained that I'd missed my plane because I'd decided to stay. That's all I'd managed to get out before Mum erupted into a raging rant.

Dad had cut her short and excused himself to another room to finish our conversation. "Trinity, I trust you to make the right choices. We'll talk again soon. Take care of yourself."

But now she was calling again. I nearly poked my eye out applying mascara when my phone rang. My heart raced. Fuck. Her timing was always horrendous. Arlowe was waiting to leave and his friends were meeting us so there was no time for a drawn out lecture. But, ignoring her call would fuel her fury. That was not an option.

I called out to Arlowe, who sat on the edge of the bed tying his Vans. "Babe, I'm sorry but my Mum is ringing. I promise I'll keep it short."

"Ohh. Take your time, beautiful."

I took a deep breath before I tried to sound cheery. "Mum, I'm so glad you called."

"Thank you. It's good to hear your voice." She sounded as relaxed as she normally did after a bottle of Shiraz. It was only 9 a.m. back home—definitely too early for her to be in the wine.

I spoke cautiously. "It's good to hear yours. How are you?"

"I'm better now. Are you ready to explain why you delayed your return *again*?"

Underneath the calm, she was seething. This was not the ideal time to explain, but if I didn't she might hold it against me for months. She might anyway.

"I wanted to explain when I called before."

"I'm sorry I lost my temper. I was just really looking forward to your return. I had a party planned. All your friends were coming 'round tonight."

I winced. As laid back and hippie as she could be, she took party planning seriously. She'd gone to a lot of trouble to make it special and I'd shat on her plans. "Oh. I'm so sorry, Mum. Calling them all to cancel must've been dreadful."

I felt as guilty for not having told Evie myself as I did for ruining Mum's party. She'd be pissed at me now, too. Balling on our roomie arrangement that we were both excited for was a bitch move.

Mum's annoyance was apparent when she shot back, "Especially when they asked what happened and I had no answers."

"I feel terrible about that, all of it. I'm sorry to do that to you guys so last minute. It just happened."

"*What* just happened?"

They didn't know any of the gory details of my break-up with Diego. I'd told her I'd been dating a guy while I was in Peru, which I could tell had made them both happy. They'd accepted my bisexuality and supported me completely to be authentic to myself, but I knew she secretly hoped I'd settle down with a man and have a family. Of course, she'd rather that I be in Australia than on the other side of the world, so she was ecstatic when I announced that I was coming home. Never did she have any idea that I'd had my heart broken into a million pieces. So she might not appreciate how monumental my simple explanation was. "I fell in love?"

"I knew it. This is over a boy?" Her incredulous tone soon shifted to scorn. "Or is it a girl?"

"His name is Arlowe. I can't wait for you to meet him."

I bit my lip through her long pause. She sounded annoyed. "How long are you planning to carry on with this?"

That was a good question. "As long as it lasts."

"Jesus, Trinity."

I was glad I couldn't see her face. She must be gutted. "I'm sorry, but I couldn't leave without giving this a chance. He might be the one, Mum."

Her voice softened. "If a man has you acting this erratically, he must be special. Tell me about Arlowe."

"He is special. He's pretty perfect." I told her about him giving up a corporate career to save his favorite surf shop from closing.

"Good on him. At least he doesn't think like an American."

I chuckled, relieved that she was focusing on the positive. "No, he doesn't. And he's even more romantic than the Italians. He came to the airport and begged me to stay."

"Really?" I could tell she was smiling. Arlowe already had her smitten.

"Yeah. He ran to the gate just before I boarded the plane. It was quite dramatic."

"He gets points for theatrics."

"You should have seen the Bomb Squad around his Jeep when we left. He almost got arrested for leaving his car on the curb while he rushed in to catch me."

She almost giggled. "This sounds like a film."

"Yep, just like one of those cheesy Rom-Coms we love. But I didn't stay because he made such a show. I stayed because I realized that we both feel the same."

"Oh, Trinity. I'm so bloody sad that you're not here. But I haven't heard you sound so happy in months. Part of why I was so anxious for you to get home is that you'd been sounding so down. I was afraid you were losing your spark. Sometimes seeing too much too soon can leave you jaded. At your age, you should still see the good in the world. Hopefully you never lose that, but I wanted you to at least make it to your thirties before you do."

I remembered the quote she'd emphasized when we read *The Diary of Anne Frank* together, before our trip to Amsterdam when I was thirteen, the same one I'd recounted with the old man in the shitty hotel in Miami Beach. "Don't worry, Mum. In spite of everything, I still believe people are good at heart."

"Aww, you remember Anne Frank."

"Of course I do. I remember everything you've taught me."

She was silent for long enough I was afraid she might cry. "I love you, Trinity. And I miss you."

"I miss you, too, Mum." I bit my lower lip. This could easily become a moment for a deep conversation. I had to nip it in the bud. "I'd love to tell you more but we're late to meet Arlowe's friends for dinner. Can we FaceTime later?"

"Oh, yes, of course. I look forward to meeting this American anomaly."

I chuckled. Arlowe was certainly that. "Me, too. You will love him as much as I do."

Arlowe smiled up from the couch, waiting patiently with Kai on his lap. "Everything okay?"

"Everything's great. She took the news better than I hoped."

"So she's not ready to hire an international hitman to take me out?"

Dante might do that—only if I asked him to, of course. But not my parents. I chuckled at the thought. "We're Australian. We don't have guns. We don't think that way."

He grinned. "Lucky for me."

"She doesn't want to kill you. She wants to meet you. I told her we'll FaceTime soon."

"You'll have to help me prep for that."

"It will be fine. Trust me. She will succumb to your charm as easily as I did. She's already impressed by the lengths you went to to convince me to stay."

"Good that she doesn't take me for a raging lunatic. I wouldn't blame her."

"Quite the contrary." I noticed he still wasn't moving. I gestured with my hands. "Aren't we late to meet your friends?"

"A little. It's no big deal. But you're right, we should go."

Arlowe opened my door for me to climb into the Jeep before he slid into the driver's seat. "You like oysters?"

"I love oysters."

"They have other stuff, too, but if you're going to Shuck's, it's a shame not to have their specialty."

The name rang a bell. "Is that the raw bar a block or so off the beach?"

"The one and only."

"I went there once. The bartender was nice." The assholes who'd tried to pick me up, not so much, but he didn't need to hear that.

"Jules? She's great."

Of course he'd know her. She knew all the locals. "Seemed like it."

Jules smiled coyly as we approached. A guy seated at the bar had just started to turn his head when Arlowe's arm wrapped around his shoulder. His mouth twisted to a grin. "I'd almost given up on you."

"Sorry, I was detained."

Arlowe's friend glanced my way and grinned. "Understandable."

"Get your mind out of the gutter, Toby. Trinity had a call."

Toby did a double take. "Wait, you're Trinity?" He looked at Arlowe, surprised. "Why didn't you tell me?"

Arlowe shrugged. "I'm telling you now."

Jules beamed at me from behind the bar. "You stayed."

"This guy wouldn't let me go." I leaned into Arlowe's shoulder as he slipped his hand around my waist.

She grinned from ear to ear. "Oh my God, I can't believe it worked."

My brow creased. "What worked?" Was there another sinister plot I didn't know I was involved in? I thought I'd left that behind in Guatemala and Peru.

Arlowe interjected. "I was here the night before I went to the airport. These guys helped convince me I should go find you."

"So you two are responsible for the great stunt." I slid onto the stool beside Toby.

Jules took a tall blue bottle from the top shelf and set four shot glasses on the bar. "Oh, no. It was his idea. We just gave him a little encouragement. Back to the great stunt…there must be a story there."

We took the tequila shots before Arlowe recounted a short version of the long story. Jules touched her chest when he finished. "That's so romantic."

Arlowe grinned. "Especially since it didn't end with me spending the night in a Miami jail."

Jules chuckled as she collected the shot glasses. "Although, that would have been an interesting plot twist."

Toby laughed. "I told you, dude, chick flicks."

"I'm glad this one had a happy ending." Jules winked at me. "Beer?"

"Yes, please. And I'm pretty happy about the ending myself."

Arlowe's hand tightened around my waist. "Sounds like we all are. That's what we're celebrating. Should we start with a couple dozen on the half shell?"

Toby bombarded me with questions while we ate. By the time we finished, he knew my entire travel itinerary including all the surf spots along the coast where I'd worked.

He stared at me in awe. "It's really cool you'd just pick up and move to the US."

"Well, that certainly wasn't the plan, but you only live once."

Jules grinned. "And it's not every day a guy chases you down and nearly gets arrested to tell you how he feels."

I wiggled my eyebrows at Arlowe. "Very true. I couldn't let that effort go to waste."

"I have to say, I've seen Arlowe with more women than I can count."

Arlowe held up his hand and leaned across me, shooting Toby a warning glare. "We can do without that."

"Relax, brother. I was going to say that I've seen you with girls, but none that I've never seen you give a shit about." Toby turned to me. "He was so distraught the other night, I didn't have the heart to give him a hard time for acting so pathetic."

"Really?" I grinned at Arlowe before leaning back into his chest.

"Alright, that's enough. You're making me sound like a pussy."

Toby shirked off Arlowe's concern. "Chicks dig that shit."

"This badass chick can smell weakness. Don't make me look bad."

After he'd shown me his Dom side, there was no risk of that. "Going to extraordinary measures to get what you want is anything but weak."

Toby grinned. "What'd I tell you?"

Arlowe rolled his eyes then changed the subject. "How's your training going?" He turned to me to clarify. "Toby competes on the national circuit."

"Wow, that's pretty cool. Do you have to travel to train?" The waves in Jupiter weren't consistent enough for high-level practice.

"Yeah. I'm heading up to Cocoa Beach tomorrow. It's supposed to be a good few days. You guys should come."

"We have a dinner with my folks tomorrow, and we're busy

281

as fuck at the shop. Trinity and I both have students for the next four days."

"That's great, bro. Glad to hear it."

Jules handed Arlowe another beer. "What happened with the job?"

"I turned it down. I've got everything I want right here." My cheeks warmed as my stomach fluttered.

Jules was jubilant. "Thank God! You'd have been miserable."

"That's exactly what Trinity told me, many times."

"Good choice," agreed Toby. "You ought to start training with me. You've still got the moves."

"Trinity should start training with you. She'd have a chance at the podium."

Toby's brow lifted as he looked me up and down. "You're that good?"

Arlowe beamed. "She's fucking phenomenal."

The butterflies in my stomach flew up into my chest. I wasn't sure about the podium, but Arlowe definitely put me on a pedestal. "He exaggerates. And I think I have enough on my plate with work and starting uni in January—if my visa gets sorted."

Toby smiled. "Your boss is easily persuaded. Keep it in mind."

I chuckled. "Thanks, I will."

Arlowe and Toby proceeded to talk about people I didn't know, so I excused myself from between them and moved a few stools down to chat with Jules. "I can't remember from our previous conversation...do you surf?"

"I mess around. Mostly I just party with the surfers."

"That's the best part."

She grinned. "It's been a solid system so far."

"Do you have a boyfriend?"

She shook her head adamantly. "Noooo. I don't want one of those. But I have a couple of friends that keep me busy."

"I know that feeling. Careful, you might end up with one when you least expect it." I took the last swig of beer and set the bottle on the bar.

"You ended up with a good one."

I looked over at Arlowe. The angle of his jaw in his profile made me wet. "I think so."

"Trust me. I've known him for ten years. He's a great guy." She set a fresh beer in front of me and poured us each a shot. "He told me what happened with the other chick. I'm not making excuses for him, because it was totally his fault. He should have told her he wasn't interested. But being a dumbass is different than being an asshole."

"I agree. What is with the whole ghosting thing though?"

"Fucking pussies." She handed me a shot. "Here's to the good ones out there."

I chuckled to myself, thinking of the good pussies *and* the good men out there. "To the good ones." The tequila went down smooth, taking me back to the Mezcal bar days. The seven months since I'd left Antigua had passed in a flash but felt like another lifetime.

"Arlowe is not the cheating kind. A lot of girls suspected that he's not the marrying kind either. But I figured that one day there'd be a woman who'd capture his heart. He was always casual because he didn't really care. Not because he was an asshole, though. He just had't met you yet."

I held up my hand. "Let's not get ahead of ourselves."

She grinned. "Oh, you're in deep. I can tell."

I'd been afraid of getting in so deep I'd drown. But she was right, it was too late.

Jules must've seen the fear in my face. "Don't worry. You can trust him."

Arlowe and I had both been guarding our hearts. It was scary as hell, but trusting him was the only way to open my heart. "It's either trust him or go home. And I'm not going anywhere—for now."

"That makes me so happy. You have no idea." She looked down at the glass she was drying before finding my gaze. "We should be friends."

I grinned, touched by her openness. "I think that's already happening."

"You're the coolest chick I've met in a long time. Most of my friends are guys."

She was so cute, I just couldn't. "Same. And you're the coolest chick I've met in town, so, yes, please, let's be friends!"

"I'm off Wednesday and Thursday. Will Arlowe let you come have a beer next Wednesday?"

I picked up on her sarcasm. My needing permission was preposterous. But asking him would be fun. He might make me do something to earn it. I blinked back to reality to keep my mind from wandering further down that exciting rabbit hole. "He lets me out when I behave."

"Great! It's a date."

~

Arlowe's hand slipped off the gearshift onto my knee. "Did you have fun tonight, beautiful?"

"I had a blast. Toby is super chill and, you're right, Jules is the best. I think we'll be good friends."

"I bet you will."

"What's that supposed to mean?" I grinned, pretty sure there was a sexual insinuation in there somewhere.

"I mean...she's cool and fun and wild like you. You'll make great friends."

"It's funny, when I first met her, I thought she was into me."

"That's entirely possible. Quite likely, I'd say."

My brow cocked. "Really? I didn't think she was into girls. She said as much, if I remember correctly."

Arlowe chuckled. "She's played with girls. I have friends who've witnessed it firsthand."

I giggled. "Friends, huh?"

"Yeah, friends. Jules and I have always just been friends. But she gets wild."

A girl after my heart. "Interesting." My gaydar wasn't broken after all.

I was quiet as we sat through a red light. Arlowe prodded,

half-jokingly. "Are you thinking about a threesome with Jules?"

Heat rose to my cheeks. "It might have crossed my mind. But that's just me."

"I know. I fucking love it." The white of Arlowe's grin glowed in the darkness of night.

He loved me for who I was. The feeling was mutual.

CHAPTER 31

ARLOWE

*D*read started to creep in as we wrapped up the day at the shop. I was excited to share the news that Trinity was staying, but how my dad would take my decision to turn down the job was anybody's guess. The uneasy feeling in my gut was familiar. It always came when I was afraid to disappoint him.

Trinity smiled as she handed me my keys. "Are we going straight to your parents' house?"

"Sure, unless you need to stop home first." Home. My house felt like a home now that it was ours.

"Nope, I'm good."

"Grab your pussy then."

"I'd rather you grab my pussy." Trinity grinned as she lifted Kai to her carrier.

I shook my head and chuckled. We really were made for each other. "Don't you worry, I plan on it. But don't make me think about that before we go to my parents' please."

~

The house smelled like my favorite dish. "Chicken and dumplings?"

Mom wiped her hands on her apron and smiled. "With turnip greens and cornbread."

Just how I liked it. I leaned over to kiss her on the cheek. She smiled up into my eyes. "And banana pudding for dessert."

She turned to Trinity. "I was surprised—pleasantly—when Arlowe said you were coming. I thought you'd gone already."

Trinity glanced my way with a question in her eyes. Hadn't I told them? I grinned. "I wouldn't let her leave." I slipped my hand around her waist and pulled her in close to my side.

My mother eyed us, the first time she'd seen us *together* together. "That might be one of the smartest things you've ever done."

I knew she'd approve. "You're not wrong."

"Oh, I know." Mom took Trinity's cheeks between her hands. "I'm delighted."

Dad came in from the garage. "Delighted to see these two?" He patted my back. "Of course we are." He was unusually chipper. That would soon change when he heard that I turned down the job. Better to focus on the good news.

"How nice you're still here." Dad hugged Trinity.

"Your son can be very persuasive."

Dad grinned. "He learned that from his mother." He glanced at the cat carrier. "You kept the kitty?"

"Of course he did!" Mom took the canvas bag from Trinity's

hands. "Let's see that little cutie." She unzipped the flap and pulled Kai out. "Look how much you've grown!"

"She eats nonstop." Trinity beamed.

"Speaking of eating…" I nodded toward the kitchen. "Is there anything I can do to help?"

Mom shook her head. "Nope. It's ready."

Trinity's hand squeezed my knee after we took our seats around the table. I groaned as the first bite of dumplings melted in my mouth. "Your Southern cooking is the best, Mom."

She smiled proudly. "It's what I do."

"You do a lot more than Southern food well, but you know it's my favorite."

"That's why I made it." My mom winked as she sipped her tea.

Our dinner conversation inevitably ended back on the storm. It was all anyone had talked about for over three weeks. "Kate called again and said the Keys escaped the brunt of it. The wedding is on."

"Yeah, she told me. Looks like Christmas in the Keys!"

Mom smiled. "That is going to be something else." She was anxious to meet Sally and get her hands on that baby. The wedding was a bonus. She looked to Trinity. "Are you going home for Christmas or will you be joining us?"

I answered with a full mouth, even though I'd been taught better manners than that. "She's not going anywhere."

Trinity looked surprised. "Oh, I hadn't thought about the

holidays. My parents will want me to come home, I'm sure, but I'd rather go to the Keys."

I grinned. "Two weeks in Paradise on Zayne's dime is a no-brainer."

"Two weeks? Wow, I wouldn't want to pass that up. I'll have to see, but I'm certainly going to try."

Dad changed the subject. "How's the shop since the storm?"

I wondered if he doubted Trinity would be around that long. "Back to normal. We've been crazy busy."

He smiled. "That's great! What's Slim going to do when you start that new job? Rely on Trinity?"

I avoided his question by posing one to Mom. "Didn't I hear you say that there's banana pudding for dessert?"

She looked nervously at my Dad but answered quickly. "I sure did. I'll bring it right out."

I always appreciated that Mom knew when I needed a buffer. "I'll help."

Trinity eyed me curiously as I stood. She'd picked up on my hesitation. "Slim can count on me. It doesn't feel like work." She knew how to skirt subjects she wanted to avoid.

I heard Dad chuckle as I followed Mom to the kitchen. "That's a blessing." Hopefully he'd say the same when I told him I was staying at the shop.

I waited until Dad had a mouthful of banana pudding to get back to his question. The sweet dessert might make the news easier to digest. "I turned down the job."

You could have heard a pin drop in the silence while Dad blinked, confused. "You did?".

Trinity's hand moved to my knee under the table. She knew this wasn't easy.

"Yeah. Business is good. I don't need to leave, nor do I want to. I love my job." Saying it outloud made it feel even truer. Especially now that Trinity was staying. "I don't need something to fall back on. I've got everything I want and need right now."

Dad pressed his lips together and nodded, thinking for a moment before he responded. "Few people can say that. Very few."

My eyes narrowed. Was that a positive response? "Trading my lifestyle for a corporate job would make me miserable."

"Well, we don't want that. If you're happy, then you're doing the right thing."

I glanced at Mom who looked as surprised as I was at his calm. Had he gotten medical marijuana? Whatever the reason, I'd take it. I let out a breath I didn't realize I'd been holding. "I couldn't be happier."

Mom nodded as she smiled. "You're happier than I've ever seen you, that's for certain." She winked at Trinity. "You're good for him."

Trinity grinned as she squeezed my knee tighter. "I hope so. He's good for me, too."

I kept waiting for Dad's disappointment to surface, but he seemed buoyant. Our conversation flowed easily and they were as smitten with Trinity as I was.

Mom and Dad walked us to the front door. Dad surprised me by pulling me into a hug. "I'm proud of you, son. It takes courage to follow your heart. You've always been better at that than I."

I was almost speechless. "Thanks, Dad. That means a lot." Probably more than it should.

Once we were in the Jeep, Trinity smiled warmly. "That went surprisingly well."

"No kidding. That might be the first time my father has ever treated me like an adult."

"What he said was true. It does take courage to follow your heart."

"It's easy to follow my heart now that it's in your hands."

Trinity's blue eyes sparkled in the orange-red twilight. "You're a sap."

"See what you do to me, woman." She didn't know it yet, but I planned to spend the next fifty years showing her—if she'd let me.

*****

Did someone say wedding on Paradise Key??? Arlowe's sisters will be there with all the gang in Christmas in Paradise.

And if you haven't read Trinity's adventures with Lena and Dante, you'll find them in the Unholy Trinity duet!

ACKNOWLEDGMENTS

This book wouldn't have happened without the love and support of my two amazing teenage sons. They are as proud of me as I am of them, and that's about all I can hope for in life.

Special thanks to my editor, Ethan Freckleton, whose insight helped make this book far better than before he took his red pen to it.

And a big shout out to my BFF, Keri Peyton, for all the listening and talking about my characters like they're our friends.

I am eternally grateful to the plethora of fellow authors who continue to offer advice and support. One day, I will pay it forward.

ABOUT THE AUTHOR

Macy is a foul-mouthed tennis addict whose sweet side comes out with her two teenage sons. Strong, smart heroines inspire her as much as hard-bodied heroes with hearts of gold.

When she's not on the tennis court or locked in her writing cave, you'll find Macy on the beach with a sunset cocktail or out on the boat near their home in the Florida Keys.

Connect with Macy, and get exclusive content and special offers at www.macybutler.com

ALSO BY MACY BUTLER

Paradise Found— Kate's wedding happens here!

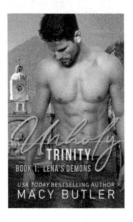

Unholy Trinity- Trinity's adventures in Guatemala

Taming Kate- Kate and Zayne's sizzling story

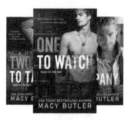

Happier Ever After- Sally's story (and meet Kate!!)